OUT-OF-TOWN SUSPECTS

Addie begrudgingly folded her arms and stared at the board. "Now we need motives for murder," she said as she wrote . . .

Money or Greed
Revenge
Fear
Crimes of Passion
Personal Vendetta
Jealousy
Anger
Hatred
Self-defense and in-defense

"Although, I don't think that last one really fits here because poisoning indicates premeditation, not spur-of-the-moment or a reaction."

"Don't forget blackmail, power plays, and whistle-blowing." Paige pointed to the board.

"Right," said Addie, scribbling those on the list.

"Wow," said Paige, reading the list. "It's sad to think all those are the reasons why people justify murdering someone."

Addie scanned the board. "Yes, but you know what's missing when I look at all these possible motives for murder?"

"What?"

"We're the only two people on the board without a probable motive, and yet we're Turner's number one suspects . . ."

Books by Lauren Elliott

MURDER BY THE BOOK

PROLOGUE TO MURDER

MURDER IN THE FIRST EDITION

PROOF OF MURDER

A PAGE MARKED FOR MURDER

UNDER THE COVER OF MURDER

TO THE TOME OF MURDER

A MARGIN FOR MURDER

Published by Kensington Publishing Corp.

A MARGIN for MURDER

Lauren Elliott

Kensington Publishing Corp.
www.kensingtonbooks.com

KENSINGTON BOOKS are published by

Kensington Publishing Corp.
119 West 40th Street
New York, NY 10018

All Kensington titles, imprints, and distributed lines are available at special quantity discounts for bulk purchases for sales promotion, premiums, fund-raising, educational, or institutional use.

Special book excerpts or customized printings can also be created to fit specific needs. For details, write or phone the office of the Kensington Sales Manager: Attn.: Sales Department. Kensington Publishing Corp., 119 West 40th Street, New York, NY 10018. Phone: 1-800-221-2647.

The K and Teapot logo is a trademark of Kensington Publishing Corp.

First Printing: May 2022
ISBN: 978-1-4967-3513-3

ISBN: 978-1-4967-3517-1 (ebook)

10 9 8 7 6 5 4 3 2 1

Printed in the United States of America

Chapter 1

Addie Greyborne stood on the sidewalk, gazing into one of the display windows of her book and curio shop, Beyond the Page. However, she wasn't admiring the classic romance book selection embellished by a watering can, multiple butterflies, and clusters of spring bouquets that her assistant manager, Paige Stringer, and shop assistant, Catherine Lewis, painstakingly spent hours creating. No, her mind replayed the last words Simon Emerson had said to her that morning.

Promise me that you'll get back to Greyborne Harbor in time for the special birthday dinner I have planned for you tomorrow evening.

Then he'd swept her into his arms and kissed her like they had never kissed before—a scene that played out right now in her mind, very much like one directly out of the pages of the romance novels in her window.

Her gaze settled on her own reflection in the glass. Sunlight glistened off her diamond-encircled emerald earrings, and she softly smiled. Even the thought of his words and that embrace sent her heart racing as she studied the mirrored image of the earrings. They were the ones he had given her as a gift last Christmas.

She recalled how hard she had tried Christmas morning to hide her disappointment when he produced a small blue jeweler's box, revealing the earrings instead of the ring she truly wanted. Thankfully, Paige had warned her. Bless her heart. Otherwise, there might have been tears and a whole lot of embarrassment.

"Perhaps tomorrow," she whispered.

"Earth to Addie." An annoyingly chipper voice broke through her thoughts, bringing her back from her dream world.

Addie stared blankly at her best friend, Serena Ludlow, and dropped her gaze to her friend's heavily extended abdomen before making eye contact again. Addie could tell by the set of Serena's jaw that she expected an answer. "What did you say before that?"

"I . . . asked . . . *you* if Paige is ready to go? I have the Wrangler all gassed up." She waved the keys in Addie's face. "We'd better hit the road soon or we'll miss the sale."

Addie took a deep breath and tried to switch gears in her mind to focus on Serena's words. "We've been through this already. There's no way you can come with us."

"Why not?" Her bottom lip trembled, and tears formed in the corners of her round, brown eyes.

"Because you're due to have your baby any day now." Serena crossed her arms over her heaving chest, and her blotched, freckled face tilted into a pout. "I don't believe that, so you shouldn't either."

"But that's what Doctor Dowdy told you two days ago at your last exam, isn't it, and he's your doctor and should know these things."

"Doctor Dowdy-Shmoudy. I don't think he knows anything anymore." Her voice quivered with tears. "First, he tells me I'm due in late June—well over a full month from now—and then suddenly he says *any day now*." She thrust her hands on her rounded hips. "You tell me if that's a doctor who knows what he's talking about. Besides," she huffed, "I'm tired of missing out on all the fun."

"Aw, hon," Addie cooed and stroked her hands up and down her friend's sundress-exposed arms. "I know this is hard on you, but remember, you're building an amazing little Serena or Zach inside you right now. You're doing something that's far more important than I am with going to this book sale and haggling over prices."

"I can haggle better than you. You've seen me at garage and estate sales, so you need me with you today, right?"

"Yes, you are the best negotiator I've ever seen. By me saying no today, I'm thinking of you. This is an old library. There's lots of flights of stairs to hike up, and from what I've been told, there isn't any air-conditioning in the building. You'd be miserable and hate every minute of it." Addie placed her fingertip under Serena's chin and tipped her downcast face up, forcing Serena to look into her eyes. "Don't you see? After all the times you've looked out for me, this time, I'm looking out for you."

"Yeah, I suppose you are. No air-conditioning, really?" Serena shuddered. "I don't think I could handle that." She cradled her bulging tummy.

"That's right." Addie studied her friend's face in case her words brought on another round of tears. "The building's too old, and to refit it would cost a fortune. It's one of the many reasons why the library is being closed down." She eyed Serena, who, from the way she gnawed on her bottom lip, was still fighting back hormonally-charged tears. "I hear it's stuffy, and the air's filled with dust motes—*ghastly* is one way a customer described it."

Of course, that wasn't entirely true, but Addie knew the more horrible it sounded the less likely Serena would feel she was being excluded from an adventure. Besides, what if she went into labor when they were on the highway? The mere thought gave Addie the heebie-jeebies. What did she know about delivering a baby?

The closest she ever came to something like that was when Carolyn, her friend and Simon's sister, had her last baby in the back room of Martha Stringer's bakery. Even then, Martha had relegated Addie to keeping watch for the ambulance and told her to phone Carolyn's husband, Pete, from the front of the store. Martha helped with the delivery, not her, so she wouldn't have a clue what was expected.

"And you promise you'll be back tomorrow?" Serena sniffled.

"Yes. We're not staying for the entire weekend sale, so I promise, we'll be back tomorrow by noon."

"I still don't understand why you have to stay the night, anyway. It's only about a fifteen-minute drive from Pen Hollow. You could be back tonight for dinner." Serena's eyes filled with hope.

Addie fought her inner eye roll. They had been over

this for the past two days. Serena's raging hormones or not, the whole conversation was becoming tiresome, but she bit her tongue. Anything she said at this point, even reminding her friend again that Paige wanted to treat Addie to a mini pre-birthday excursion, wouldn't matter right now. They'd still continue to go around and round in circles. Clearly, her friend had lost all sense of recall and comprehension. She glanced at Serena's tummy and sighed, struggling to find the words that might end this tired conversation once and for all. To Addie's relief, Paige popped her blond curly head out of the front door of Beyond the Page.

"The Mini's filled and in the back. Should I gather up Pippi's toys so we can head out now?" Paige's gaze flicked from Addie to a teary-eyed Serena. "Or not?" She stepped out onto the sidewalk. "Is everything okay?"

Addie looked fleetingly from Serena to Paige and gave a helpless shrug when Serena's tears renewed and rolled down her splotchy cheeks.

"Oh no, sweetie, what's the matter?" cried Paige, hurrying to Serena's side.

"I just feel so useless and left out of everything," she sobbed.

"You're not either of those, and you know it. You're doing something very, very important right now." Paige wrapped her arms as best she could around Serena and held her close.

"That's what Addie said, but I feel so sidelined, and I hate it."

"It won't last forever, and you'll see, soon enough you'll be back to being one of the Three Musketeers," Paige murmured softly.

"That's easy for you to say," Serena said, stiffening as

she pulled away from Paige. "You have a mother that takes your little girl whenever you want, plus four sisters that take her on holidays with them whenever they go away. I have no one. I'll be left out for the rest of my life." Serena swiped at the tears tumbling down her cheeks.

"Serena, that's not true." Addie stroked her friend's heaving back. "You have a whole village of people here that love you, and your parents will dote on your baby, not to mention your brother. He's already such a proud uncle."

"Do you really think the high-and-mighty Police Chief Marc Chandler will change dirty diapers and walk the floors at night with a screaming baby?" Serena's eyes flashed. "I think not, and as for my doting parents, it seems once I was safely married off, they decided it was time to travel and see the world. I'll be lucky if they pop in for a visit at Christmas."

"You have us and Catherine," said Paige meekly.

"Yes," echoed Addie, "and we're not going anywhere."

"But if you help me with the baby so I can have an adventure or two, who will I be having an adventure with?"

And . . . here they were . . . talking in circles again just as Addie predicted.

"Look," said Paige, "I know right now it seems your life has ended, but believe me. It's only Mother Nature's way of preparing you for the incredible new adventure you're about to embark on. All these mixed emotions you're feeling right now will become nothing more than a hazy, distant memory the moment that you finally get to hold this precious little baby in your arms for the very first time."

Addie stared at Paige, and a wave of pride and awe surged through her. This meek, mild-mannered young girl, who wouldn't say boo when she had first come to work for Addie, had blossomed into a highly aware, intelligent young woman.

"Paige is right," said Addie, "and she knows what's she's talking about, so you need to listen to her."

Serena looked at Paige and shrugged. "I guess you would know better than anyone about what I'm going through."

"I have a good idea even though we each deal with this process differently. Just remember, each step through this is only a phase and soon passes onto the next one. Today you feel lonely and left out. Tomorrow, and I am being completely honest here, you might feel overwhelmed and at your wits' end with no sleep because the baby has days and nights mixed up. But remember that no matter what, each phase only lasts a short time, and then a new one starts and in time, it's all just your normal life. You'll take it all in stride because when you gaze into your little one's eyes, you will see nothing but pure love."

Serena wrapped her arms around Paige. When she pulled back, Serena had something on her face that Addie hadn't seen for a few weeks. A smile.

"Here, you guys take my Wrangler in case you find loads of books at the sale. It holds more than the Mini does." Serena dangled the keys in front of Paige, who glanced questioningly over at Addie.

Addie nodded, and Paige scooped the keys into her hand.

"Thank you, Serena," said Addie. "It will really be a big help if we don't have to arrange to ship too many books back from the sale. Paige will give you the keys for the Mini, so you have something to drive today."

"Not sure I could fit behind your wheel, so I'll call Zach to pick me up when he has some spare time between patients."

"Sure, whatever, but we'll leave the keys with you just in case. Till he can get away from the naturopathic clinic, why don't you come inside and keep Catherine company? She's not used to running the bookstore by herself, and since you're on maternity leave from your tea shop, you can give her a hand—from your perch at the counter, of course." Addie laughed as they made their way inside the bookstore.

At the sound of Addie's voice and the overhead bells tinkling, Pippi shot out from behind the counter and clickety-clacked her pin-like nails across the wooden floorboards to Addie's side.

"I think," chuckled Catherine from behind the Victorian bar Addie used as a sales and coffee counter, "that your little friend knows something's going on." Her silver-highlighted bob swung freely with her laughter.

"Hey there girl, do you sense an outing in the making?" Addie bent down and scratched the little Yorkipoo behind the ear.

"Are you sure you want to take her?" asked Catherine. "It is only for one night, so she's more than welcome to stay with me."

"What do you think about staying with Auntie Catherine?" Addie looked down at the ball of fluff by her foot.

Pippi's ears perked, and her head cocked to the side as she looked over at Catherine then at Addie. She let out a little yip and danced gopher style on her back legs, her front paws scouring the air to get to Addie's arms.

"I guess that answers that question." Addie laughed while she scooped Pippi up and cuddled her.

"It's just that I know it will be a long afternoon for the little thing, and I don't want you to have to worry about her while you're trying to shop."

"I know," said Addie, nestling her face into the silky fur behind Pippi's head. "I have the doggie carrier, and she likes the cozy comfort it brings her. She'll be fine. Besides, I really don't like waking up and not having her beside me, like when she adopted my cousin last fall and didn't sleep with me for a week."

"But that was different," said Serena. "She knew your cousin needed her."

"I know," said Addie, "but I need her too." She chuckled and ducked her face away from the lapping pink tongue searching out her lips.

After giving last-minute instructions to Catherine, Addie transferred her overnight luggage, Pippi—stowed safely in her carrier—and Pippi's things, including Baxter, her favorite toy bear, from the Mini into Serena's Wrangler. As Paige pulled away from the alley parking space, Addie settled in the passenger seat and waved farewell to a misty-eyed Serena and beaming Catherine.

"I sure hope Catherine doesn't feel overwhelmed running the shop by herself for the rest of the day," said Paige as they pulled out onto Birch Road.

"It's not her I'm worried about." Addie swiveled in her seat to look back up the alley. "I don't ever recall Serena being so disagreeable and ornery as she has been these last few weeks, do you?"

"She's at the final stages of her pregnancy and feeling a bit like a beached whale, I imagine."

"Yes, but when Carolyn had her last one, she wasn't so disagreeable."

"You're forgetting that was Carolyn's fourth, and she knew what to expect. This is Serena's first, and I'm pretty sure, on top of being tired of lumbering around, deep down she's petrified."

"You're right. The whole thing must be very scary for a new mom."

"It is. But you'll see when she and Zach get to hold that little baby and finally get settled into a routine, it won't take long for the same old Serena we all love to return to us."

"I hope you're right. This new version of her is a little terrifying." Addie settled back and prepared to enjoy the drive, but when they came to the intersection on the highway, Addie's eyes bulged, and she grabbed the dash. "What are you doing?"

"Umm . . . driving to Pen Hollow? Remember?"

"I know where we're going, silly, but why are you going this way?"

"Because this way takes fifteen minutes."

"But the other highway is far more scenic," cried Addie. "So let's take it."

"Why would we spend an hour getting there when we can be there in a flash this way? Don't forget my sister's neighbor has to give us the key, and she has to be at the doctor at ten, so we don't want to miss her this morning. Besides, didn't you say you had arranged with the head librarian for us to shop earlier than the noon sale start or something?"

"Yes, but . . ." Addie's fingers tightened around the armrest on the door panel. The mental vision of the switchback curve that would greet them at the top of Cliff Side Road sent her mind reeling. Her hand glowed white on the armrest. She struggled to force air into her lungs. This was why Addie had always avoided the short trip to Pen Hollow. It was a too painful reminder of the day her father died on this very highway.

Chapter 2

Addie couldn't move. She was frozen in time—the time Marc had brought her up here so they could take a look at the scene of her father's accident for themselves because something in the state police report hadn't sat right with either of them. That's when she had peered over the guardrail down the three-hundred-foot drop where her father's car had crashed onto the rocks below.

"Isn't the scenery up here amazing," said Paige, her attention focused steadfastly on the winding road before them.

Addie squeezed her eyes shut and shook her head as she fought the lump growing in the back of her throat and the pressure in her chest that was rising to meet it. Certain she was going to vomit, she pawed at the closed window and frantically pressed the button to open it.

"When we get to the top here, look over the railing. I'm sure you'll agree with me that this route is just as scenic as the other longer drive up the coast. Look, now! You can see the entire peninsula Pen Hollow sits on. Isn't it beautiful? I just love coming here," Paige said excitedly as she slowed down to make the sharp, hairpin curve. "Should I stop so we can get a picture?"

"No, just go!"

"What's wrong?" asked Paige, glancing over at Addie. "Why are you so—Oh jeez, in all my excitement about going to Pen Hollow for the night, I completely forgot. I'm sorry. Keep your eyes closed. We'll be down to the intersection at the bottom in a minute. Hold on. Can you ever forgive me for my stupidity?"

"Just drive," Addie sputtered, squeezing her eyes shut.

After what seemed like an eternity to Addie, but in actuality was only moments later, Paige's soothing voice broke through the noise in Addie's mind. "See, we're down at the bottom and just up ahead is the intersection of Coast Highway and the road onto the peninsula."

Addie hesitantly peered through her thick dark lashes and glimpsed the blurred image of a huge stop sign. "Okay, thanks," she hoarsely whispered and blew out the breath she'd been holding.

Curious to see how Pippi had fared on the harrowing switchback ride, Addie glanced into the back seat where her little furry friend was securely seat-belted in her doggy carrier. Pippi's face poked out of the circular opening of her enclosure, revealing eyes closed in sleep. A wave of envy swept through Addie. *Wouldn't it be wonderful to be a dog during moments like this?*

The Wrangler came to a smooth stop at the crossroads

and out of habit, Addie checked left and then right—all clear—but there they sat. Questioningly, she glanced over at Paige, whose hands gripped the steering wheel.

"Addie," she choked huskily, "I don't know where to begin in apologizing to you. I never even thought. Emma and I make this drive almost every Sunday when Logan works, so I can spend the day with my sister, Brianna, and her kids. It didn't occur to me until it was too late that was the road—" She swallowed hard. "The road where—"

"It's okay, don't worry." Addie reached over and patted Paige's hand. "It was a long time ago, and I have to learn to face my fears. Maybe being forced to do it today will help me bury another ghost from my past. I'm fine now. Let's just get to that book sale and later, since you've spent so much time in Pen Hollow, you can be my tour guide. What do you say?"

Paige's somber face lit up, and she gave Addie an impish grin. "I say, let's have some fun this weekend doing what we both love to do best. After all, it is your mini-birthday getaway."

"That's the spirit." Addie grinned as Paige pulled out onto the peninsula roadway. Addie glanced out her window when they came round a curve on the road. An involuntary shiver quivered up her spine as the base of the cliff on the seaward side of the peninsula came into view.

The landmass distinctly widened as brightly colored, small, wood-clad houses poked out of the tree groves and replaced the coastal view. Addie stretched out her still tightened fingers from the harrowing ride. "Are those the summer cottages you told me about, the ones you dreamed of buying someday?"

"Yes, the smaller, more affordable ones are on your side, what some call the sea side of the road. But, if you look to your left through the trees that lead down to the bay side of the peninsula, you can just make out the rooftops of some of the mansions that were built here back in the nineteenth century. I'd love one of those, but they're a little out of any budget I might ever have in this lifetime."

Addie craned her neck to get a glimpse, but apart from some towering turrets peeking through the foliage, and an odd gabled roofline, she really couldn't see much of the houses. "From what you've told me before, it sounds like this cape has quite the past?"

"Yeah, it does, and I would have loved to have seen it during its heyday."

"It's heyday?"

"Yeah, according to what Brianna told me, back around the late eighteen hundreds, an adventurous family from Boston stumbled on the sleepy little fishing village of Pen Hollow and fell in love with the unspoiled area. It didn't take them long to build a summer estate home. Many of their friends followed, and it became the best-kept secret of the then Boston aristocracy. It didn't hurt either that the land was cheaper and they could buy bigger lots and build larger summer homes than they could on places like Cape Cod."

"It sounds like there's lots of money here."

"Yes, and old money at that. Although with the shifting economy these days, some can't afford to have two houses anymore, so a few live here year-round. Most owners, though, still come out around Easter to start opening their summer houses for the season."

"What about these smaller cottages on my side? Are they lived in year-round?"

"No, they're mainly just seasonal holiday homes and

belong to families in the region." Paige shifted in the driver's seat. "Just wait until we come around this next curve. You'll see how the landscape abruptly changes." She slowed down for the sharp corner. "Now, look out my side. What do you see?"

Addie bobbed her head to see past Paige and gasped. "It's so different. What happened to the trees? And the water in the bay . . . it's as smooth as glass."

"On this side of the peninsula, there are miles of soft sandy beaches, but when we get around this point up ahead, and then drive past the amusement park and board-walk, you won't believe the change on the sea side of the peninsula. It's like a different world on that side."

Addie scanned her surroundings as they passed the amusement park. "Is the park fairly new?"

"No, it was built back around 1910, and it's so cool. There are all sorts of old-style rides. Like the wooden Ferris wheel you can sort of make out in the distance. There's also a beautiful antique merry-go-round and some old-fashioned midway games on the boardwalk, along with the cool little store-like stalls and food vendors. It's sort of like stepping back in time to an old market and fair, and one of the reasons it's still such a big attraction. Very different and old-world like."

"It sounds like a lot of fun."

"It is." Paige grinned. "Emma and I brought Logan last Sunday for the May Day grand opening. That's the festival that really kicks off the summer season. We all had a blast, and even Logan, who doesn't go in much for rides and games, had fun."

Addie smiled at the mental image her mind conjured up of Paige's little girl, running around the amusement park with her tiny fingers tucked inside Paige's fire-fighter boyfriend's big burly hand.

"It was especially nice," added Paige, "because Emma has the run of the park with her cousins, who are a little older. Graham is ten and Chelsea is twelve, so it also gave Logan and me some much-needed time alone to play at being kids ourselves. I made him take me on every ride and play all the midway games." Paige giggled.

"I had no idea all this was just a short drive from Grey-borne Harbor," Addie said wistfully. "But there's not many cars in the parking lot. Is it usually busier?"

"It's not even ten yet, and we missed the first on-slaught of holidaymakers last weekend. With this good weather, though, I suspect more will be arriving today."

Addie craned her neck to see past Paige and get a better view as the midway slipped from sight.

Paige grinned. "It's one of the reasons I wanted us to stay overnight. I thought after we're finished at the sale, I could treat you to an early birthday dinner, and then we could come back here for a dessert of mini donuts or something, and I could show you around."

"That sounds like fun. I even saw a few rides I might go on." Addie patted her belly full of pre-ride butterflies.

"Yeah, and tonight will give you a better idea of what it's really like here during the high season, because I imagine it being Friday and with this great weather, it will be packed."

"I wonder if that's why the library picked this week-end to hold the closing-out sale. It sure would help drum up book sales if seasonal homeowners are in town too."

"Probably. The library has been here for nearly a hun-dred years, and for those families that come to holiday year after year, well . . . they'd be disappointed to miss out on it. Although, I think that's why my sister and her family picked this week to go away on vacation."

"Is she not a fan of the library?"

"The complete opposite. As a member of the library committee and chairperson of the local book club, the whole idea of the library closing broke her heart. She just couldn't face it."

"That's too bad," Addie said as she absently scanned the sandy dunes and windswept landscape. "Is this the only road into the village?"

"No, we could have turned into the village a couple miles back, but I wanted to bring you this way so you could get a clearer picture of the whole peninsula."

"Is this way like a ring road or something?"

"Yeah, sort of." Paige slowed down for a curve when the waterfront came into view in front of the Wrangler. "We came out to the sand spit on the bay side of the peninsula, and now we're heading back up the sea side. The village starts just up here past this grove of trees."

"I just can't get over the extremes in landscape."

They whizzed past the tree grove. A stone seawall towered over the road on the left, and without warning, a huge Atlantic wave splashed over the top, sending spray out onto the road.

"I see why this is called Sea Spray Drive," Addie said with a laugh as Paige swerved the car to avoid the deluge of water. "Does this happen often?"

"It does on this short stretch. Up here, where the village starts"—Paige jerked her head toward the upcoming village sign—"the beach below the seawall is a lot wider, so it's not as much of an issue."

"That's good. Otherwise, I could envision one head-on collision after another."

"I know, duck-the-waves is an ongoing game here." Paige laughed.

"You really seem to feel at home on the peninsula"— Addie grinned at her friend—"and it's clear how much you love being here. I'm surprised you didn't move to Pen Hollow when you left Boston instead of going back to Greyborne Harbor."

Paige slowed their speed as they passed the WELCOME TO THE VILLAGE OF PEN HOLLOW sign. "Believe me, if there was work here, I would have."

Brightly painted, historic-appearing clapboard buildings dotted the roadway, each boasting a unique seaside resort experience, and Addie looked questioningly over at Paige. "But look at all the cool shops. There must be tons of work here."

"Yeah, there are lots of shops, but don't forget, this is still very much a seasonal town. The merchants depend on the busy summer season to carry them through the leaner winter months when they have to lay off all their staff just to make it through until the next season. It's a vicious cycle of hiring and layoffs. That's the only way they can survive."

"That's too bad. Does it make it harder to find staff for the open season?"

"No, there's tons of college kids and teenage vacationers who come with their parents who are dying for what work they can get."

"I guess it's sort of a win-win situation, then?"

"Yes, for people looking for seasonal work; not for people like me, who need full-time employment."

"Yeah, I can see that." Addie was amused by some of the attention-grabbing names on the signs over the shops. "Not that I'd want to lose you, but you just seem to be in your element here. I don't think I've ever seen you come so alive before."

"Truth be known, I feel like I'm home whenever I'm here, that's for sure, but I think it has more to do with Brianna. Out of all my sisters, Bree and I are the closest, and she was the most supportive when I was having Emma." Paige looked fleetingly at Addie. "You know, she never judged me for not being married to Brett, Emma's father, like a couple of the others did."

Addie recalled what she could about Emma's father, and how he, a university professor, had taken advantage of a young and very naïve freshman. The situation had caused a rift that lasted a few years between Paige and her mother, Martha. Even Paige's older sister, Mellissa, who was great with Emma, had never supported Paige's decision to raise a child on her own. Addie snorted. *Like Mellissa's life is perfect. Pot to kettle.*

She gazed out the window and gasped. "Slow down!"

"Why? What?" Paige cried and slammed on the brakes.

"Did you see that guy by the lamppost, who was handing the flower basket up to the woman on the ladder?"

Paige checked the reflection behind them in the rearview mirror and nodded. "Why, who is he?"

Addie tried to pivot around in her seat, but her seat belt locked and pinned her tight. "No way." She sat back. "It can't be him."

"*Who* are we talking about?" Paige asked, exasperated, and stepped on the accelerator when the car behind them honked.

"Never mind me." Addie waved her off. "Just somebody who looked a lot like a guy I used to know." Addie took a quick peek in her sideview mirror as Paige continued to drive.

"Who?"

"My old high school boyfriend."

Chapter 3

"No, don't turn around," squealed Addie as Paige slowed the Wrangler and flipped on the left-turn indicator.

"Are you sure? I can just make a U-turn here at the corner, and we could drive back for one more look. Then at least you'd know for certain."

"No," Addie said, checking the time on the dashboard clock. "It's nearly ten, and we don't want to miss Bree's neighbor."

"But what if it is him? Don't you want to say hello after all these years?"

"There's no way it was." Addie dismissively waved her hand. "I'm just seeing things. The drive over Cliff Side Road must have stirred up more than one ghost from my past today. Besides, why in the world would he turn up in Pen Hollow, of all places, after basically disappearing off the face of the earth sixteen years ago?"

"Maybe this is where he disappeared to?"

"Tony?" Addie said with a short laugh. "I doubt it, at least not the Tony I knew back then. He loved action, and the slow pace of life here would have killed him. My Tony thought Boston was even too unexciting for him. He used to love to listen to the stories my dad told him about when he worked as a police detective in New York City, and that's where Tony decided he was going after graduation, which . . ." Her voice trailed off. "Sadly, he never did, as far as I know."

"What do you mean?" Paige pulled up in front of an attractive Cape Cod two-story home.

"Two months before graduation he suddenly stopped coming to school, and no one could reach him. I tried, but his phone was disconnected. I went by his house every day for weeks, but it was locked up tight and there were never any signs of life or anyone having been there recently. Neither me nor any of our crowd ever heard from him again."

"You're kidding?"

"No, it was all pretty mysterious, and the school legally couldn't give us any information. All they would say was he was safe and not to worry. I guess with graduation coming up, most of our group took that as a good sign and just focused on the future and forgot about Tony as everyone made plans to head off in the fall to different colleges."

"Except you didn't really forget about Tony, did you?"

"I tried to find him for a while after I went to Columbia. I thought maybe he got impatient and headed to New York early, but after a while I gave up too, and went on with my life and have barely thought about him since I graduated and moved back to Boston where I met David,"—tears stung at Addie's eyes when she thought about her dead fiancée—"at least, until today. It's weird, isn't it?" She shrugged. "Oh well. I guess it's like I said, one of the ghosts from my past was stirred up in my memory today, and for some reason, it conjured up an image of him."

"So, tell me about this guy," said Paige eagerly as she shifted into park and turned off the ignition.

"There's not much to tell. It was a high school romance and was a long time ago."

"But there had to have been something special about him for you to spot some random guy on the street and the first person you thought of was this Tony."

Addie shook her head and chuckled as she opened her door. "Not really. He was a typical, gangly, seventeen-year-old boy, that's all." She paused, one foot on the grass boulevard. "Except his smile." She sighed. "It lit up a room. I guess that's what reminded me of him. It was the way that man smiled up at the woman as he handed her the hanging flower basket."

"I still think we should have gone back so you could see if it was him or not," said Paige, getting out on the driver's side. She opened the back of the Wrangler. "You take Pippi in to Bree's, and I'll grab our bags."

Addie, doggie carrier already shouldered, came around to the back of the car. "Sounds like a plan to me." She laughed and closed the hatch after Paige had their two overnight bags firmly in hand.

"Yoo-hoo, Paige!" called a small voice from the front porch of the colonial bungalow next door.

Paige waved at the pear-shaped, gray-haired woman sporting a colorfully flowered dress. "Hi, Mrs. Price, it's nice to see you again."

"I've told you before, my dear, please call me Valerie. We've known each other far too long for such formalities." She smoothed her hands over a bright, sunflower-yellow apron.

"Yes, ma'am . . . er . . . I mean, Valerie," Paige said with a little giggle.

"Perfect timing. I've just got home and have made a pot of tea. Come in, come in." She stood back, motioning toward the door.

Addie glanced at Paige questioningly. Paige frowned. "But don't you have an appointment at ten?"

"Goodness, dear, as soon as your sister called to tell me you would be staying at her house while they're away and you'd pick up the key this morning, I had my doctor get me in early. I've just gotten back, so there's no rush. Now come in and take a load off before you head out again."

Addie gestured with her head at Pippi.

"My friend Addie, here, has her dog with us, so I think we'll just freshen up before we head over to the book sale."

"Nonsense, you can bring the pup in with you." Valerie headed down the porch steps, her gaze glued on the little whiskered face peeping out of the dog carrier's circular opening. "Hello, my little friend." Valerie held her hand out for Pippi to take a sniff. Pippi licked the woman's arthritic, knobbed fingers, yipped, and tried to squeeze her head out of the front opening. Addie laughed, set the carrier down, unzipped the top zipper, retrieved her furry little friend, and released her into Valerie's outstretched hands. "Come here. Oh my, aren't you just the cutest little thing I've ever seen." She cradled Pippi close and laughed as a tiny pink tongue lapped at her flushed cheeks.

Addie rose to her feet. "Hi, I'm Paige's friend, Addie Greyborne."

"Well, Addie, you have a very special little friend here, don't you?" She stroked the back of Pippi's head. "Yes, she does, doesn't she, and I think I even have a treat inside for you." Valerie started back toward the porch.

Stunned, Addie looked at Paige and opened her mouth to protest—

"We'd love to come in," said Paige, "but maybe after the book sale, if you're going to be home?"

Valerie tsked. "Surely you can give an old woman a few moments of indulgence before you run off. Can't they, sweetie?" She nuzzled Pippi's head under her chin. "Come along now."

"Do something," Addie whispered to Paige.

Paige stepped forward. "We'd love to accept, but we really do have to go."

"Yes," said Addie, sliding up to Paige's side. "We promised the librarian we'd be there around ten thirty."

Valerie stopped short. "Patricia Seagram?"

"Yes, I think that's her name."

"Yes, well, then you best not keep her waiting. The poor thing is having one heck of a time dealing with all this closing stuff these days, and if she's left waiting? Well"—Valerie glanced down at Pippi in her arms—"I certainly don't want to be the cause of her having a stroke or something. But why don't you leave your friend here with me while you attend the sale?"

"We couldn't impose on you like that," said Addie, taking a step to retrieve Pippi.

"It's not an imposition at all. My niece Laurel is a veterinarian, you know, and she's been telling me for months I should get a pup of my own. Spending the day with this one might be all the encouragement I need to do just that." She grinned. "And who knows, maybe I'll just steal you away from your mommy, and you can come live with me. What do you think about that?" Valerie cooed and rubbed Pippi behind her ear. Pippi's tail wagged and thumped Valerie. "See, she likes me, so why don't you girls run off and enjoy the sale. Pippi and I can play outside in my garden all afternoon, and you won't have to worry about her."

"Are you sure it wouldn't be an imposition?" asked Paige.

"Pish posh." Valerie shook her head. "None at all, and"—she glanced at Addie—"I was only teasing, my dear, about stealing her from you. I promise she'll be here when you get back."

Paige glanced sideways at Addie. "What do you think?"

"I think if you don't mind then . . ." She gazed at Pippi's little pink tongue hanging out the side of her mouth. If dogs could smile, then she definitely was. "I think that sounds fine. Thank you. I did hear there's no air-conditioning in the building, and the day is shoring up to be a hot one, so it's probably for the best."

"Exactly," said Valerie. "Although that doggie bag looks cozy, I image it would get a might warm, and we don't need this little one getting sick, do we?" She buried her face into the silky fur at the back of Pippi's head.

"Then it's settled. You girls go on and enjoy your day, and we'll stay here and keep nice and cool in my yard. She can help me dig out my flower beds. How does that sound?" She laughed when Pippi squirmed excitedly in her arms.

Satisfied Pippi would be well cared-for, and key in hand, Paige and Addie headed up the flowerbed-lined sidewalk of the Cape Cod next door. After stepping into Brianna's small foyer, Addie knew instantly that the original character features of the house had been maintained, even though the home had undergone a contemporary remodel sometime in the past few years. The brick fireplace in the living room held all the charm of a home built well over a hundred years ago, but over the mantel, instead of a portrait depicting the master or mistress of the house, hung a wide-screen television. A comfy-looking beige sectional sofa, one just perfect for a family to curl up on while enjoying a Friday evening movie marathon, faced the fireplace.

"Nice, isn't it?" Paige grinned and set their overnight bags down in the entrance to the living room.

"Very homey and exactly the style I would expect your sister to create for her family."

"Her husband, Darren, is so busy with his job as a state trooper that he leaves all the home decorating to Bree and never complains about any of the changes she makes. This is all her."

"I can see it. Even though I've only met her a few times, you can tell she's very much a family-first person, and this room especially reflects that. It's lived in, not kept as a showpiece." Addie studied the comfortable furnishings throughout the room and into what she could see of the adjoining dining room. "Yes, very nice and very comfortable. I can see why you and Emma enjoy coming here."

"That's Bree, the homemaker. So, I was thinking, I really can't stand the idea of sleeping in her and Darren's bed. So I thought I'd take Graham's room, and you could have Chelsea's. How does that sound?"

"Fine, whatever you want."

"Good, we can take our bags up later, but it is nearly ten thirty, so . . ."

"Yes, you heard what Valerie said, and I sure don't want to be the cause of this Patricia having a stroke either."

"No, I knew the library closing wasn't sitting well with the village, but I guess when we planned this, I really didn't stop to think about what it meant to the individuals. Bree wasn't pleased, but for people like Patricia it must be hitting especially hard. I heard she's been the librarian for over thirty years."

"Yikes." Addie winced. "This might be a tough day, so we'd better be careful not to show our enthusiasm about buying any of the books too much, right?"

"Agreed."

Chapter 4

When Addie and Paige got to the library, they made their way up the crumbling sandstone steps past the two pitted columns on either side of the weathered oak door. It was clear that this old building with its peeling paint trim and weather-beaten brick exterior had seen better days.

"Ready to spend some money?" Addie gave the heavy door a heave-ho.

"As long as it's yours." Paige snickered and followed in behind her. "Remember, don't show too much excitement over what we find. This sale is hard on the whole village, and Bree would never let me visit again if people started calling us the Greyborne Harbor Vultures."

"I'll try," Addie said with a short laugh, "but you know me when I come across a good book sale."

"Just try and restrain yourself, for once, please, for Bree's sake."

"Yes, I promise to behave. I'm not heartless, you know."

"I know you aren't, but I also know how singularly focused you become when books are involved, especially old books like we'll most likely find here . . . Wow!" Paige sputtered when they stepped onto the small landing. An age-darkened oak-carved banister curved upstairs, and an equally grand staircase led down to an inviting set of oak-framed French doors at the bottom. "Which way do you think we'll find Patricia?"

Addie pointed to the book sale sign. "Down seems to be the best place to start. If she's not there, then we can head up."

They trotted down the wide, wooden stairs to the lower level, pushed through the double-wide doors, and stumbled to a halt. "Whoa." Addie gave the large room a once-over. "Talk about stepping back in time."

"In all the times I've been to Pen Hollow, I can't believe I never made time to come in here. It's beautiful." Paige sighed. "Or, at least, it would have been at one time. Looks and smells like it's seen better days though."

Addie wriggled her nose. "I'd call it Eau de Musty with subtle undertones of old book and leather. But, wow, look through the arched doorway into the reading room." She dropped her voice and gestured. "That fireplace must cover the entire wall!"

Paige peered around the corner and clucked her tongue. "From what Bree told me, the furnace conked out early last winter, so that's probably the only heating source they had this past year. Sad, when you think of the damage it must have done to some of the books, judging by the odors in here, anyway."

"Yeah, we'll have to be careful about what we purchase. Check all the books for mildew damage before you get too excited about them."

A lump grew in the back of Addie's throat. "It really is sad to see such an elegant old building filled with all these books descend into—Look at that library table!" Addie darted over to the wall by the arched reading room entrance and waved Paige over. "This is an authentic Renaissance Revival library table from the late eighteen hundreds. Wouldn't it be a perfect display table in the bookstore?"

Addie scanned the room and dashed over to a bookshelf. "Come see this. It's an Italian Neoclassical bookcase from the early nineteen hundreds." Addie gaped as she once again scanned the room. "Look, there's a Gustav Stickley library table over against that wall and a Craftsman bookcase complete with sliding-glass doors. I'd say that both pieces are from the early nineteen hundreds." Her hands reverently covered her chest. "Ah, just look at that brown leather French Beech Sofa. That's from the early nineteen hundreds." She swooned. "Oh, wouldn't all these pieces be just perfect in the bookstore?"

"Sure, if you want to expand into my mom's bakery, maybe."

"Ooh-ooh, that's a good idea. I wonder if she'd mind."

Paige snorted and shook her head. "I really do hope you're joking."

"Maybe, maybe not." Addie gave her a sly wink. "It's a thought, anyway. But, seriously, I wonder if the furnishings are for sale too?"

"And here I was thinking we came for books," Paige croaked mockingly.

"Excuse me, I couldn't help but overhear you." A compact woman approached them and waved her hand, adorned with a showy gold bracelet, around the room. "Yes, everything you see is for sale. Books, bookcases, tables, and yes, even that leather loveseat you were admiring. It all has to be gone by the end of the month for demolition."

"Demolition?" Addie's jaw dropped. "But wouldn't this building be classified as a heritage site?"

"No more than any other old building in the village. Unfortunately, the State of Massachusetts says they're a dime a dozen here on the peninsula."

"But it's beautiful, or at least it could be. Please tell me the town council at least petitioned the state to have it designated."

"Yes, but they aren't giving any money for the upgrades required, and the library association lost our major benefactor, so"—the woman gave a half shrug—"it's become a town eyesore and has to go. Like I said, everything is for sale, and I should know. I'm Luella Higgins, the mayor, president of the town council, and the head of the library committee. You are?" She looked questioningly at them as she extended her well-manicured hand in greeting. "Say, I know you, don't I?" She withdrew her hand and studied Paige.

"Yes, I work at Beyond the Page Books and Cur—"

"Ooh, yes, that charming little bookshop in Greyborne Harbor. I remember you now."

"Yeah, we've met a few times when you dropped in."

Paige gestured to Addie. "This is Addie Greyborne. She owns it."

Luella took a step back, removed her dark-framed glasses, and tapped one of the temple arms on her chin as she considered Addie. "No, you don't look familiar. I don't believe we've met." She extended her hand in greeting. "Judging by your last name, though, is it safe to assume you are one of those silent owners? You know, one of those people who put up the money but don't get involved in the day-to-day operations of the business?"

"Umm, far from it," Addie said, taken aback as she hesitantly returned the woman's offer of a handshake. "I guess it's just come down to timing, as I do have to be out of the store on occasion. Which"—Addie bit back the scathing rebuke she wanted to utter, pasted a smile on her face instead, and glanced at Paige—"is why I make certain I hire only the very best team to look after my shop on those occasions when business takes me elsewhere."

"I see." Luella nodded and shoved her glasses back on. "Well, like I said, if you want any of the furnishings, or finishings such as the fireplace mantel or wrought-iron grates, please make an offer. It all has to go."

"I think we'll browse a bit and make some notes on the books and furniture we'd be interested in. When we've decided, should we speak to you or Patricia Seagram? After all, she was the one who invited us and gave permission for our early viewing." Addie knew her tone came across a bit edgier than it should, but this woman really had rubbed her the wrong way. Patricia had been such a sweetheart when they had spoken on the phone, and she hoped Luella would pass them off to her to haggle over the final prices.

"The larger or bulk buys, which I assume will be in

your case, should go through me. Patricia's duties as the librarian will end as soon as the books are cleared out, and I *depend* on her to make sure that happens by the end of this weekend's sale." Luella visibly shivered. "I really don't want to go to all the bother of holding another one of these." She sighed heavily. "So no, she'll be occupied filling shelves and ringing in sales for the next few days."

The woman swayed on her feet as though she was torn between going in two different directions. "I just had a thought." She stopped wavering and focused on Addie. "Since it's clear by your interest in the tables and bookcases that you have more in mind than just purchasing books to replenish your shop, would you be interested in seeing the bookmobile bus that we also have for sale?"

Addie was dumbfounded, and by the blank look on Paige's face, it was clear she was too.

"Well then," said Luella briskly, "I'll leave you to mull that over. I'll be in the back corner by the service elevator when you decide." She whirled around and strutted across the wooden floor. Her heels echoed a *clickety-clack* with each step.

"Well." Addie released a harsh breath. "That sure came out of the blue, didn't it?"

"It sure did, and I know for certain that a bookmobile won't fit in the back of Serena's Wrangler, if you're thinking what I think you are." Paige gave a half laugh. "You are considering it, aren't you?"

"Of course I am."

Paige's brows rose in horror.

"Not the Wrangler thing, silly." Addie scoffed teasingly. "But remember when we talked about finding a way to attend all of the area festivals and events to sell our books and spread the word about Beyond the Page?"

"Yeah, and if I recall, there were a couple of bottles of wine involved that night too."

"Yes, but before the wine kicked in and things got crazy, didn't we consider all the options?"

"Yes . . . we did, and we decided that hauling books, tables, an event tent, and setting up for each weekend would be more trouble than it was worth . . ."

"And . . . ?"

"And . . . with a bus that was stocked and all ready to go that we'd just have to park, we *could* hit all the festivals during tourist season!"

"Yes," squealed Addie. "That's exactly the thought that ran through my mind as soon as Luella mentioned it."

"Do you think we could manage it?"

"I don't know why not." Addie took Paige's hands between hers. "Just think about it. How hard can it be for us to refit a bookmobile into a traveling bookstore?"

"It would be a great way to get out of town for weekends during the summer," Paige said wistfully.

"That was my thinking too. We could take turns, and if it was a big festival where we knew it would be busy, Catherine could look after the bookshop so we could both go."

"You don't think she'll want to go too?"

"She might, and we could work out a schedule between the three of us."

"So, what are you thinking?" Paige said breathlessly.

"I'm thinking it wouldn't hurt to at least take a look at it."

"Yes!" Paige said with an excited fist pump.

* * *

As instructed by Luella, Addie turned the Wrangler onto the access road running beside the town council building, drove through the open gate of the secured parking lot, pulled around the back of the building, and stopped. "The gate was open, so she has to be here by now." Addie scanned the lot filled with an array of vehicles marked with the Pen Hollow municipal crest.

"There"—Paige pointed—"down there by the fence in front of the fire engine."

Addie pulled into the parking space on the far side of the bus, where Luella stood waiting for them. Addie turned off the ignition and hopped out onto the graveled lot.

"The painted mural across the bottom is absolutely charming." Addie nodded her approval as she walked around the front of the refurbished school bus. The word BOOKMOBILE ran across the hood in bold blue letters. When they climbed into the bus, Addie's eyes lit up. "It's perfect!"

Behind the driver's seat, a short checkout counter had been built in. Running the entire length of the bus on both sides were floor-to-roof bookshelves filled with—from what Addie could see—every category of books one would find in a regular library or bookstore. However, one thing concerned her. None of the bookshelves had brackets on the front of them to hold the books in place while traveling. A vision of the books flying into the aisle and she or Paige having to re-shelve them after every trip flashed through her mind.

The look on her face must have told Luella she had misgivings, and Luella quickly dropped into the driver's seat and turned over the ignition, which caught on the first try. She smiled at Addie. "It's just had a major tune-up and the annual maintenance work completed. Everything is in perfect running order, and I have the paperwork to show it. You wouldn't have to worry about any initial repairs or problems that might occur, if you're worried about that."

"That's not what crossed my mind." Addie glanced at Paige, who was already combing through a section of books by the door. "How do the books stay shelved when the bus is in motion?"

"Ah, so that's it." Luella checked the parking brake and got out of the seat, leaving the engine idling. "This is the best part. It's a little something we had installed with a generous donation from our old benefactor." She edged behind the checkout counter, flipped open the top of a metal box on the end of the adjoining bookcase, and pressed two buttons. The hum of a hydraulic motor filled the bus. From the top casing of the bookshelves, a metal shutter began to roll down, covering the bookcases. When it was secured against the floor, Luella turned a small handle marked *Locked* and closed the plate cover. "There, all the books are tucked in nice and snug."

Addie couldn't find the words to express her amazement. It was the same kind of system she had seen used for window security, and it worked perfectly here to secure the books in place. "Well, I'll be," was all she could manage.

Luella pressed the two buttons opening the shutters. "I have to pick up some papers from my office inside and take them back to the library, so why don't I leave you two to discuss what you want to do." As she made her way around the desk, she reached into the pocket of her blue blazer and pulled out a piece of paper. "I took the

liberty of jotting down the asking price," she said, handing it to Addie.

No matter what it says, don't let her see your reaction.
Addie blew out a shallow breath as she unfolded the
paper and glanced at the figures written on it. *Keep it together.* "We'll need a few minutes to discuss this," Addie
said, straining to keep her voice even.

"Of course, you two can mull that over, and I'll catch
up with you back here in a few minutes, and you can let
me know what you've decided." She started down the
steps and stopped. "Did I mention before that the bus is to
be sold as is and with all the books it's currently stocked
with? That should help you see that price there"—she
motioned to the paper clutched in Addie's hand—"is
more than fair, I should think."

With that bit of news added to sweeten the deal, Luella
power walked across the parking lot and in through the
back doors of the municipal building.

"Do you hear that?"

"What?" asked Paige.

"My heart pounding like a jackhammer." Addie thrust
the piece of paper into Paige's hand.

Chapter 5

"I think we've struck gold with this bus, don't you?" asked Addie. "I know the price is steep, and it will eat up nearly two years of my budgeted operating expenses. But with what we can make off this inventory and the increased advertising that attending the festivals will bring to the store, we'll be able to recoup the initial investment probably by the end of festival season this Thanksgiving."

"Provided, of course, the weather holds out," replied Paige absently as she checked out the titles down the aisle behind her.

"Yes, the weather. Something we have to consider as a variable but can't really factor into the plan as a constant." Addie tapped her finger on spine covers as she moved down the length of the bus. "Well, if not by Thanksgiving, then at least by early next year, so it's a win-win, don't you think?"

"Yeah, we'd have to remove the library bar codes first and then sell all these at a reduced price because they're stamped inside with *Property of the Pen Hollow Library Association*. See?" She flashed a title page in front of Addie's face. "But still, with what's here and what we'll probably find over at the library, we should make up the cost quickly." Paige placed the book on the shelf. "After all, most of the budget was allocated to purchasing new inventory anyway, and, well, inventory we will have with all these." She scanned the wall of books.

"Did you notice," Addie muttered almost to herself, "that the bottom shelves are filled with picture books, and the shelf above is easy reader chapter books, and they go up in degree of difficulty to the top rows, which are all classics and bestselling novels? Whoever organized these sure has a pulse on what readers are looking for and what height certain books should be placed at." She cocked her head to the side and paused when one title jumped out at her.

"Well, well, what do we have here?" Addie pulled a brown leather-bound book from the shelf and whistled. "Paige, come look at this. It's a first edition of Wilkie Collins's *The Woman in White*."

"You're kidding," cried Paige. "I just saw *The Murders in the Rue Morgue* by Edgar Allan Poe on this shelf." She pointed to one of the books she had just glanced at.

"Did it have a library stamp?"

"I didn't notice because I just assumed it would." She retrieved it from its slot and flipped to the title page. "No."

"Neither does this one." Addie stared curiously at Paige. "I wonder why."

Paige darted up the aisle toward the midsection. "I wonder if the copy I saw back here of *The Strange Case of Dr. Jekyll and Mr. Hyde* by Robert Louis Stevenson has a stamp." She tapped over spine titles and plucked the leather-bound book from its place. "No." She shook her head and fixed her stunned gaze on Addie. "It doesn't either."

"That's so odd." Addie took the book from her hand. "Look, it's a first edition too."

"Is there an inscription inside?"

"That won't explain why they're not bar coded or have the library stamps though."

"No, but maybe if there's a name inside, we could track down the person, and they could explain how these three books ended up here with the library books," said Paige.

"You're right, because they most likely got mixed up with their library returns."

"They are probably frantic, thinking they lost these somewhere."

"Yeah, that's the only explanation that makes sense."

"I wonder if there's more." Addie retraced her steps and looked closely at the titles and bindings. "Which of these don't look like the others?" she mused, scanning the books from the top shelf to the bottom shelves of each section. "Bingo! Here's another one!" She pulled a blue cloth-covered book from the second from the bottom row and flipped to the title page. "And it's an inscribed first edition. Robert Louis Stevenson's *A Child's Garden of Verses*."

"Really? Fantastic. Now, maybe we can figure out

who to return these to." Paige read the inscription aloud. *"To my dearest friend, Maisie, and your beloved new baby grandson, Anthony. May this bring you both great reading enjoyment for many years to come. All my love with a hint of tear-filled envy in your new-found happiness, your loyal friend, Anita xxx."*

Addie re-read the inscription. *It can't be, can it?* "Does that say *Anita*?" She glanced at Paige.

Paige's eyes lit up with comprehension. "You don't think this Anita could be your aunt, do you?"

"I just spoke to Patricia on the phone," chimed Luella, ascending the stairs into the bookmobile. "The library is packed. The turnout is bigger than we could have hoped for, so I instructed her to put SOLD signs on the pieces of furniture you indicated you were interested in buying because she said everything is moving. An area contractor even put a bid in on the fireplace wall. He wants to dismantle it and rebuild it in a house he's refitting." She clapped her hands together. "It's just the best news possible. Unless, of course, you're going to make my day even better and tell me you've decided to buy the bus too." She glanced expectantly from Addie to Paige. Her face fell. "What is it? Have you decided not to buy it?"

"No, on the contrary, we're most interested in purchasing the bookmobile."

"Yes, it's perfect for a traveling bookstore," echoed Paige.

"Then why the glum faces?"

Addie glanced down at the book in her hand and at the three Paige held close to her chest. "You told us the bus and the entire current inventory was included in the price you quoted."

"Yes, that's right."

"In full disclosure, we found these in the mix." She held out the first edition of *A Child's Garden of Verses.*

Luella stared blankly at the book and then at Addie. "How? Where?" She pressed her hand to her throat.

"On the shelves. The only thing we could think of was that when someone returned their library books, they must have accidentally put these in with them."

Luella shook her head and slid the book from Addie's fingers. "No, and I'm shocked." She turned the book over in her hand. "This book along with three others were donated to the library late last fall by our old benefactor, Mrs. Maisie Radcliff. They were to be sold at our past annual Christmas fundraiser."

"Do you mean these three books?" Paige held out the three she held in her hands.

Luella stared at them and then glanced up at Addie. "Yes, I'm stunned. Where did you say you found them?"

"Here." Addie waved her hand, motioning toward the shelves.

"Mixed in with the library books?"

Addie nodded.

"That's just so odd." Clearly confused, Luella stared at the bookshelves and then back at the books. "When we started to set up for the auction, these books were nowhere to be found. Of course, we panicked. Mrs. Radcliffe had been so good to the library committee for several years, and these books are worth a lot of money. We called the police, but the sheriff couldn't find any evidence of theft. Long story short, we held the auction; but without these, the funds we brought in was a drop in the bucket compared to what we needed to raise for renovations."

Addie pointed to *A Child's Garden of Verses.* "Do you know anything about the inscription written inside this one?"

Luella flipped to the title page and shook her head. "It's inscribed to Maisie, so it had to have been a friend of hers."

"Did you ever meet a woman named Anita Greyborne?"

"Can't say as I did. Judging by the name I'd say she's a relative of yours, is that right?"

"Yes, she was my great-aunt, and since Greyborne Harbor is close by, I wondered if this Anita could be her." Addie couldn't believe it. Could this inscription really have been written by her great-aunt, the same aunt whose estate she had inherited? Was Maisie the link her father had to Pen Hollow and perhaps the reason he had been traveling here when he was killed that fateful foggy evening?

"Sorry, I can't help," Luella said breathlessly. "Well, I'll have to get these back to the library and decide what to do with them now."

"If you sold them at auction now, would it be enough money to save the library from closing?" Addie glanced around the bus, knowing what her answer might mean to them about the sale of the bus.

"Not even close. Unfortunately, the money these might bring wouldn't even make a dent in the estimated costs of bringing the building up to code, paying continued operating expenses and maintenance of the building, or this budget drainer on wheels." She scowled. "It was the worst purchase we ever made from a budgetary standpoint. I should have had better sense than to allow Mrs. Radcliff and Patricia to talk me into it."

This comment had Addie second-guessing her decision to purchase the bookmobile. Was Luella implying it was a bad investment and was going to eat into her annual operating expenses?

"Don't get me wrong," said Luella, shoving the books into her large red-leather satchel. "The bookmobile was the perfect solution for the small fishing villages up and down the coast, to bring them the gift of reading. Some of those people had never before set foot in a bookstore, let alone a library."

Paige gave Addie's arm a nudge. "Something for us to keep in mind when we hit the road with this," she whispered.

"However, little did I know at the time that after Maisie passed away, her grandson would revoke the annual bursary endowment she bequeathed to the library, and we wouldn't have the funding for the library upkeep, let alone the operating cost of this!" She waved her hand as she stomped down the steps of the bus onto the parking lot pad. "I'll meet you back at the library so you can sign the paperwork, but first I have to get some answers from Patricia and her assistant, Bea, about these books and how they might have ended up on the shelves."

Addie and Paige arrived back at the library. As soon as they set foot on the landing, they were hit with a barrage of voices echoing up from the sale area below and the sound of shrill voices resonating down the stairs from the second floor. Addie no longer had to wonder what it would be like to be between two walls of colliding thunder.

"It sounds busy down there," said Paige, staring down the staircase. "I hope we're not too late to pick up some decent books."

Addie glanced upstairs to the raised voices echoing through the glass door at the top. "What do you think that's all about?"

Paige headed down the stairs "If I can hazard a guess, I'd say Luella is on a rampage about the books and is looking for answers."

"Yeah, and we know now it wasn't a patron that accidentally returned them, so my guess is she thinks Patricia must have mis-shelved them."

"But do you really think Patricia would make an error like that? Luella said she's been the head librarian here for over thirty years."

"You'd think after all that time she would know what library property was and what wasn't."

"You'd think so, wouldn't you?" said Paige thoughtfully. "Plus, Patricia would also have known the books were earmarked for the Christmas auction. So that means—"

"Someone took them at Christmas," said Addie, "and hid them in the bookmobile. Knowing full well they wouldn't be discovered until about this time of year because it was in storage all winter."

"It would have to have been someone who would be preparing the bus for the weekly seasonal runs."

"We need to find out who conducted the bookmobile runs."

"Addie, I know you love a good mystery, but does it really matter?"

Addie paused mid-step and studied Paige. "No, I suppose it doesn't. After all, no one died."

"Exactly. This seems like an internal issue and best left to Luella and Patricia to figure out. Clearly, a mistake was made when stocking the bus, and it's as simple as that."

"You're right. It just seems weird to me, but I'm glad we discovered the books when we did. If we hadn't and tried to sell them later, we could have ended up on the suspect list; she did say it had been reported to the police," Addie said with a short laugh as she continued her descent.

Above them a door slammed. Heavy footsteps clopped on the stairs behind them.

"Is it true?" shrieked a gray-haired, birdlike woman as she whipped herself around the banister railing onto the top of the landing.

Stunned, Addie stopped and gazed up at her. "You mean about the books?"

"Not just the books but the whole darn bookmobile," the woman hissed, and took a step down toward Addie.

"Patricia, stop that!" cried Luella from above. "It's not Miss Greyborne's fault. Like I told you already, the town council approved the payment for the bus and continues to pay for all the fuel and maintenance expenses. Therefore, we can do whatever it takes to recoup the money, and that includes selling it. Now, go find your assistant, Bea, like I instructed, and then both of you get back up here so we can figure out how Mrs. Radcliff's books ended up on that bus!"

"I already told you," hissed Patricia through a tightened jaw. "I have no idea how they got there. They must have somehow gotten mixed up with the library loan books and then mis-shelved. It was clearly an error when we were stocking the bus last winter. Which, I remind you, is when you told me that no matter what happened with the library, we would still operate the bookmobile because providing services to outlying communities was important to the memory of Maisie Radcliff and something we could do to honor her."

"Why in the world would we continue to fund the bookmobile when it is such a drain on town finances? Now, go and find Bea." Luella turned on her heel and slammed the upstairs door behind her.

Patricia glared at Addie as she stomped down the stairs past her and dashed into the library hall.

When she was out of earshot, Addie looked at Paige. "What do you make of all that?"

"I'm not sure, you?"

"I'm wondering if Patricia did know the books were there . . . Maybe she was even the person who hid them on the bus."

"But why would she sabotage the auction that would have helped the library?"

"I don't think the auction itself would have helped much, by the bits and pieces I've put together. Regardless of the fundraising, without Maisie Radcliff's money, the library was going to have to close."

"And since Patricia was head librarian, she would have known that."

"Yes, so perhaps hiding the books was her way of making sure there would be a nest egg for her to continue to run the bookmobile or pay for her retirement after she lost her job."

"She does seem more upset about the discovery of the books and hearing we bought the bus than the actual closing of the library."

"Yes, I expect she's scrambling now to figure out her next steps. Keep your eyes open. I get the feeling she's a feisty one, and I don't think she'll go down without a fight."

Chapter 6

Addie scribbled her signature on the bottom line where Luella had indicated, smiled with satisfaction, and handed the pen to Patricia to witness it.

Patricia begrudgingly snatched the pen from her fingers, scrawled her name on the appropriate line, and then dropped the pen on the desk. "I want it to be known that I do this under protest."

"Yes, Patricia," Luella said with an exasperated eye roll. "Your protest is duly noted." She glanced at Addie. "That only leaves the matter of the money exchange." She slid a piece of paper across the desk toward her. "This contains the library banking info you'll need to conduct the transfer of funds."

Addie retrieved her cell phone from her handbag, glanced at the paper, tapped in the information, reread her message, and pressed Send. "There. The total paid includes the purchase price of the bus and contents, as per our discussion, and the addition made to the sales contract for the two library tables, two bookcases, and the French Beech Sofa that we discussed earlier." Addie dropped her phone back in her bag. "You should get the verification notice within a few minutes."

"Thank you." Luella rubbed her hands together, grinning like a Cheshire cat. "Now, any books you're interested in, you can pay Patricia or one of the volunteers downstairs at the desk. Are there any questions?" She glanced from Addie to Paige.

"I think"—Addie pinned her expectant gaze on the woman—"that only leaves the matter of a copy of the sales receipt, the keys, and the registration papers so I can make arrangements with my insurance company as soon as possible."

"Right. Yes, you will need those, won't you? I'll make a photocopy of this for you." She turned to the small copier behind the desk, inserted the paper, and pressed the copy button. "The registration is in the bus. I was thinking that since I've already made arrangements for the local news station to be here to interview me after the potluck we're throwing for the volunteers, we could do an on-air ceremony of me handing over the keys to you."

Addie shifted uncomfortably, her thoughts immediately going to Pippi, who was still at Brianna's neighbor's house. "We really didn't plan on making an evening of it."

"I know it'll make for a long day. However, with all the turmoil the library closure has caused its patrons and volunteers, we wanted to give something back to them that might help lessen the blow. The dinner tonight is in honor of them, to show our appreciation. Plus, a televised event like this would be a great public relations story for your bookstore in Greyborne Harbor, while giving our community a glimmer of hope that all was not lost in this whole mess."

"I can phone Valerie," said Paige, looking hopefully at Addie. "I'm sure she won't mind watching Pippi for a few more hours, because Luella is right about the press coverage. It would be a big boon for the bookstore."

"I know. It's just that . . . okay . . . sure, as long as my dog sitter doesn't object."

"Wonderful. Some of the volunteers will be starting to set up for the dinner shortly, and then at six, we'll close the doors for the day, I'll grab a quick bite, and then head over to the parking lot to collect your bus and we can do the key ceremony."

Patricia harrumphed, spun on her heel, and marched out the door.

"Don't mind her," said Luella, waving her off. She pasted a smile on her aesthetically enhanced ruby lips. "Why don't the two of you run along now and head back down to the sale. I have some paperwork to look after, and I'll join you at the dinner." She fluttered her fingers, shooing them off, and slid into the chair behind the desk. "You can close the door behind you, thank you."

"I guess we've just been dismissed." Paige chuckled, closing the door. "I'll call Valerie now and let her know what's going on. We have to eat anyway and with any luck this won't run too long, then we stop and get Pippi and head out to the amusement park for some fun."

"Okay, but if Valerie even sounds a wee bit reluctant," said Addie, "tell her we'll be right back to get Pippi. I really do appreciate her taking her for the day and don't want to impose any more than we already have."

Paige nodded, tapped in the number, and stepped outside the entrance door to the second-floor main hall and meeting room.

A group of volunteers bustled about setting up buffet tables and arranging chairs into smaller conversation groupings. Addie glanced into the small kitchen where a hefty woman slid a foil-covered pan into an oven. Addie noted a number of other foiled-covered pans sat on the counter, and someone had arranged an assortment of yummy-looking dessert dishes on a side table.

"That's a lot of food," Addie called out.

The woman, sporting a hairnet over her salt-and-pepper hair, glanced over her shoulder at Addie. Her eyebrow arched.

"Sorry." Addie held out her hand. "I'm Addie, from Greyborne Harbor."

"Gretchen, the kitchen volunteer. Nice to meet you." She wiped her hand on her apron in response to Addie's extended hand. "What did you say when you came in? I'm a little hard of hearing in my right ear."

"I said that's a lot of food."

"Yes, and judging by the dishes that were dropped off, I think the turnout tonight will be much larger than we expected."

"Are these all donations then?"

"Oh yes, everyone attending the dinner was asked to contribute at least one dish, and judging by what's here, I think a few of them brought more than one. It looks like we might even have leftovers, which will be a first."

She turned back to the counter, picked up another pan, and slid it into the oven. "The trick is going to be to keep everything warm that should be served hot, and everything cool that is supposed to be." She mopped her brow with the corner of her apron. "Gad, it's like an oven in here already. Dang air-conditioning."

"We're all set," said Paige, sliding up to Addie's side. "Valerie said they had a wonderful afternoon in the garden and have just headed inside for her to start dinner. So, no problem, she loves the company and said for us to enjoy our evening. Feel better?"

"Yes, I do, and now that I smell all the delicious aromas coming out of the kitchen, I realized we haven't eaten today, and I'm starving." She laughed when her stomach rumbled in agreement.

Paige glanced at her phone before she tossed it into her bag. "There's still time for us to go down and see if we can add to our book purchases, because the dinner's not going to start for another hour. Then, we can do something about that." She gave a pointed look at Addie's grumbling tummy.

"All right, but I have to be careful. I've already spent enough money for the day. As it stands, my accountant is going to have a stroke when he sees how much money I just transferred out," Addie said with a tentative laugh.

An hour later, and another box filled with books secured in the back of the Wrangler along with the smaller of the two library tables, Paige and Addie took their place in the lineup at the buffet tables.

"I do feel guilty about eating any of this when we didn't make a contribution." Addie eyed the assortment of food displayed on the table in front of them.

"Guilty enough not to eat?" Paige grinned.

"Not even close," Addie said, stabbing a serving fork into a delicious-looking Swedish meatball and plopping it onto her paper plate.

"Addie." Luella's tawny-brown head of loose-flowing hair poked between her and Paige. "Do you like chocolate mint?"

Addie pulled back and stared at her. "Um, yes, why?"

"It's just that"—she waved her gravy-stained empty plate—"I'm on to dessert now, and see the crystal dish of chocolates there in the middle of the table?"

Addie nodded.

"The serving tongs seem to have disappeared, and there, right on top, is a delicious-looking chocolate mint patty. But I'm not a fan of those, and I want the chocolate-covered cherry one right under it, but I don't want to poke around for it in the dish with my fingers. Could you, please?"

"I see." Addie chuckled and plucked the mint patty from the dish and set it on the edge of her plate.

Luella excitedly removed the chocolate-covered cherry from the dish and popped it into her mouth and closed her eyes. A smile of deep satisfaction crossed over her face. "Mm . . . perfection. There, now I'm done eating." She dabbed a napkin to the corner of her lip. "The television crews just arrived and are outside setting up. So, I'll head over to the parking lot to pick up the bus. I should be back in about fifteen minutes, and hopefully by then they'll be ready to roll." She turned on her heel, sashayed into the office, and called back over her shoulder, "See you downstairs then."

Luella grabbed her red leather satchel from behind the desk, removed the four books they had discovered earlier, shouldered her handbag, closed the office door, and marched off toward the staircase.

"I guess it's officially going to happen," Addie whispered to Paige.

"I thought it was already official."

"It is, but in fifteen minutes there will be documented video evidence, and, boy, I'm going to need to re-watch that over and over again until it sinks in how much money I spent today."

"Fifteen minutes?" cried Paige in protest. "I'll never get through this plate of food by then."

"Start shoveling," said Addie with a short laugh as she brought a forkful up to her lips.

"Addie? Addie Greyborne? Is that you?"

She spun around and gaped. A striking, stubble-chinned man with a lustrous head of brown-sugar-colored hair smiled at her. She snapped her mouth shut and stared into a pair of jewel-like cognac-brown eyes. "Tony?"

"I can't believe it. What are you doing in Pen Hollow?"

"Me?" she cried, dropping her plate on the end corner of the buffet table. "What about you?"

"I'm here on business."

"Me too, but what—I can't believe—this is so weird after all these years."

"I know, right?" He trailed his fingers through his wavy hair. "I never thought I'd see you again, and yet here we are in Pen Hollow of all places."

"What happened to you? I mean . . . wow! I can't believe this." She looked at Paige and then back at Tony. "It's so weird. I thought I saw you earlier today and then decided I must be seeing things."

Paige squealed. "I told you we should have gone back to see if it was him."

"Umm, Tony, this is my friend Paige."

He nodded in greeting.

"She's right though," said Addie, trying to formulate her thoughts. "I guess we should have gone back, but I couldn't believe it was really you I saw because you just disappeared senior year, not a word, a letter, a call, nothing. You fell off the face of the earth it seemed."

"Ah, yes, that was an interesting year. Let's get out of here and grab a drink over at the hotel bar, and I can tell you my long story of woe, and you can fill me in on the last sixteen years of your life. How does that sound?"

"Oh, Tony, really, there's nothing better that I'd like to do, but this evening isn't a good time, you see—"

"It's okay." He waved his hands. "You don't need to explain. After all this time, I can't expect you to change your plans instantly for me."

"It's not that I don't want to catch up. It's just that tonight's not a good night."

"Look, I'll be in town for another month or so before I head back to England. We can get together another time."

"I thought I detected a bit of an English accent."

"Yes, it's where I call home now, but my grandmother passed away last Christmas, and there are a number of loose ends I've had to tie up. It's taking longer than I figured it would."

"Maisie Radcliff, the benefactor of the library association, was your grandmother?"

"Yes, and *was* the benefactor to be more precise. Things have changed since she—"

"Addie," interrupted Patricia. "I see you've met our local bestselling author."

Addie stared blankly at Tony.

"Anthony Radcliff?" Patricia said, giving Addie a curious look.

"You're *the* Anthony Radcliff?" Addie stared wide-mouthed at him. "The mysterious author of some of my favorite gothic horror novels?"

"Guilty as charged." He grinned impishly. "But don't feel bad for not recognizing me as him. I don't like being in the limelight, so I don't allow photos of me to be published." His high cheekbones turned a rosy shade of red.

Addie staggered a step back. "I can see that we do have a lot of catching up to do."

"Patricia." Bea, the brown-haired, skittish, mouselike assistant librarian, pulled on her blouse sleeve. "I hate to interrupt, but the sheriff called and asked if you can go to the corner of Sea Spray Drive and the town council building."

Patricia swiped at her assistant's hand as though it were an annoying insect. "Can't you see I'm busy?"

"But he said it's important," Bea said, her eyes filling with tears.

"What on earth could be so important? Did Luella forget the bus keys or something? If that's it, I'm not going anywhere. Why in the world would I want to be a party to her selling *our* bookmobile out from under us?"

"That's just the thing." Bea choked back a trickle of tears. "I guess there's been an accident and . . . Luella's dead."

Chapter 7

Addie stared into the sink of steaming, bubbly water. Her mind and hands were disjointed in thought and action. She couldn't shake the sheriff's news and the sick grumblings in the pit of her stomach over what happened this evening. *Luella's dead and the bookmobile is a write-off.*

"Addie, you've been washing the same pan for over five minutes. I'm fairly certain it's clean by now."

She gave Tony a weak smile. "I suppose you're right." She rinsed it and handed it to him to dry.

"Even though I love spending this time with you, which is the only reason why I volunteered to help clean up after the dinner came to such an abrupt end, I hadn't counted on receiving the silent treatment, especially when we have so much catching up to do." He wiped the pan with a dish towel and stacked it on the sideboard by the large farmhouse sink.

"I know, and I'm sorry. It's been so long, and we do have a lot to talk about. But I'm just sick about what happened this evening. It's all so sad and . . . never mind." She shook her head, rinsed another pan, and handed it to him.

"If you ask me, the real tragedy is in the damage to the bus you had the pleasure of owning for all of an hour."

"Tony!"

"It's true, isn't it? Hadn't you just paid for it? That's a big financial hit for you."

"Yes, and that's unfortunate, but the real tragedy is a woman *died* tonight."

"Did you know her well?"

"No, I only met her today, but that's not the point."

"If you knew her like the rest of us did, you wouldn't be so heartbroken over her death." He moved the stack of pans from the side table to a space on the counter by the stove.

Addie stared at the back of his head. Did he just say what she thought he did? "So you're saying she deserved to die?"

"That's not what I meant. It's only that Luella rubbed a lot of people the wrong way, and I was one of them."

"I had picked up on the fact that she did blame Maisie's grandson for the loss of funding to the library and that's why it had to close."

"That's not the half of it." He came to her side and slipped another pot from her water-pruned fingertips. "Did she tell you that when I arrived in December because my grandmother's health had taken a sudden turn for the worse, I discovered that she'd just changed her will? Under Luella's convincing, my grandmother not only donated some very pricy first editions to the library, but she also set up a healthy bequest to them, guaranteeing annual future funding."

"I heard your grandmother was a big supporter of the library association and felt it important for them to be able to continue to operate. Wasn't it her goal to keep libraries open with the state cutting funding to them?"

"I imagine that Luella left out the part that in her last years, my grandmother suffered from progressive dementia and could easily be persuaded by every charlatan that crossed her path. Let me tell you, Luella was the worst, because over the years my grandmother had come to trust her. In the end, that woman took advantage of that. I hope this accident calls for an investigation into Luella Higgins's financial records." He slammed the pan on the counter. "I don't believe for one minute that all the money she convinced my grandmother to hand over went into the library accounts. That's why, when my power of attorney was enacted due to Maisie's health and mental state, I put a stop to it. Especially when I discovered that the rare books she had donated went missing. Does that sound like everything was on the up-and-up to you? No, I'd say Luella took those books, sold them, and pocketed the money."

"Then you didn't hear?"

"Hear what?" he snapped.

"Paige and I found those missing books this afternoon mixed in with the library books on the bookmobile."

"What! No, I hadn't heard. I have a hard time believing that though."

"Are you trying to tell me we didn't, and they're not sitting on Luella's desk over there in the office right now?"

"No, that's not what I meant. It's just that when the books were discovered missing, the sheriff conducted a thorough investigation. I should know. I made certain of it as I wasn't happy at all about the first edition books being donated in the first place."

"Did he check the bus?"

"Yes, and he had his deputies search the entire library."

"That means the books were shelved after the investigation."

"What did you say?"

"Nothing, it just seems weird they didn't turn up then, but Paige and I found all four of them today."

Paige bustled through the kitchen door, juggling two large plastic-wrapped platters in her hands. "Tony, can you open the fridge for me?"

He darted to the door and flung it open. "Yikes, will those fit?"

"I hope so. They're the last of the food to be saved." Paige managed to maneuver the platters into the overflowing fridge and closed the door. "Fingers crossed they don't crash to the floor when the next person opens it."

"That's a lot of leftovers," said Addie, rinsing the last pan. "It's a good idea, though, to save it until tomorrow and serve a lunch buffet for the volunteers since their appreciation dinner was cut short. It's hard to believe that this tragedy happened. I mean, the parking lot is only a few blocks away and . . ."

Paige leaned against the wall by the door and crossed her arms. "Wanna hear the weirdest thing?"

"It gets weirder?" asked Addie.

"Yes, I overheard one of the deputies telling Patricia that when Luella pulled out of the parking lot access road into traffic, she never made the left turn onto Sea Spray Drive to come back to the library."

"What do you mean?"

"He said she went straight ahead and smashed into the sea wall, head-on, and was traveling at a high speed."

Addie looked at Tony and then at Paige. "That doesn't make sense. Why would she shoot straight across two lanes of traffic?"

Paige shrugged. "Got me, but that's what he said."

"Does he think it was mechanical failure?" Tony asked, drying the last pan as Addie let the water out of the sink.

"I don't know. They're going to do a mechanical check, of course, but it sure sounds like it to me. Which makes me grateful that nothing happened to us while we—well, you know, drove it back to Greyborne Harbor."

"The news just gets better and better, doesn't it? I took Luella at her word about the recent maintenance performed on the bus and—" Addie slammed her fist on the counter. "If he's right—" A sick feeling in her tummy rose and met with a lump in her throat. She gasped. "One of us could have been killed driving it home!"

"The deputy also told her that they suspect drugs or alcohol might have contributed. So her body's been sent to the area coroner for testing."

"Is Pen Hollow in Essex County?"

Paige nodded.

"Then that's still Simon's jurisdiction, right?"

"Yes," said Paige, "and am I horrible to hope he finds

out that one of those tests comes back positive? Just to know that she didn't knowingly sell us a mechanically defective vehicle."

"No, not horrible, as I hate to think she lied about the mechanical inspection." She glanced at Paige and Tony. "Did either of you see her drink anything other than coffee tonight?"

"No," said Tony, "but that doesn't mean she wasn't popping pills on the sly or didn't have a bottle hidden in her desk. She is pretty tightly wound most of the time and was getting a lot of flak about closing the library, so maybe . . ." He shrugged.

"I guess." Addie wiped off the sideboard beside the sink. "We'll just have to wait to see what Simon's report comes back with."

"Do you always refer to the area coroner by his given name?"

"What do you mean?"

"I mean it seems rather familiar, or is Greyborne Harbor such a small town that everyone refers to each other that casually?"

"Simon is the love of Addie's life, and he has something special planned for her tomorrow night. Isn't that right, Addie?" Paige winked mischievously.

"Would that something special include putting a ring on that bare finger?" He glanced at Addie's left hand. "If truth be known, the thought strikes an arrow deep into my heart." His hands shot to his chest, and he feigned being shot in the chest.

"What? After all these years, now you're telling me you'd be heartbroken if I was to marry someone else?" She hurled the soggy dishcloth at him. "You're just as incorrigible now as you were back in high school." She laughed when the cloth caught the side of his head and spewed water down his face.

"Really, Addie, that's how you want to play this? You and this doctor friend of yours are breaking my heart and . . . and . . ." He snatched the damp kitchen towel hanging from a rod, twirled it in his hands corkscrew style, and snapped it out like a whip. She spun away, the towel just missing thwacking her bottom. "I loved you. We were going to get married. I guess when I saw you here tonight, and I noticed you're not wearing a ring, it meant we were truly fated to keep our promise to each other. That's why we're both here after sixteen years."

"What promise?"

"You don't remember?"

Addie shook her head.

"Well, by my calculations, and if memory serves me right, it's almost your thirty-fifth birthday, right?"

"You remember when my birthday is?"

"Of course, it's two months to the day after mine, re-member?"

"That's right."

"And we made a pact that if we were both single when we were thirty-five, we'd marry each other."

"Yes, but we were kids then and so much has changed. Besides, how can you hold me to that when you disap-peared on me without a word? I thought you were dead or something."

The laughter disappeared from his eyes. "Not me, my parents."

"I'm so sorry. I never knew."

"No one did."

"I can't believe that was something everyone wasn't talking about."

"The authorities wanted the incident kept quiet because of the international implications and the possible diplomatic fallout that would ensue."

"You're kidding?"

"So I had to cut ties with everyone I knew in case I slipped up, and had to come here to Pen Hollow to live with my grandmother, and, well . . ."

"Tony, I wish I had known."

"There was no way you could."

"Can you talk about it now?"

"Yes, but"—he glanced around—"not here. I'll tell you later."

Addie nodded in agreement. "Then tell me how you ever started a writing career. I don't recall you ever having those aspirations in high school."

"When I couldn't reach out to my friends, I found that writing really helped me not to feel so alone. My mind went to some pretty dark places," he said with a short laugh. "I guess that's why I started writing gothic mystery tales, plus I was trying to make sense out of my parents' deaths."

"In any case—" Addie grimaced, unsure of her next words. "I guess if there is a silver lining to what happened—if there could be one—you've been the hottest author on the bestsellers list for the last five years. According to what I read in the *New York Times*, three of your books have been optioned for movies," she said, adding a lighthearted lilt to her voice, hoping it would dispel the haunted look clouding his eyes.

"Addie," said Patricia, poking her head into the kitchen. "Are you nearly finished in here?"

"Um, yes." She looked at the peevish woman. "I think we're almost done. Are you waiting to lock up?"

"I have to run. My cat needs feeding. Jody and Bea are just finishing up mopping the floors. Bea has a key and will lock up as soon as you're ready to go."

"Okay, thanks, we'll just be a minute." Addie glanced at Paige as Patricia bustled out the door and marched across the meeting room. "Is it just me or doesn't she seem fazed in the least about Luella's death?"

"I told you," said Tony, "not many people around here will be sad at her passing. But it is late, and I should go too." He reached into the inside pocket of his navy blazer and removed a small notepad. "A tool of the writer." He laughed at the surprised look on Addie's face. "I always carry one of these. You just never know when you'll get an idea for a book. Jot down your phone number, and I'll call you tomorrow so we can arrange to get together while you're in town."

"I'm afraid we're leaving tomorrow."

"What time?"

"We had hoped about noon. Paige has a little girl she has to get home to, and I—"

"You have a doctor who is planning on slipping a ring on that bare finger of yours tomorrow night for your birthday surprise, right?"

A hot blush crept up Addie's collar to her cheeks. "Well, I don't know about that, but, yes, I have plans for dinner."

"Oh, come on." Paige laughed and hung the dish towels on the rod to dry. "You know what Simon has planned for you. He's been dying to propose since Christmas."

Addie scribbled her number on the notepad and handed it back to Tony. "We could meet for an early lunch. At least do some catching up."

"Great, I'll call you in the morning." He kissed her

cheek lightly and turned to Paige. "It was a pleasure to meet you, and I hope you'll join us for lunch too."

"I'd love to. I've read all your books and . . . no, maybe I shouldn't. I'd just be a fan girl and ask you so many questions. This is your time to catch up with an old friend, so no, I don't think I will. Thanks, anyway."

"Until tomorrow." Tony saluted Addie and turned away, but then stopped, spun around, and in one sweeping motion pulled Addie into his arms and placed a passionate kiss on her lips.

Addie's eyes flew wide. She pulled away and wiped the back of her hand over her lips. "What are you doing?"

Tony gazed into her eyes. "Something I've wanted to do since the very moment I saw you tonight."

"But I told you—"

He placed a finger over her lips, quieting her. "I know I shouldn't have, and I do apologize. It was a silly impulse. I guess you brought out the seventeen-year-old in me. So, until tomorrow, my old friend." He lightly kissed the back of her hand and turned and hurried off.

"Are you okay, Addie?"

"What will I tell Simon?" She grabbed the edge of the counter when her knees buckled, and touched her fingers to her lips.

"That an old high school friend got over exuberant and kissed you, but that I was there and can swear you never kissed him back."

Addie clutched at the counter edge and tried to wrap her head around what just happened. "I have to cancel the lunch tomorrow. There's no way I can go. Tony seems to have the wrong idea about us seeing each other again."

"Don't jump to conclusions. He did just apologize and call you 'old friend,' so why pass up the chance to catch up with him before you see what his true intentions are? If it makes you feel better, I can tag along too."

"Would you mind?"

"Not at all." Paige smiled over at her as she put a baking pan in a cupboard. "I've never met a famous author before, and I promise I'll sit there quiet as a church mouse while you two talk. I'll even put my fingers in my ears so I can't hear a word."

"There's nothing we're going to talk about that you shouldn't hear, and I'll make sure to set Mr. Famous Author straight about how I feel after sixteen years."

"Then it's settled. You have your reunion, and I'll chaperone."

"Yeah, even after that I would like to hear what's been going on, and he did seem remorseful about the . . . well, you know." Addie straightened herself up and came to terms with what just occurred. "Yes, I really do want to see him again after all this time, and as long as you come too, it should be fine."

"Good," said Paige. "Then first thing in the morning, we can head over to the sheriff's office and inspect the damage on the bus and figure out what to do about it. Then we can meet Tony for lunch, and as soon as we're finished eating, we can head back to Greyborne Harbor."

"Sounds like a plan." Addie flipped off the light in the kitchen. She glanced around the meeting room. "I wonder where Bea and Jody are?"

"Probably making sure everything is okay for the night, downstairs in the library, before they lock up."

"You're right." Addie shouldered her bag and stopped. "That's weird."

"What is?"

"Luella's office door is slightly open."

"I don't think it's her office. I think it's just the library office."

"I know, but those first edition books are in there and"—Addie pushed the door open—"they're gone."

"Someone must have put them away for the night." Paige poked her head under Addie's arm. "Probably Patricia before she left."

"You're right, but I'm going to ask her tomorrow. Remember, I have a hunch about their disappearance last winter, and that hunch tells me Patricia knows more about the books than she's saying, so—"

"You also remember this is an internal issue that doesn't involve us, so keep your busybody sleuthing nose out of it." Paige shooed Addie toward the exit.

Chapter 8

"Mmm, it smells good in here," said Addie absently as she walked into the kitchen, her head down as she scrolled through her phone.

"Happy birthday!" cried Paige. "I hope cinnamon flapjacks with apple butter are still your favorite."

"Weird."

"What's weird? The cinnamon pancakes or my cooking?"

"Not that, and thank you." Addie glanced up and gave Paige an appreciative smile. "It's just that I have two missed calls this morning from Simon . . . shoot! I put my phone on airplane mode for the dinner last night and forgot to turn it back on."

"He called me this morning too and said to have you phone him as soon as you were up."

"He called you? Hmm, I wonder what's so important."

"He probably just wants to wish you happy birthday and make sure you'll be back in time for that *special* dinner he has planned." She giggled and piled flapjacks onto two plates and set them on the island.

"Yeah, I guess you'd be the one to call since he couldn't reach me. Anyway, it all looks great." She smiled at the vase filled with fresh cut flowers Paige had arranged for the birthday breakfast. "Sorry, but I'll be back in a minute." Addie punched in the number and headed back out into the hallway.

"Don't be long. This will get cold, and we're going to need some fortification before we see what's left of the bookmobile," Paige called out, her muffled words hinting that she had shoveled a forkful of pancake into her mouth.

When Addie returned to the kitchen moments later and spied syrup dribbling down the corners of Paige's mouth, she knew her suspicions had been correct. "You just couldn't wait for me, could you?" She laughed and pulled up one of the counter stools.

Paige shook her head and downed a large gulp of orange juice. "No." She sputtered juice escaping from the corner of her mouth. "I don't know about you, but half a meatball for dinner last night and the box of stale crackers we found in the cupboard when we got back from the library just didn't do the culinary trick yesterday."

"I know. I've never been so hungry in my life." Addie scooped up a mouthful and purred. "These are amazing. Thank you. Best birthday breakfast ever."

"I guess when you're starving, anything tastes good."

"Don't sell yourself short. You definitely inherited your mother's cooking genes."

Paige grinned. "Thanks, but that was a short call with

Simon. What did he want? Was it to wish you happy birthday?"

"No, there was no answer." Addie sipped her juice and glanced around the kitchen. "Is there any coffee?"

"I haven't been able to find the coffeepot yet. Bree and Darren are tea drinkers now—at least, Darren is when he's home. I imagine when he's working, he guzzles the station coffee by the gallon. But last year my sister got on this no-caffeine kick, so she's stored the coffeemaker somewhere. I'll look again later." She shrugged and scraped the last of her flapjacks and syrup into her mouth. "Until I find it, there's a coffee shop down on Sea Spray that we can stop at on our way to the sheriff's office." She rinsed her plate and put it in the dishwasher.

"Perfect! As much as I like tea now that Serena has me onto it, I still can't start my day without a good kick of hot java." Addie rinsed her plate and placed it and the cutlery into the dishwasher and glanced over her shoulder at the doggie dish filled with kibble. "Why hasn't Pippi eaten her breakfast yet?"

Paige glanced at the bowl then at the back door off the kitchen. "Oh dear, I got so wrapped up in making the flapjacks, I completely forgot about her being outside," she said and dashed to the door, flinging it open. "Pippi, come on girl, breakfast time."

No response.

"Pippi, here girl, come on." Paige clucked her tongue. "Come on, time to eat . . ."

Addie grabbed the bowl of kibble and scooted past Paige in the doorway and shook it as she raced down the back stairs. "Here girl, come on, breakfast time." She glanced up at Paige. "I thought the yard was fenced?"

"It is, but . . ."

"But what?"

"Pippi's so small maybe she found an opening somewhere."

Addie gasped and raced to the side of the house. "Pippi, here girl, come on, come see Mommy." She shook the dish of kibble, hoping her little friend would hear the sound of food and come running.

"Yoo-hoo, over here," called Valerie from the front corner of the fence between the two yards. There was Pippi standing gopher style, balancing on her hind legs, as Valerie dropped pieces of kibble over the fence to her.

Paige raced around the house and thwacked into the back side of Addie. "What the—Oh, hi, Valerie."

"I hope you don't mind. There were a few pieces of her food left over from her dinner last night, and I thought she might like a little treat."

"No, I don't mind, I just hope she wasn't bothering you."

"Not in the least. She's such a sweetie, aren't you girl?"

Pippi yipped and scratched her front paws in the air, begging for another piece of kibble.

"Oh, Pippi, you're so spoiled, but come here. We have to get going." Addie scooped her furry friend into her arms. "Say good-bye to the nice lady."

Pippi yipped.

"Aw, I'm going to miss you, little friend." Valerie reached over the fence and patted Pippi's head. "You tell your mommy that you're welcome to come and stay with me anytime, do you hear?"

Pippi's pink little tongue lapped across the woman's hand.

"I mean it," said Valerie. "Whenever you need a dog

sitter, I'd be happy to help out. Having her around made me see that my niece is right. Since my George passed, a little friend like this is exactly what I'm missing in my life." She scruffled the fur behind Pippi's ears. "So, who knows, perhaps when you came back again, I'll have a little playmate for you. How does that sound?"

"Thank you for the offer, but we really have to get going."

"Are you heading back to Greyborne Harbor now?"

"No, we have a couple of stops to make first."

"Yeah," said Paige, "and the first one's at the sheriff's office."

"The sheriff's office? Whatever for?"

"Um . . ." Addie shifted Pippi into the crook of her arm. "I'm not sure if you heard about what happened last evening."

"You mean that nasty business about Luella and the crash?"

Addie nodded.

"Yes, Jody Pettigrew called me this morning and told me. It's too bad, of course, but I can't say that I'm all that upset about it. I do hope now that she's gone, Patricia will be able to save the library from closing."

"How would she do that? According to Luella, they lost their funding, and from the little the state contributes, there isn't near enough to pay the building repairs and cover the operational costs."

"Patricia's a smart cookie. She's probably got a card or two up her sleeve, if I know her like I do."

"Or a book," whispered Addie to Paige.

"But why do you have to see the sheriff if she was killed in an accident?"

"Sadly, we had just purchased the bookmobile, and Luella had gone to the town parking lot to retrieve it for us and—"

"Oh . . . I see. I bet that didn't sit well with Patricia, did it?" She shook her head. "I don't think the sale of the bookmobile would have been a popular move with many of the folks around here. It was the library's pride and joy. But I sure hope that old goat of a sheriff isn't saying you're somehow responsible as the owners of the bus."

"I don't think so." Addie glanced questioningly at Paige. "But I guess we'll find out soon."

"So, you're heading over there now?"

"Yes, and then we're meeting an old friend of Addie's for her birthday lunch before we head back to Greyborne Harbor."

"Oh my, it's your birthday? How wonderful." Valerie glanced at Pippi, then at Addie. "Surely you don't want the bother of looking after her while you're talking to the old goat and then trying to have a nice lunch. Why not leave her with me until you're ready to head home?"

"We couldn't impose on you again."

"Nonsense, it's not an imposition," said Valerie, reaching over the fence with outstretched arms.

"If you're sure?"

"Yes, my niece is coming later this afternoon to take me to the library sale, and I'm sure you'll be done by then. Now, skedaddle, and enjoy your birthday lunch." She cuddled Pippi into her chest. "We'll be just fine, don't worry."

"Okay, thanks. Oh, and here's her breakfast."

Valerie took the dish with her free hand and held the bowl up to Pippi's face so she could take a nibble.

* * *

"Valerie sure has taken to Pippi, hasn't she," said Paige as she pulled into an angled parking spot in front the sheriff's office.

"You have to admit Pippi is lovable. I don't think I've ever met anyone who didn't take to her." Addie flung the passenger door open and hopped out onto the curb. She glanced past the SHERIFF'S OFFICE sign and scanned the stone building and its adjacent STAFF AND OFFICIAL VISITORS ONLY parking lot and gasped. "Isn't that Simon's Tesla parked in that visitor spot?"

"It sure looks like it," said Paige, joining her on the sidewalk. "When I talked to him he never said a word about coming to Pen Hollow this morning. Did he say anything to you in his messages?"

"No, not a word."

"But then again," added Paige, "he can't be the only person on the East Coast that drives a silver Tesla sport coupe, right?"

"Right. That's a pretty fancy hotel we passed back there. I'm sure it belongs to one of their guests who just happens to have police business." Addie eyed the car again, shrugged, and followed Paige through the door of the station.

"Good morning. May I help you?" A fresh-faced deputy rose to his feet from behind a desk by the front counter.

Addie slid her sunglasses up on her head and glanced around the small room. No Simon. There was no one except the young officer and a more seasoned-looking deputy at a back corner desk of the communal office space.

"Good morning." She smiled and approached the counter. "My name is Addie Greyborne, and I understand that a bookmobile bus I purchased yesterday was involved in a crash. I was wondering if you'd completed the mechanical inspection and are ready to release it?" she asked hopefully. "I'd like to make arrangements to have it towed back to Greyborne Harbor."

His steely eyes narrowed. "You mean the fatality accident yesterday evening?" He picked up a file folder from his desk and dropped it on the countertop.

"Yes, sadly, that's the one, but if you're not finished inspecting it, could I, at least, take some photos for my insurance company?" She glanced at Paige. "Fingers crossed they'll cover the damages even though I'd only purchased it less than an hour before the accident."

The deputy opened the folder and thumbed through the papers. "Addie Greyborne, you say?"

"Yes."

"Just a moment." He peered over at the door with a gold sign engraved with Sheriff Jack Turner.

"I have the paperwork to prove it's mine if there's an issue with the registration." She retrieved the bill of sale from her satchel and passed it across the desk to him.

He scanned it, glanced up at her, and then again at the door. "Please have a seat." He motioned to four chairs against the wall. "I'll be back in a minute." He knocked on the sheriff's door and, at the entry command by a gruff voice, slipped inside and closed the door behind him.

Addie strained to get a view of who was in the room, but the young deputy was too quick for her. She sat down beside Paige and moaned. "I suddenly got a funny feeling about this. I sure hope Valerie wasn't right about this sheriff holding me responsible for the accident and blaming me as being a negligent owner or something if they discovered any mechanical issues with the bus."

"How could he? You owned it for an hour, and besides, Luella said there was paperwork to back up her claim everything was in good running order." Paige squeezed her hand reassuringly. "If there were mechanical issues with the bus, it would fall back on the library or the mechanic, not you."

"I hope you're right," Addie said, resting her head against the wall behind her chair. Unable to shake the edgy feeling in her gut, she stared at the sheriff's door so long the name etched in the gold-plated sign began swirling.

Chapter 9

Addie sat upright at the sound of the sheriff's office door opening. This time the deputy left it ajar as he approached the counter, giving Addie a clear line of sight past him. "Simon? Marc? What the . . . ?" She rose to her feet as the door closed. "What's going on?" She glanced at the deputy.

"Have a seat, please. Sheriff Turner will be out in a minute."

"But why are Chief Chandler and Doctor Emerson here?'"

"Please, miss." He waved his hand toward the chairs. "Have a seat."

"But . . ."

"Sit down, please." His eyes were grim but determined, and Addie knew this was a standoff she wasn't going to win.

"Did you see that?" Addie hissed in Paige's ear as she reluctantly dropped back onto the chair. "He's worse than any of the desk sergeants the Greyborne Harbor Police Department have, that's for sure." She crossed her arms and frowned, shooting daggers at the young deputy with her glare.

"Have you ever met Sheriff Turner?" whispered Paige from behind her cupped hand.

"No, why?"

"When you do, you'll understand why he's following orders to the letter."

"But Simon and Marc are in the office."

"So?"

"So? I'm the owner of the bus. I have a right to know what's going on."

"Do you?"

"Well, yes."

"You're not in Kansas anymore, Dorothy. This is Sheriff Turner's town, and like the Wizard, he makes his own rules."

The door opened and a medium-height, barrel-chested man with a graying crew cut, donned in the typical sheriff's department beige shirt and brown trousers, stalked out and headed for the coffeemaker along the back wall. He filled two Styrofoam cups, mixed creamer and sugar into one, left the other black, and sauntered back into his office. Simon reached over behind him and closed the door without even a glance in Addie's direction.

"Ha, of all the nerve!" She turned her dagger glare onto the closed door. "This is all very weird, don't you think?"

"It's your birthday. Of course, it's weird." Paige sighed and yawned.

"What does that mean?"

"It means that if things are going to go sideways and get weird on us, they will on your birthday. It's sort of a Murphy's Law."

"I don't think this weirdness has anything to do with an old adage."

"What then? Or are you just upset because you didn't know Simon was going to be here?"

"Don't forget he's here with Marc. That alone is weirdness. They're like oil and water and have been as long as they've known each other."

"Yeah, except they work together."

"Yes, *work* being the key word. So, what are the two of them doing here in Pen Hollow this morning? Luella's death was due to a motor vehicle accident, wasn't it?"

Paige pushed herself upright in the chair and stared at Addie. "I see what you're getting at. If it was an accident, then why would Simon—"

"And . . . Marc, even though this is out of his jurisdiction—"

"Be with him?"

"Exactly. The fact that they're in Sheriff Turner's office tells us Simon didn't just show up in town this morning to surprise me on my birthday."

"Unless they got arrested on their way in for speeding or something. He does drive a sport coupe."

"But—and I'll repeat the weird part again—he and Marc *aren't* friends outside of work. There's no way the two of them would go on a nice friendly outing to Pen Hollow for the day." Addie peered again at the closed door. "Unless it is work related, and Simon found something in the autopsy that showed Luella's death wasn't an accident."

Paige rolled her eyes. "You know, not every death is a murder."

"I know." Addie folded her arms and leaned her head back against the wall. "But why else would the two of them be here . . . *together*."

"It looks like we're about to find out," said Paige, rising. "And judging by the looks on their faces . . ."

"No one is happy about whatever was said in there," said Addie, joining her.

"Miss Greyborne." Sheriff Turner waved her over to the counter. His tone sounded more perturbed than one would expect upon meeting a stranger. "I understand from Deputy Roberts here that you're the owner of the bookmobile that was involved in the fatality collision yesterday at approximately six forty-five p.m." He glanced over his shoulder at a stone-faced Marc.

"Yes."

"Can I assume that as substantiated by *several* witnesses that you were also in attendance at the dinner which took place at the library prior to the accident?"

Addie gazed over at Simon and detected an ever-so-slight head nod. Was he encouraging her to answer or was he finally giving her some recognition? "Yes, we were there."

Sheriff Turner's unwavering gaze flitted from Paige to Addie. "There have been some developments in this case, and your bus will not be released until the investigation is complete." His large chest rose as he filled his lungs with a deep wheezing breath. He tapped the counter with a chapped knuckle. "Also, don't leave town until this matter has been concluded." With those words, he brushed past Marc and Simon and marched back into his office.

Addie jerked at the slamming door and glanced in stunned silence at Simon.

"We have to talk," he whispered, glancing at Deputy Roberts. "Let's go somewhere and grab a coffee."

His tone, cool and businesslike, was more a command than a coffee invitation, so she nodded and she and Paige followed Simon and Marc out onto the street.

She stopped. "I'm not taking another step until one of you tells us what's going on and—"

"And why we can't leave town," interjected Paige. Her voice teetered on panic and rose to a sharp shrill. "I have to get back to Emma this afternoon. Mellissa has to work at the B&B this evening."

Marc hooked his thumbs into the belt tabs of his jeans. "Perhaps your sister could bring her here, at least until this is cleared up."

"Until what is cleared up?" Addie pinned Simon with a mystified look and then glanced at a silent Marc. His ticking jaw had her sleuthing wires buzzing. "I only asked to see the bus so we could take photos. Hopefully, my insurance company will pay something for the damages."

"That's all you said to the deputy when you came in?" Curiosity glinted in Marc's eyes.

"Yes. Oh, I also asked him if they were done with the mechanical inspection, and if it was ready to be released so I could make arrangements to have it hauled back to Greyborne Harbor as that piece of scrap metal apparently belongs to me."

"Yeah, for a whole hour," said Paige, more like a huffy sidebar as her gaze flitted from Simon to Marc.

"I thought you were coming here for a book sale," said Simon.

"We did. We were."

Marc fixed a bewildered gaze on Addie. "Then how in the world did you end up as the owner of a bookmobile?"

"Long story."

"Since you two aren't going anywhere, I think we have time." Marc crossed his arms over his broad, denim-clad chest.

"Have they found a mechanical issue with the bus? Is that what this is all about? Because Luella Higgins informed me that it had just had its annual maintenance work completed, and she had the paperwork to prove it. Surely the sheriff isn't going to try to hold me responsible for the accident, is he?" She glanced at Simon. "Is that why you're here this morning? Did he find something in his inspection? Did you come to talk to him about the possibility of . . . whatever defect caused the accident, killing her?"

"Not . . . exactly . . ." said Marc hesitantly as a couple passed by them on the sidewalk. "This probably isn't the best place to discuss it. Maybe we should go somewhere more private. Are you staying at Bree's?"

"Yes, why?"

"Maybe we should go there and talk."

"Wait a minute." Addie's hands flew up in a stop motion. "We're not going anywhere until you tell us what's going on and why the two of you are here."

"Addie, please," pleaded Simon. "It's for the best."

"Is it? In case you forgot, today is my birthday, and so far, the day has been a disaster. Paige and I have plans for lunch, and if I can salvage anything out of this day, I would like to go ahead with those plans."

Simon looked at Marc and shrugged his shoulders.

"Just tell her." Marc kicked at a pebble on the side-walk.

"Okay, Addie, Paige, both of you take a deep breath."

"You're scaring me, Simon."

He let out a harsh breath and stared into her eyes. "We're just the messengers here, remember that." He glanced over his shoulder at Marc, who was standing stone-faced, staring at them. "I called Sheriff Turner first thing this morning—" He smiled at a woman walking past with her dog. When she was well past them, he continued. "I told him about some anomalies I discovered in the autopsy."

"And?" said Addie curiously.

"And it seems the accident was not the cause of death."

"What was then? A heart attack?"

"Yes and no." He sucked in a deep breath. "The heart attack was caused by poisoning."

Addie reeled backward and thudded against the hood of the Wrangler. "She was poisoned?"

"Yes," said Marc, "and shortly after Simon called Turner with the preliminary report, the sheriff called him back and said, if that was the case, then he already had two suspects in mind."

"He does? Fantastic! Who?"

Simon glanced at Marc and then at Addie and Paige.

"Not us?" Paige cried.

"She's wrong, right?" asked Addie, her gaze darting from one to the other.

"I'm afraid not," said Simon. "Turner said after taking statements last night from some of those in attendance at the dinner, the two out-of-towners that showed up at the last minute were at the top of his list of suspects. He sounded quite pleased with himself too."

"Which is why Simon and I jumped in the car and came right here to meet with him. We've spent the better part of the last hour trying to convince him that neither of you would be guilty of murder."

"Did you?"

"We thought we had until the deputy came in and showed him the bill of sale for the bookmobile. Now he thinks he has found the motive—"

"But we've convinced him to continue the investigation and look at all options, because as far as we knew"— Simon glanced over at Marc—"you only came to buy books and not the bus. What motive would that be for murder?"

"Yeah, I'd like to hear why he thinks that would be a motive for us to kill Luella and not someone else who perhaps didn't want the sale of the bus or the library closure to go through."

"We offered every explanation we could think of, but he's a small-town sheriff and feels that no one in *his* town would commit murder, so he's convinced it had to be the two of you."

"I can't believe this."

"Well, you'd better, and we'd better get this solved as fast as we can, or he's going to railroad you just for being outsiders."

Chapter 10

"Do you know what the poison was or the source?" asked Addie, trying to wrap her head around the news Marc and Simon had just given her and Paige.

"No, the prelims look like probable aconitine though, but I can't be certain until I get the final results."

"Aconitine?" said Addie, looking at Paige. "Why does that sound familiar?"

"It does to me too, but I can't think from where."

"Where the heck would she have come across that?" Addie asked. "Would it have been in something she ate?"

"Most likely," said Simon. "If I recall correctly, it's a poison derived from the monkshood plant."

"That's it," cried Paige. "Sometimes monkshood is called wolfsbane."

"Yes." Addie snapped her fingers. "You're right. It's

called that because the tips of hunters' arrows were dipped in a solution of it to kill wolves."

"True," said Simon, "but since I found no evidence of her having been shot by an arrow, and it generally kills rather quickly, I have to rule out any contact or ingestion earlier in the day. It must have been in one of the food dishes at the dinner."

"Turner told us," added Marc, "that he's already sent deputies over to the library to shut down the upstairs rooms where the dinner took place."

"Yeah," said Simon. "I guess a woman named Patricia Seagram told him there was leftover food in the fridge, so I'm heading over there now to take some samples and run more tests."

"Are you going back to Greyborne Harbor afterward to perform the tests?" Addie's gaze flitted from Marc to Simon.

"No, the sheriff was *good* enough to make arrangements for me to use the lab at the medical clinic. He said it was to save driving time in case more than one trip was required."

"But if you ask me," piped in Marc, "I think it's more of a matter of him wanting to keep an eye on any developments and be Johnny-on-the-spot when there's enough evidence for an arrest. He's itching to end the final months of his career with an open-and-shut murder conviction, and he believes he has the two suspects in hand."

"Why would we want to kill a woman we just met in a town that we don't live in? It doesn't make sense."

"No, it doesn't," said Marc, "and there appears to be no evidence so far implicating you two, only suspicion."

"So, he's fishing?"

"Yes," said Marc, "and he was also told that you and

Paige were responsible for packing up most of the food and putting it away last night. Now he thinks you tried to cover your tracks and tampered with whatever evidence there might have been."

"But what would our motive be?"

"I think he was struggling with that too," said Simon, "until you showed up with the sales receipt and wanted to ship the bus back to Greyborne Harbor as soon as possible. Now he thinks it had something to do with some first edition books you found hidden in the bookmobile."

"We turned those over to Luella as soon as we found them."

"Where are they now?" asked Marc.

Addie glanced at Paige and dropped her gaze. "I don't know. She took them back to the library office. I saw her put them on the desk, but when we were leaving last night, I noticed the door was open. I peeked in, and the books were gone."

"It's my understanding," said Marc, "those were the same books that went missing last Christmas and that he conducted a month-long investigation trying to find them."

Paige nodded. "That's what we were told too."

"Unfortunately"—Marc dropped his voice as he glanced back at the station house door—"he finds it strange that you two found them when his deputies couldn't. It seems this Patricia told Sheriff Turner that she never actually saw the books yesterday, but was told they had been found, so it's only your word they were turned in."

Addie slumped back against the hood of the Wrangler and crossed her arms. "If my hunch is right about who took those books in the first place, then it also tells me that Patricia is trying to make us look guilty of not only theft but of murder too."

"It does, doesn't it? But why?" asked Simon.

Addie told them about the disagreement they witnessed between her and Luella, how Patricia blamed Addie for the loss of the bus, and how Patricia insisted that the town council had promised it to her and Bea so they could carry on with servicing the outlying communities. When Addie finished retelling the exchange of words she and Paige had overheard, she glanced hopefully at Simon and Marc. "Well, what do you think? Because if anyone had a motive to kill Luella it would be Patricia Seagram."

Paige interjected with what Bree's neighbor had said to them that morning about having a card up her sleeve to save the library.

"See, now don't you agree?" Addie said, excitement building inside her. "She's the one he should be focusing on."

"We can talk about other suspects later," said Simon. "Marc and I should head over to the library and get some samples. If we can trace the contaminated dish to the person who brought it, that might give us a lead."

"Tell Sheriff Turner that Paige and I had nothing to do with setting up the food. We were downstairs at the sale during that time."

"Yes," said Marc, "but apparently you didn't eat any of it yourselves, which Turner finds suspicious and keeps you at the top of his suspect list."

"We didn't have time to eat. We were at the back of the food line, and by the time we filled our plates, I ran into . . . an old friend. We got chatting, then we heard the news about the crash, and the dinner was pretty much over. We helped clean up. I felt it was the least we could do after that. The volunteers were upset as they all knew Luella, and Paige and I had been last-minute dinner invitees."

Marc's brow rose. "Who invited you to the dinner?"

"Luella. She had arranged for a news crew to be there to interview her about the library closing. When I bought the bus, she thought doing an on-air ceremony with her handing over the bookmobile keys would be good public relations for the town and my bookstore."

"Look, right now, go for your lunch and sit tight. Between Marc and me, we'll figure this out."

"The problem will be getting Turner to follow up on any of this," Marc said, "because he's convinced it was the work of an outsider. He's been friends with these people throughout his thirty-year career, and I'm afraid he's lost all objectivity."

"Okay," said Addie. "I guess we start by gathering samples of all the dishes brought to the dinner. When we find something that tests positive, we can find out who brought it—"

"Addie." Simon placed his hands on her shoulders. "I'm afraid there's no *we* here. You are on his suspect list, and having you involved with any collection of samples will jeopardize the findings."

Marc nodded in agreement. "He's already leery about our involvement because of our involvement with you." His ears reddened. "I meant us knowing you."

"What are we supposed to do? Nothing? Sit back and wait until he drums up some concocted evidence so he can charge us with murder?"

"Not if we can help it. That's why Marc is here working as a civilian because Pen Hollow is out of his jurisdiction."

"Yeah," said Marc, "I've known Turner for a lot of years, and for the most part, he's a good cop, but he seems to have made up his mind on this one for some reason. When Simon told me what he said after he got the lab results, I thought I'd better tag along and make sure he goes by the book on this one, approaching retirement or not. Trust us, we won't let you two be the final gold stars on his badge."

"That's right." Simon glanced uncomfortably at Marc and then locked his gaze on Addie. "I'll get samples of everything there, and we'll find out what poisoned her, and it will prove that you two couldn't have had anything to do with it."

"If you ask me," said Paige, "it was her own poisonous personality that killed her."

"Paige?" Stunned by the force of her words, Addie looked at her. "That's not like you."

"Sorry, but this has turned into a nightmare, and on your birthday of all days."

Addie glanced awkwardly at Marc and Simon. Was that sympathy she saw in their eyes? She waved off Paige's comment. "Ah, it doesn't matter. When you get to my age, birthdays come and go."

"No, she's right. This is supposed to be your special day. Why don't you and Paige head off to that lunch you said you'd planned, and Marc and I will get to work clearing all this nonsense up."

"I don't feel like eating now." Addie took her phone out of her bag. "I'm going to call Tony and cancel."

"Tony?" Simon pinned her with a curious look.

"Yes, the old friend I ran into last night. We were supposed to meet for lunch at the hotel."

"Hotel?"

"Yes, in the dining room."

"Should I be worried?" whispered Simon, leaning into her.

"No, I haven't seen or heard from him since high school. He's here on business, and we thought it might be nice to catch up." She fixed her steady gaze on his probing one. "Paige was coming as a chaperone, if that's what's bothering you."

"He's a famous author," piped in Paige.

"He is, is he?" Simon pulled back from Addie. "Well, you two run along and enjoy your luncheon then."

The strained look on Simon's face told Addie that he was struggling to keep his tone even and cheery, but the hollow look in his eyes also told her he felt anything but.

Marc glanced apologetically at Addie and placed his hand on Simon's arm. "Turner just pulled out of the parking lot. We should get over there before he starts issuing warrants."

"Yeah, you're right," said Simon, threading a hand through shocks of his black hair. "Enjoy your lunch. I'll call you when we're done."

"I just told you, I'm going to cancel."

"No, you should go," he said as he backed away. "Have some fun on your birthday, enjoy yourself." He stalked off with Marc toward his car in the visitors' parking lot.

"Hmm," said Paige. "I'd say Simon is a wee bit jealous, wouldn't you?"

"I have to introduce him to Tony so he can see there's nothing to be jealous about."

"After Tony's performance last night?" Paige mimicked Tony's antics of being shot in the heart. "Oh, and that kiss, even though you didn't appear to return it." She winked slyly. "Do you really think that's a good idea?"

"I see what you mean. I can't promise Tony will behave. He never could in school either. Always the class clown and thought he was funny, but he generally ended up pushing things too far."

"Let's go to our lunch as planned, and you can explain to him why we're stuck here. Let him know in no uncertain terms that you'll be busy clearing our names so he doesn't get any other ideas as to why you're hanging around town. Then catch up and say goodbye."

"No." Addie retrieved her phone from her bag. "I can't deal with a trip down memory lane or reliving all the tragedies of my life these past sixteen years."

"It hasn't all been tragic, has it?"

"No, not all of it." Addie squeezed Paige's hand. "But my head's not into a reunion right now." Her thumbs flew over the small keypad. "There, done, canceled. Now I need to find some paper and get some of these facts down so I can start putting this crazy puzzle together."

"I have a better idea. Come on, let's go back to Bree's. There's something there that's exactly what we need."

Addie snuggled Pippi under her chin and stroked the fine, silky fur on the back of her head. "Sorry to cut your playdate short, sweetie, but Mommy missed you so much, and I needed a cuddle today. I think you missed me too, didn't you?" she cooed, and laughed as Pippi's tongue sought out her cheek. "Yes, Valerie's a nice lady, but there's still no one like Mommy, right?" Addie giggled when the little pink tongue made contact. "Silly girl." She bent down and set Pippi on the floor. "Now, where did Auntie Paige get to?"

"I'm here," called Paige from the stairwell. "It took me a minute to find everything we'll need. I think Graham's idea of cleaning his room means tossing everything in the closet." She came around the corner into the living room and set up two art easels with blackboard backing beside the fireplace. "What do you think? Better than nothing, right? And although it took some digging, I did manage to find these." She held out three sticks of chalk.

"Perfect. The blackboards aren't large, but they'll do the trick to keep names, events, and suspects organized for now." Addie stood back, eyeing one of the child's drawing easels.

"They used to have pads of drawing paper that attached up here under this clip, but I guess those are long gone. The kids are getting older, and I don't think either of them are aspiring artists," Paige said with a short laugh. "Anyway, at least we have chalk for the blackboard backing."

Addie slipped a piece of chalk from Paige's hand, studied the board closest to her for a moment, and wrote *Patricia*.

"I think she's our best suspect," said Paige, nodding in agreement, "but I think you can also add her assistant, Bea. They seem pretty tight, and the way Bea scurries around behind Patricia cleaning up after her, she seems like the type of employee that would do anything to make her boss happy."

"Yes, and we both know that neither of them is happy about the library closure—"

"Or Luella selling the bookmobile."

Addie scrawled *Bea* under Patricia's name.

"Although," Addie said, tapping the chalk stick on her hand. "If we're going to add names of the people who weren't happy about the library closing, we'd have to add pretty much everyone in town, wouldn't we?"

"What about Tony? He didn't seem fazed by her death."

"Tony? No, I can't see him as a suspect. He was the reason the library lost their funding. If there was any killing to be done, he'd more likely be the victim."

"You're right." Paige stretched out on the sofa and scratched Pippi with her toe.

"The library was already scheduled to close. Killing Luella now wouldn't change that. We're left with finding a possible motive." Addie frowned and studied the board. "It's clear there had to be another reason why someone wanted Luella dead."

"Yeah." Paige heaved herself off the sofa and grabbed a stick of chalk. *Bookmobile sale.* "This seemed to blind-side everyone, especially these two." She tapped the tip of the chalk under Bea and Patricia's names.

"You're right, and they didn't seem at all broken up about her death."

"Yes, but then we're back to not many people were. So, we might as well write Valerie's and Tony's names on here too."

"Yeah, okay." Addie begrudgingly folded her arms and stared at the board. "Now we need motives for murder," she said as she wrote . . .

Money or Greed
Revenge
Fear
Crimes of Passion
Personal Vendetta
Jealousy
Anger
Hatred
Self-defense and in-defense

"Although, I don't think that last one really fits here because poisoning indicates premeditation, not spur-of-the-moment or a reaction."

"Don't forget blackmail, power plays, and whistle-blowing." Paige pointed to the board.

"Right," said Addie, scribbling those on the list.

"Wow," said Paige, reading the list. "It's sad to think all those are the reasons why people justify murdering someone."

Addie scanned the board. "Yes, but you know what's missing when I look at all these possible motives for murder?"

"What?"

"We're the only two people on the board without a probable motive to kill Luella, and yet we're Turner's number one suspects."

"Which doesn't make sense?"

"I know, because we didn't even know her. Unless we're some sort of psychopaths or sociopaths who go around killing willy-nilly, we should be the last two he could pin a motive for murder on."

"Then our job here is to somehow prove that to him, before he railroads us for being outsiders."

Chapter 11

"Okay, we're going to have to dig around in Luella's past because there has to be something there that would tell us why she was murdered. I don't buy the whole library closing thing. It's the one motive that doesn't fit since it was a done deal and had been in the works for a while. Whoever killed her wouldn't have waited until the eleventh hour to do it if that was the reasoning behind it." Addie studied the list of motives. "No, it has to be something in her past and could very well be any one of these." She tapped the chalk on the motive list. "And my money is on the first edition books and their sudden disappearance and unexpected reappearance being somehow connected to Luella's murder."

"Maybe, but where do we start? We don't know any of these people in town. We can hardly walk up to them and start asking questions about Luella's past, can we?"

"No, we can't." Addie snapped her fingers. "Yes, we can. We know one person, and that person might be a good place to start."

"Who?"

"Valerie!"

"But I barely know her. I mean I do know her, but we're not really close. We chat over the fence and there's always a 'good morning' or 'afternoon' when Bree and I come and go. That's about the extent of our friendship."

"Ah, yes, but we have the perfect Trojan horse." Addie pointed to Pippi, her head propped up on Baxter, sleeping soundly in her doggie bed.

"But what would we say? 'Hi, you said to bring Pippi back anytime for a visit so here we are, and what can you tell us about Luella that might have gotten her killed?'" Paige flopped on the sofa. "No, I don't think that's gonna work. It's a small town, and she'll tell everyone we're snooping around and asking questions about an upstanding member of the community, the mayor, no less. If Turner hears about it, you can guarantee he'll find a way to use that against us and say we're interfering in the investigation to take the heat off us. Remember, he's not Marc, who, if I'm not mistaken by his being here today and the way he looked at you, still has feelings for you." She shook her head. "No, Turner definitely won't be as tolerant of your Miss Snoopy methods."

Addie rolled her eyes. "Marc and I are just friends now, that's all."

"Are you sure?" Paige pinned her with an accusatory look.

"Yes, I'm sure."

"You're sure about you, but can you be so sure about him?"

Addie hesitated. "Yes, and he knows I'm with Simon—"

"Yeah." Paige snorted. "Simon, who didn't even give you a hello kiss, not to mention a birthday kiss, and then barely acknowledged you until you mentioned Tony."

Addie took a deep breath. The reality of Simon's behavior had struck a chord in her that—if she was going to be honest—had bothered her too. "Simon's got clearing our names on his mind, that's all. I'm sure later when he's not so laser-focused, he'll apologize and—"

"Well, tonight was supposed to be your special birthday dinner, and judging by what I saw today, I bet once *again* there's no ring in his pocket."

"What's with you right now?"

"Because . . . because . . ." Paige's voice quivered with tears. "It's your birthday today, and he already ruined one special day for you last Christmas. I really had hoped this time he would do what I thought he really wanted to do. But now I think I'm wrong, and he's going to wreck another special day for you."

"Oh, sweetie." Addie sat down beside her on the sofa and placed her arm around Paige's shaking shoulders. "Don't worry about me. Birthdays come and go. Nothing is ruined. I'm here with you, and you made me a spectacular breakfast. It's been perfect."

"Perfect? How does being on the top of a suspect list make it perfect?"

Addie thought for a moment. "Well, it kind of has become our thing, hasn't it?" She chuckled.

"But what about Simon?"

"I think Simon is giving me a birthday present by being here and trying to clear my name. What better gift could he give me, really? Think about it."

"I guess you're right. I'm just feeling sad for you."

"Well, don't. I'm a big girl, and Simon and I will work this out."

"But he says he loves you so much and told you he'd wait for you to put all your ghosts to rest, and yesterday you even faced your father's ghost on Cliff Side Road, but he couldn't even kiss you when he saw you."

"I get the feeling that you're bothered by more than what's going on with me and Simon right now, am I right?"

"I guess." Paige flung her head back on the sofa. "It's just that this is such a mess. Besides ruining your birthday, my sister lives in this town, my brother-in-law is a state trooper stationed here, and me and one of my best friends are murder suspects in the death of a woman we just met. Now we have to get all Nancy Drew about it and start looking for skeletons in closets in a murder investigation that should have nothing to do with us."

"I know. It doesn't seem right or fair, but it's our reality right now. We have to do what we can to figure out who might have wanted Luella dead." Addie glanced at the board. "And the best place to start is to learn who the victim was, because that's where we're going to find out who the killer is. Come on." She rose and held out her hand to Paige. "Let's go wheedle an invitation to tea."

Paige seized Addie's hand and pulled herself to her feet. "I hope this doesn't backfire on us and my sister ends up hating me for giving her a bad name in town."

"She'll understand. I'm pretty sure she'd rather us be known as busybodies than murderers."

Pippi jumped to her feet, yipped, and raced to the door as if she knew where they were going.

"Either she senses she's going to get more treats from

Valerie, or she really has to go for a walk badly." Addie laughed.

Addie grabbed the lead by the door just in case they were heading for a walk rather than a visit and tea. "You're not the boss of me, you know." She chuckled as she clipped the lead onto Pippi's collar and opened the door. "Now, Paige, before we wrangle an invite to tea, maybe you should tell me a little about what you know of Valerie so I can build some familiarity with her before—"

"Before you start interrogating her?"

"Well, yes, I suppose." Addie laughed and trotted down the front steps.

"Okay, her husband George passed away about four months ago—"

"Yikes."

"I know, and she's really been struggling with it. They didn't have any children, but she is really close to her niece Laurel Hill, who lost her mother, Valerie's sister, a few years ago."

"This is the veterinarian?"

"Yeah, she works at a clinic in Boston, but comes most weekends to visit. I think she's pretty concerned about her aunt right now. That's her car parked in front of the house, I see."

"Hmm, it hasn't been that long since her husband passed, so that's to be expected. Valerie is lucky to have her. What did her husband do?"

"He was a lawyer here in town."

"So she's pretty well connected in the community?"

"Yes, and more of a reason for us to be careful about how we approach this." Paige dropped her voice as they approached Valerie's front door.

"Gotcha," said Addie as Pippi dragged her up the front steps and sat, tail wagging.

"Hello! This is unexpected," said Valerie, opening the door and peering at the threesome on her porch. "Is there a problem?" Her eyes filled with concern, and she glanced down at Pippi.

"No, not at all. We were—were—" Paige glanced at Addie, a *Help Me* sign flashing in her bright blue eyes.

"We were out for a walk, and my little friend here dragged us right to your door, so we thought we'd just stop and say hello. Say hello, Pippi." Addie bent down and ruffled the fur on the back of Pippi's head. "Then we can let the nice lady get back to whatever she was doing."

"Nonsense. If this little sweetie wanted to visit me, then a visit she shall have. Come in, come in." Valerie stepped aside, giving them room to enter her small front hallway. "You're just in time to meet my niece Laurel. Would you like to join us for lunch?"

"We wouldn't want to intrude," said Addie, unclipping Pippi's lead. Unfortunately, her stomach picked that exact moment to make its own wants known and let out a horrible growl.

"It sounds to me like lunch is exactly what you need." Valerie laughed and headed down the hall to the back kitchen. "Laurel, look who dropped by for a visit," said Valerie.

Pippi scampered by her like she owned the house and came to a skidding stop beside the tall pantry cupboard and sat, wiggling her hind end as her tail thumped on the floor. Clearly, Pippi felt completely at home and no doubt knew exactly where the treats were kept. No wonder she was pulling at her lead to get to the house.

"This is Pippi, the little dog I was telling you about, and, of course, you know Paige, Bree's sister. This is her friend and Pippi's mommy, Addie."

Addie reached her hand out in greeting to the striking brunette with a lustrous mane of shoulder-length hair. "Hi, it's nice to meet you."

"Likewise." Laurel gave a radiant smile that could have lit up even the darkest room, and shook Addie's hand with more strength than its dainty features would have suggested.

"Here you go, girl." Valerie retrieved a foil package from the pantry cupboard and plucked out a small brown morsel. "Now, sit pretty for me. That's it." She laughed and dropped the treat into Pippi's waiting mouth.

"Don't worry, Addie," Laurel said with a reassuring smile. "They're health treats from my clinic. I brought them last month and told Auntie to put a few in her pockets when she goes for walks in case she runs into a friend walking their dog. Sadly, by the look of how many are left, she didn't open them until yesterday when Pippi came over."

Addie smiled as Pippi held the treat in her front paws and savoured every bite before scampering to her feet, looking for more.

"You've had enough, my friend." Addie laughed. "If she had her way, she'd down the whole package in one sitting." Addie glanced at Laurel and smiled. The look on her face as she watched her aunt with Pippi seemed to please her.

"Auntie has talked nonstop about Pippi since I got here today," Laurel said, gazing wistfully at her aunt in the kitchen where Valerie and Paige were now setting out the plates of sandwiches. "I couldn't be happier for her."

She dropped her voice. "Since my uncle died, she's been an ongoing concern for me. I've tried to convince her to get a dog because I wanted her to get out of the house and go for walks, and she's always found a reason not to. Last week she told me she might get a cat, and although I love cats, they don't require regular walking, and she needs to get out again instead of shutting herself up in the house all the time."

Addie signaled her agreement with a nod of her head, glanced down at the lead she clutched in her hand and felt a little guilty about letting Pippi out in the dog run and not walking her as much as she should.

"This visit, so far, has been a breath of fresh air and completely different to what I expected when I arrived after hearing about that nasty business with Luella Higgins. Having Pippi around has kept her mind off it, and I shudder to think what kind of state she would have been in today if she had nothing to occupy herself with except thinking about what happened. They were close friends, and I know it must be tearing her up inside."

"They were friends? Really? Funny." Addie shifted in her chair. "I got the opposite impression from her this morning."

"What's funny?" Valerie set a small sandwich plate down in front of Laurel and Addie.

Paige put one on her plate, then began tearing into her sandwich as though it was the first food she'd seen in a month, closed her eyes, and Addie could have sworn she heard her purring, and shook her head.

"Oh," said Laurel, "Addie and I were just talking about what good friends you have here in the village." She gave Addie a slight nod as though she wanted Addie to follow her lead.

"Um, yes, it must be nice to have spent most of your life in Pen Hollow and gotten to know people as well as you have."

"I could tell you stories that would curl your toes," said Valerie, plopping into her chair. "It doesn't hurt that my George was nearly everyone's lawyer at one time or another, and I know things that others don't and would pay to keep quiet. If you know what I mean." She gave Addie a sly wink and bit into her chicken-salad sandwich. "I could write a book about it, I tell you. The goings-on in this town"—she tsked—"would make a priest blush."

Addie glanced at Paige, not sure what to say next. Laurel had just confessed her aunt was good friends with Luella, but this morning Valerie had appeared anything but.

Did they have a falling out? What should she say without offending Laurel, who seemed relieved her aunt wasn't dwelling on Luella's death?

She telegraphed *Help me, Paige* under the table with a tap on Paige's shin.

Paige jerked, stared at Addie, then seemed to clue in. "It must be so hard on everyone, losing one of their own. I'm not sure how Bree's going to take it when she gets back. She worked on the library committee and on the gardening committee with Luella. Didn't you too, Valerie?" She glanced at Addie and gave a slight shrug as though to say she'd done her best.

"Don't get me started on that woman," said Valerie, taking a bite out of her sandwich.

Laurel glanced at Addie, and Addie gave her an apologetic grimace.

"She used to be one of the nicest people you could meet, was my best friend for years. Did you know she used to run the pharmacy in the shopping area just down the hill from here? You know it, Paige, the one on Sea Otter Circle."

"Um, yes," mumbled Paige, covering her full mouth.

"We had such a lovely community back then," Valerie said wistfully. "The same mayor for over twenty-five years, nothing ever changed, and the people liked it that way. Then he suddenly retired—said it was for health reasons—and moved to Florida. His nephew took over the last few months of his uncle's term. I'm sure he intended to stay in charge as long as his uncle had, but the law says we have to have elections every four years."

"And he won?" asked Addie, biting into her sandwich.

"Yes. Everyone thought he'd be like his uncle, but then everything changed. Suddenly, we had bylaws that took away our rights. There was paid street parking, and don't get me started about the charges he implemented out at the dump." She set her sandwich slice on her plate and glanced at Addie. "Well, you should know him. I understand he's now the mayor in Greyborne Harbor."

"Mayor Bryant was here before he came to us? Why didn't I know that?"

"Probably, because he left town with his tail between his legs after suffering such a devastating loss to the likes of Luella. I'm sure the fewer people that heard about what happened here, the better for him, especially given how badly she walloped him in that election."

"I had no idea." Addie scratched her head. "I mean, I don't pay much attention to politics but still . . ."

"But," said Valerie leaning forward, "that's when Luella started to change." She sat upright. A knowing look crossed her face. "I guess what they say about power corrupting really is true because it sure went to her head. She became a regular little dictator after she won by a landslide. We thought Bryant was difficult to deal with." Valerie harrumphed. "Well, she took one look at the budgets from the programs he'd implanted and decided they were good for the community and kept them plus added more tariffs and taxes to balance the books."

"Is that when she decided to close the library?"

"Yes, something I could never understand because she was chairman of the library association too, and had been for years. Overnight, it was a drain on tax dollars and had to go. Oh, she says—said—she tried to save it with Maisie Radcliff's endowment, but if you ask me, she wanted to close it because she had a developer friend interested in the property. The town stands to make a pretty penny off that land sale. I should know. My George was handling the property sale."

"Wait a minute. I thought your husband passed away four months ago?"

"He did."

"And even then she had a buyer for the land?"

"Yes, it had been in the making for months before that with some fellow from Boston Mayor Bryant had introduced her to."

"Even before Maisie passed away at Christmas?"

Valerie nodded. "And there's one other thing. Did you know Luella and Jack Turner used to be an item?"

"The sheriff?"

"Yes, not the best kept secret in town either, and it wasn't a pleasant scene when Jack's wife, Wanda, caught wind of it."

Chapter 12

"Laurel seems nice," said Addie absently, scrolling through her phone as they walked next door to Bree's house.

"Yeah, she's a hoot. I really like her. As a matter of fact, she reminds me of you in a lot of ways."

Addie lowered her phone and stared in disbelief at Paige. "Really, in what way?"

"Quick to anger, quick to laugh, breaks the rules, smart, and if I dare to say, stubborn."

"Me? Stubborn?"

"Just a teensy-weensy bit." Paige chuckled and squeezed her thumb and forefinger together. "She's also great looking, has a magnetic personality, and far-out-there sense of humor, just to name a few of the similarities. You guys could be twins."

"Wait a minute, are you saying I'm as pretty as she is? She could be the cover girl for that *All American Girl Next Door* magazine."

"Come on, Addie, you never give yourself enough credit. Why do you think you have two of the hottest men in Greyborne Harbor fawning all over you?"

"Yeah right, some fawning. I bet she's at least married though, isn't she?"

"No, and never has been."

"I find that hard to believe. She's the one you'd think men would be fawning over, as you put it."

"She's been too focused on her career, I guess."

"That sounds like someone else I know." Addie glanced back at her phone and frowned.

"Who, you?"

"No, Simon. He just sent a text saying he's still at the lab, but Marc's on his way over to fill us in."

"At least we're going to get some answers."

"Yes, and I can't wait to tell him what we learned about Luella. Like I said, the motive lies in her past, and I'd say she has one heck of one."

"And it sounds like there's more than one reason someone might have wanted her dead."

"You're right." Addie shoved her phone into the back pocket of her cropped jeans just as Marc came into sight around the corner of the street coming up from Sea Spray Drive. "It looks like we're back just in time." She gave Pippi's lead a strong tug as Pippi lunged to greet him.

"Phew, that was a bit more of a hike from the clinic than I thought it was," Marc said with a laugh as he pushed locks of his tousled, chestnut-brown hair from his forehead with the back of his hand. "I guess I've been spoiled having my cruiser at my fingertips when I'm out on a call. Not used to being the passenger." He took a quick look at Paige, then Addie. "You wouldn't happen to have any sweet tea or lemonade in the fridge, would you?"

"Actually, that sounds perfect," said Addie, reining Pippi in to steer her up the sidewalk to Bree's front door. "We just had lunch with Paige's sister's neighbor, and, boy, do we have some news for you."

"I got a bit myself. Hopefully between the four of us, we can put all this nonsense—" He stopped at the living room entrance when Addie bent down to unclip Pippi from her lead. "You've got to be kidding. Even here you manage to put together"—he waved his hand in the direction of the blackboard easels—"a crime board."

She glanced up and winced sheepishly. "Did you expect less?"

He shook his head, strolled around to the front, and read what she and Paige had written. "You know what?"

Addie raised her hand as if answering a teacher's difficult question. "Oh, oh, I know! I should keep my nose out of police business and let the police do their job." She joined him.

"Not at all. This is exactly what we need, and you've made a good start."

Addie staggered backward and feigned a swoon. "All the stress must have gotten to me. Did I actually hear Police Chief Chandler say, *Good work, Addie*?"

"No." He let out a muffled chuckle. "I did *not* say good work, I said good start."

"Same thing." She grinned coyly at him and picked up a piece of chalk.

"Okay then," said Paige uncomfortably. "I saw some sweet tea mix in the pantry, so I think I'll go and make us a batch. Come on, Pippi, let's get you some fresh water." She glanced back at Addie, shook her head, and mimicked a ring around her ring finger. "Remember, Addie, don't get too involved with crime fighting right now. You have to get ready for your dinner tonight." Her voice held an accusatory tone as she disappeared into the kitchen, Pippi at her heels.

"There's lots of time, and I think Marc needs to know what we found out." Addie gave a half shrug and turned back to the easel. "Ever since I heard that Luella was poisoned, something hasn't sat right with me."

"Why? She obviously wasn't well liked in town."

"No, she wasn't recently, but apparently up until she became mayor, she was."

"What do you mean?"

"I mean something changed, and I don't buy the whole reason everyone else was jumping to, that the library closing was the motive for murder."

"But that's the most obvious."

"Yes, but it was a done deal and had been for a long time. It got me thinking about something my father used to say."

"And that was?"

"Aside from Dad being an ex-NYPD detective before he became an antiquities reclamation agent for an insurance company, he was also an avid crime fiction reader. His favorite author was Ross Macdonald, the author of *The Moving Target*, *The Drowning Pool*, *The Barbarous Coast* and *The Chill*."

"Yes, I've read him, but wasn't his real name Kenneth Millar or something?"

"Yes, but the point is, Ross Macdonald had a great quote that Dad thought also fit well in police investigations. He kept it in mind with every tough case he worked: 'The detective isn't your main character, and neither is your villain. The main character is the corpse. The detective's job is to seek justice for the corpse. It's the corpse's story, first and foremost.'"

"How does that relate to this case?"

"Because there is no clear-cut motive for death by poisoning, which implies premeditation, not a spur-of-the-moment crime of passion as everyone seems to be focusing on."

"Which means," Marc said thoughtfully, "it has to be something that happened in Luella's past that made someone want her dead now."

"Exactly," cried Addie. "Looking into this corpse's story might reveal what is hidden in Luella's past that brought about her murder."

Addie proceeded to relay to Marc the information they had learned about Luella from Valerie and Laurel, including the affair between Luella and Turner.

"What? You're joking. He hasn't said a nice thing about that woman all day." He cracked his knuckles and stretched his neck. "Well, let's see if what we came up with can be added to this growing list of the facts as we know them. Maybe we can, at least, start figuring out how the poison was administered. That might tell us who in her past wanted her dead."

Addie primed that chalk stick against the board. "Okay, shoot."

He flipped open his notepad. "First, we got lucky. There was food left over from all of the dishes."

Addie paused writing. "Really? There were samples of everything served?"

"Yes, even from the two dishes that had the chocolates in them."

"But there were so many people there that I find it hard to believe there were leftovers from all the dishes."

"I asked the same question, and apparently the volunteers who had been working downstairs at the sale were closing up and hadn't come upstairs to eat yet. It seems the committee also planned for the news crew to eat once they'd finished filming Luella's interview and had put out the call for extra food donations. I guess because the news host wanted to stay for the dinner, so he could interview some of the volunteers to find out how they felt about the closure, to make it more of a human-interest piece."

"Okay." Addie wrote *Leftovers—samples taken and tested.* "Has Simon got results back on any of the food yet?"

"Yes, and everything has come back negative on the food."

She wrote, *Food samples all tested negative.* "Interesting, and the only thing I actually saw Luella eat was the chocolate she popped in her mouth after her dinner. Mind you, there was gravy smeared on her empty plate, so I assume she had some of the meatballs. Did anyone say they saw what assortment from the dishes she ate before that?"

He checked his notes. "Yes, it seems she ate early, and according to everyone we spoke with, she filled her own plate with a little of everything while they were finishing laying out the food. She told them she wanted to make sure she had time to eat and then get over to the municipal lot to pick up the bus and get back for the interview."

"Has anyone else taken ill from what they ate?"

"There haven't been any reports, and every volunteer who worked either at the book sale or the dinner was at the library today for their interview."

"Which means that unless the poison was in one particular meatball or just one scoop of potato salad or one biscuit, there was no way anything on the table could have poisoned her. That's why all Simon's tests have come back negative." Addie scribbled, *No one else was sick or showed signs of aconitine poisoning*. She looked over at Marc slouched in a large, pillow-backed chair, reading his notes. "That means whatever killed her was administered a different way."

He pressed his lips tight and read, "Simon said that according to the autopsy, there's no indication of an injection site or a wound."

"Okay, but if the food is turning up negative for poison, what then?"

"Deputies have taken swabs of the steering wheel and everything else on the bus. If it's not the food and not on a surface where it could have been absorbed into the skin—which, according to Simon, would mean it was in a highly concentrated form—then it's a mystery as to how the poison was administered."

"Could it have been something she breathed?"

"Not as far as Simon's tests indicate. With no evidence of an injection site and given the high concentrations in her blood stream, it was either ingested or caused by immediate contact with the highly potent poison."

Addie focused in on what she'd written. "Did she snack on something on her way to the parking lot? Was it something in the car that she might have eaten?"

"There are no signs of that, but everything in her car is also being tested."

"This doesn't make sense, does it?" Addie flopped down on the sofa and examined the board.

"No, it doesn't."

"We have no suspect, no murder weapon, an iffy motive at best, but yet a woman is dead because of aconitine poisoning."

"Here's the tea, sorry for the delay," said Paige, placing a tray set with a large glass pitcher and three tall glasses on the coffee table. "I'm afraid I got bad news for us."

"What's wrong? Did Catherine call? Has something happened at the bookstore?"

"No, nothing like that." Paige twisted her delicate hands into knots in front of her. "My sister called, and I guess the weather's been horrible. It's rained every day, and the kids are driving them nuts, so they're coming back a week early on the first flight they could get. They'll be back Monday afternoon."

"I see," said Addie, relief seeping through her. "That just means we have one-and-a-half days to figure out this whole puzzle so Turner lets us leave town. We can do that, right?" She glanced from Paige to Marc.

Marc poured himself a glass of sweet tea. "If not, the B&B Simon and I are staying at is nice. I'm pretty sure they'd have a couple more rooms after the weekend is over."

Paige's face paled. "I can't stay into next week. What about Emma? Mellissa has been able to juggle the child-care and her work schedule with my mom so far, but I'm not sure they can manage it next week too."

"I think," said Addie, her heart breaking for her friend, "that we can create enough doubt in Turner's mind before then that he'll let us go home."

"We can only hope." Paige moaned. "They're going to be so upset with me."

"If you'd like, I can talk to them and explain the situation," said Marc, setting his empty glass on the table.

"That would be great, at least then they'd know we've been held captive here and not by our choice. You saying something will really help soften the blow when none of us planned this little excursion to go on for more than one night," said Paige, relief clearly evident in her voice.

"Yeah," said Marc, "now we just have to get Turner to have an open mind and consider other suspects' evidence or, in this case, no evidence."

Addie couldn't help but miss the judgmental look Paige had in her eye as she observed Marc offering to fill Addie's glass, and decided she needed to clear the air once and for all. "Thank you"—she nodded at Marc—"but I'm curious about something."

"What's that?" Marc stopped mid-pour and met her gaze.

"Why are you here? Is it only because you know Sheriff Turner's reputation, or is there another reason?"

"What do you mean?"

"Why did you really come with Simon?" She fleetingly glanced at Paige.

"I told you guys why."

"Right, to make sure Turner followed the book, but this isn't like you to get involved in another police jurisdiction's investigation, is it?"

"Not generally. Although, it is something I'd do for a friend, and—"

"And what?" asked Paige as she hung on his words, waiting for an answer—an answer that in Addie's mind seemed to take forever to come.

"Were you afraid I'd need rescuing?" Addie blurted out.

"No." He held up his hands in an I-give-up gesture. "If there's anything I've learned about you these past few years, you're the last person who needs rescuing. I guess I just wanted to make sure you weren't going to bury Turner alongside those bones you dig up while you conduct your own investigation."

"And what makes you think I would have started an investigation?"

He glanced at the board. "Really, you have to ask that?" He sat forward and rubbed his hands together. "Look, I'm here now. I booked a couple of days off. Mayor Bryant is always nattering at me about my vacation days, so I took some. Let's all work together on this and get you guys home before Monday."

"You didn't tell Mayor Bryant where you were going, did you?' asked Addie.

"No, why?"

"That's probably a good idea because he used to be the mayor here before he went to Greyborne Harbor."

"That was a while ago though."

"Not that long ago, and it sounds like he suffered a devastating loss in the election that Luella won. Not something he'd want to advertise as he makes his way up the political ladder. Plus, he probably still has ties here. I think he might even belong on our suspect list."

"Was he in town last night for the dinner?" asked Marc.

"I didn't see him, but that doesn't mean he didn't put someone else up to it."

"Like a hit man?" Marc said with a little snicker.

Addie rolled her eyes. "Or a business associate, who maybe got carried away. It seems there was a land developer friend of his who was in negotiations with Luella over the library property."

"Interesting. Let me follow up on that one."

"This is ridiculous." Paige huffed. "Sheriff Turner has no evidence implicating us as suspects. I resent that we have to jump through all these hoops to prove there is no evidence linking us to the murder, something he should have done right from the beginning."

"Unless he's also one that should be on the suspect list. Remember what I said about the motive probably being something—or someone—in Luella's past."

"Yeah, you might be right," said Marc. "He tries to pass off his theory as being in disbelief that someone in his small town is a killer, but he's too bound and determined to find proof that you're responsible. He's not going to ease up. He's like a dog with a bone right now."

"Hmm." Paige glanced sideways at Addie. "That sounds like someone else I know."

"Who, me? At least I let up when I can't find evidence proving one of the suspects is guilty, and look at other suspects. He's not even willing to admit there are any other suspects." She glanced over at Marc. "Has he ever run a murder investigation before?"

"A couple, I think. However, there haven't been many here on the peninsula. I think the last one was about ten years ago. It turned out to be the wife of a cheating husband who tried to make it look like the girlfriend did it. There have been a few through the years, with the first one I recall reading about way back in the 1950s or thereabout. A young guy from Boston. They found his body dressed in a scarecrow costume and pinned up on the scarecrow post."

"Ugh."

"I know. It was over Halloween weekend and very weird, from what I recall reading about it."

"Then there was my father's 'accident' "—Addie waggled her fingers in air quotes—"but I guess that was the state police, not him."

"Oh no, he was also involved in that investigation, and the one who pushed for the ruling on it being accidental, which is one of the reasons I decided to tag along on this trip." He stared at Addie. "I didn't want him sweeping another murder under the rug and adding to the notches on his belt. To be honest, I think if the DA were to go back through the files for the last thirty years, he'd find that a lot of the deaths here on the peninsula ruled as accidents might have been murders."

"Are you saying he's a crooked cop?"

"Not at all. He's a lazy cop and doesn't want to take on a case that might tarnish his stellar reputation. That's why he's pushing to convict you two. He thinks because you're outsiders, he can slide it by, and no one will take a closer look."

"He really didn't know what he was getting himself into when you and Simon showed up, did he?" Paige chuckled.

"No, and he's scrambling now, but at least he's making sure he covers all his bases and dotting his i's and crossing his t's. I shudder to think what turn this investigation would take if Simon and I weren't here."

"Yeah," sighed Addie as she stared at Pippi asleep in her bed. "I guess we should be more grateful for your involvement." She glanced over at Paige and gave her a weak smile. "Because I don't think orange jumpsuits really are the fashion statement we want to make for the rest of our lives, right?"

Chapter 13

Addie tidied up the living room, returning the tea tray to the kitchen when Pippi barked. She popped her head through the doorway from the kitchen to see what the fuss was, expecting to see Marc or Paige retrieving something one of them had forgotten after they left for dinner. She was surprised to see the living room empty. She glanced at Pippi and shrugged. Then she heard the knock and Pippi yipped again. "I guess I should know by now that you don't bark unless there's a reason to." She chuckled as she passed her little friend in the front hall and flung the front door open.

"Simon, come in and sit down. You look horrible," cried Addie. "Not horrible . . . you know, tired."

"Thanks, I am. Turner wore me out today," Simon said, placing a glancing kiss on her cheek as he entered the hallway and closed the door behind him. "He wouldn't back off and hovered over my shoulder questioning me on every finding. Even about who should be collecting the samples of food from the library."

"Normally that would be the police, wouldn't it?" Addie steered Simon into the living room, sat him on the overstuffed chair, pulled up the foot stool, and took a seat herself.

"Yes, and he was right. His department should oversee the collection, but I don't trust him not to tamper with it. He's too determined to find evidence that will point to you and Paige."

"You mean besides testing everything, you also collected all the samples?"

"Yes, with play-by-play instructions being transmitted in my ear all morning. Like I had no idea what I was doing. The most frustrating part is everything came up negative, making Turner more unhappy and disagreeable. Not a fun day."

"If everything tested negative, are we free to go home now?" asked Addie.

"That's the thing. He said anyone who attended the dinner and was there before or after is not allowed to leave the peninsula until something turns up that indicates the source of the poison, and I'm sorry to say it, but I agree. It's the only way to narrow down the pool of suspects."

"Is he looking at other suspects finally?"

"No, I got the sense though that he was being very careful in how he worded his *stay in place* order, as not to make it look like he was still only focused on the two of you. I think he wants to give the impression he's being open-minded about the investigation, but he's not really, if you know what I mean. To be honest with you, he has blinders on for some reason."

"Some reason is right." Addie studied the blackboard and mentally ran through the clues they'd written down earlier. "I guess then we have to find the evidence and prove to him that there is no way we're guilty."

"I'm trying on my end."

"I know you are and thank you," she murmured and leaned in for a kiss, but he yawned and turned his head in that moment, her lips only faintly brushing his cheek. Addie pulled back and stared at him.

"Sorry." He glanced sheepishly away. "I guess I'm more exhausted than I thought I was."

No matter how badly she wanted him to take her in his arms and hold her, so they could talk about their day, she had never begged for a kiss in her life and wasn't about to do that now either.

"Yeah, we've all had a long day," Addie said, fully aware that by Simon's shifting in the chair that her disappointment had reflected in the bite of her words. She sat rigid as she struggled to refocus on the board. "There's no evidence at the library," she said, fighting to keep her tone even, "and he hasn't come by and checked out our belongings or the house to see if he can find traces of 'evidence.' To make it worse, from the time we were in Luella's office with her and Patricia, signing the bookmobile purchase papers, and for the hour leading up to the start of the dinner, witnesses place us downstairs, but yet, he still sees us as the *only* suspects."

Simon laid his head on the back of the chair and sighed. "I know it's stupid. Don't worry, though, because he has nothing that would get an indictment from the DA.

That's probably why he hasn't conducted a search here yet. He doesn't have any evidence to prove a warrant is necessary."

"That makes sense. The DA and any judge he'd take it to would laugh at him."

"I think he knows it, but that's why we have to make sure we follow the book. Any slipup and he'll be all over it."

Addie's text alert pinged

"Is that Marc?" asked Simon, lifting his head.

"It's . . . um . . . Tony. He wants to know if I can make dinner since I canceled lunch."

"Are you going to go?"

"No. You told me you had something special planned for dinner tonight, and since it's my birthday for a few more hours anyway, I was sort of hoping we could still celebrate, at least a little."

"I'm sorry, but I'm exhausted. Can we do a rain check for when things settle down? Right now, I only want a scotch, a hot shower, and a bed, because tomorrow is going to be another killer day with Turner at my heels."

"Oh, sure . . . yeah. You've had a long day. We'll do it another time."

"Thank you." He heaved himself to his feet and kissed her cheek. "Right now, I'm going to head over to the B&B and do exactly what I said I was. I assume that's where Marc is already."

She shook her head. "He and Paige went out to get dinner. I told them I thought we had plans so I waited here for you."

"I'm truly sorry your special day turned out like this, but—"

"It's okay. Really." Of course that's not what she

wanted to say, but what was the point in arguing about it? He was clearly too tired to celebrate her day, and besides, she had enough on her plate tonight as she considered her current situation and Sheriff Turner's attitude.

"We'll make another day special soon. I promise," he whispered. His lips sought out hers as he stroked her cheek. "It'll be a better celebration when I haven't been working nearly thirty-six hours straight, and I can manage to get some sleep. I swear."

"I know, goodnight." She closed the door, leaned her back against it, and as tears rolled down her cheeks she slid down the door.

There on the entryway flooring, she cradled Pippi to her chest and sobbed. She knew in her heart she was being selfish. He had good reason for being tired, between working his scheduled shifts in the emergency department, his coroner's duties with Luella's body, and now trying to help Addie out with this mess; and it was only a birthday. But that wasn't what her tears stemmed from. It was the fact he had told her it would be a "special dinner," and now it was put off. That's what gnawed at her chest. She glanced at her ring-less finger. Couldn't they have still had a "special" evening without going to dinner? Or maybe that wasn't what he meant by special at all, and she was off in a renewed bout of tears.

After what seemed like hours, Addie jerked her head up, drew in a deep breath, swiped at her damp cheeks, and fished her phone out of her back pocket. "Silly, presumptuous woman," she scoffed to herself. "He probably had no intention of proposing, and I've been living in a contemporary romance fantasy novel. Get your head screwed on right, Addie, smarten up and get on with your life."

Her thumbs flew over the keyboard. *I'd love to meet you for dinner. Eight o'clock in the hotel dining room sound good?*

She waited and waited for the sacred *ping*.

Perfect, see you then.

After strolling through the spacious Art Deco lobby, Addie hesitated at the entrance to the equally elaborate hotel dining room. She smoothed a hand over her designer dress made by her cousin. A wave of relief swept through her. Thank goodness she had thrown it in for the dinner Paige planned to take her out for. Of course, that was before the invitation to the potluck and the start of the craziest journey she had ever been on.

The room was truly a step back in time to the 1920s and 1930s, the days of the Hollywood elite. Their signed portraits even adorned the walls. To her right over the maître d's desk was a photograph of Vivian Leigh and Clark Gable sitting at one of the restaurant's tables. Farther along the wall over a circular booth there was another of Charlie Chaplin and—Addie smiled—of James Stewart and another of—her knees went weak—Cary Grant. Directly across the spacious room a large, regal black-and-white portrait of one of Hollywood's most beloved actresses, Katharine Hepburn, stared back at her.

Paige was right when she said she would have loved to have been in Pen Hollow during its heyday. Who would have thought that that this tranquil little village would have been the premier vacation retreat of some of the richest and most glamorous people of the day?

Addie took a steadying breath, smoothed the front of her royal-blue sundress, and smiled at the maître d' when he took her name and gestured at her to follow him. As he led her through the expansive room, she couldn't help but notice that most of the guests were dressed more for a night out in Los Angeles or New York, and she hoped her dress with the two front pockets, tight bodice, and flowing 1950s-style skirt was fancy enough so she wouldn't stand out and embarrass Tony. After all, he was a famous author and probably had a reputation to maintain. She chuckled inwardly at her own silliness. *Since when have I cared about putting on airs?* Even so, she was relieved when the maître d' led her through the open French doors at the far end of the dining room out to a patio table.

Tony jumped to his feet, and his eyes swept over her. "You look beautiful." He smiled and kissed her cheek.

With his words and the look on his face, she knew she'd done all right. After all, her cousin Kalea was an up-and-coming international designer. Why had she worried in the first place? "You clean up pretty well yourself." She laughed and took a seat in the chair the maître d' pulled out for her. She eyed Tony and couldn't help smiling. Who would have ever thought the gangly seventeen-year-old boy she once knew could rock a navy Hugo Boss blazer?

"I hope you don't mind." He poured her a glass of white wine. "I took the liberty of ordering this while I waited."

"No, it's fine. I hope I didn't keep you waiting long?"

"No, I arrived early. That way if you were going to cancel on me again, I could plead the fact I was already here and was getting some stares from other diners and felt awkward. You'd have to join me then."

"I thought you learned years ago that guilt trips don't work on me," she said lightheartedly. "You do remember that after my mother died, I was raised by my grand-mother, right, and she was the queen of guilt trips. I learned to let them roll off of me at an early age, or I would have spent my entire life with my bags packed ready to go on a guilt trip." She laughed.

"Yes, your grandmother was something else, wasn't she? One look from her and I'd be squirming in my Doc Martens, feeling like a petulant five-year-old."

"Ah, she wasn't as bad as all that. She actually liked you."

"Liked me?" Tony choked on his sip of wine and wiped his chin with a napkin. "If that's how she treated your boyfriends she liked, well, I can see why you're not married."

"What's your excuse, or are you going to blame my grandmother for scaring you off women?"

"Not at all. She was a challenge much like you are, and if you recall, I like nothing better than a good chal-lenge." He took a sip and gazed into Addie's eyes over the rim of his glass. "Since then, I guess I just haven't found a woman who challenged me the same way." He shrugged. "But enough about me." He leaned on the table and held her gaze. "Tell me what the last sixteen years of your life have been like. I thought of calling you several times after my career took off and I moved to England. You were the one person from my past I wanted to share my news with, but I decided that would be crazy. You probably hated me for disappearing like I did and were most likely married with four children. I'd be the last per-son you wanted to hear from."

She reached across the table and squeezed his hand re-assuringly. "Never. I would have loved to have heard from you. But don't get the wrong idea; I haven't been pining over you all these years. I almost got married once."

Addie went on to give him a very abridged version of her life since high school. How after graduate school she secured an internship at the Smithsonian, which led to her job as the curator's assistant at the Boston Public Library, and her engagement to David. How she was selected from a list of over three hundred applicants to participate in a six-month work exchange program with the British Museum and then how shortly after she returned from London, David was murdered.

After revealing that soul wound, she took a deep breath and regrouped her thoughts before telling him about the suspicious death of her father and the inheritance she received from her great-aunt, which was what took her to Greyborne Harbor. "So that's been my life in a nutshell. Rather dull, really," she said with a weak laugh.

"Dull? It's anything but. I am sorry to hear about your fiancé, but your father too? How horrible. That must have been a very traumatic time. I always liked your dad."

"He liked you too." She dropped her gaze. "It's taken me a long time to put all those ghosts to rest because it seems that since then . . . well, I've become a magnet for murder."

Tony stopped swirling his wine in his glass, held it up to the light of the table candle, and studied the contents. "Should I be worried?"

"Hardly," she said with a giggle. "It's not me doing the murdering, but murder cases seem to fall at my feet and sometimes quite literally. But enough about me. I'm dying to hear how you went from easygoing, laid-back, Doc Marten-, earring-, and frayed-jeans-wearing Tony Radcliff to Anthony Radcliff, bestselling author of gothic horror, wearing—if I'm not mistaken—a Patek Philippe Calatrava watch." She gestured to his silver and rose gold watch.

He glanced at his wrist and gave a short laugh. "No, you're not mistaken, and this was a gift from my agent when we signed the movie deal for my latest book."

They chatted through dinner service as he explained to her that the writing thing came about purely by accident. He only delved into it as personal therapy to help him come to terms with the death of his parents, who, as he had mentioned, were killed while conducting an archeological dig in the Middle East. That's why he had to leave school so suddenly and why he had been told by authorities that he couldn't contact her or anyone else to tell them what happened and where he went. He had been a wreck when he came to live in Pen Hollow with his grandmother.

By the way he glossed over his own personal tragedies, Addie suspected that, like her, there was a lot being unsaid. She also figured there might be a good story in there somewhere, and perhaps she'd read about it in one of his novels someday.

He pushed his empty plate away and refilled their wineglasses. "Look, as comfortable as we are both trying to keep this dinner by reminiscing and catching up, I think we both have to admit there is something we have skirted around."

"What do you mean?"

"Something that both of us have avoided mentioning."

"I'm still lost." She took a sip of her wine, hoping her cheeks weren't as flushed as they felt.

"The kiss."

"The kiss . . . um . . . Oh yes, I suppose we should talk about that." She met his gaze and sucked in a slow breath. "Tony, I told you. I'm in a very happy—" Her words almost choked her. "In a very happy relationship right now, and I think we just need to forget about that little incident."

"That's the thing. I can't."

"But you and I were so long ago."

"Please let me explain."

"Okay."

"When I first saw you last night, I wanted to sweep you into my arms and hold you for the rest of our lives. Just seeing you brought back the person I used to be, the person I miss. I thought if I could make you see me like you looked at me sixteen years ago, I'd have a shot. If I kissed you, you might realize you were meant to be with me, your first love, or at least that's what you told me at the time."

"Yes, that was and is still true. You will always be my first love."

"So, I took a wild chance and kissed you, and . . ."

"And?" She squirmed in her chair. Her cheeks felt rather fiery. "I'm sorry—"

"No, I'm sorry. I should never have kissed you without your inviting it, but it was the best thing that could have happened."

"Why?" She was clearly confused. He seemed to be talking in circles.

"Because it made me realize that what we had was a first-love infatuation or whatever it is when you're seventeen. Kissing you last night was a little like kissing my sister . . . if I had one."

"Your sister?"

"Yes, but I don't mean it as an insult to your kissing abilities." He softly chuckled. "You see, through all those years when I was feeling trapped and alone, I'd fantasize about us. Wondering what would have happened if I had contacted you after my parents died and told you where I was and why. I wondered if things would have turned out differently, and if we would have eventually married as we planned. It ate at my heart to think I had let the best thing in my life slip away from me when I had already lost so much. Well . . . that kiss made me see that what we really are, and were, was best friends, soul mates or life mates of a sort, but not love mates."

"I could hug you right now." She grinned. "You have no idea how relieved I am to hear that. I felt the same way last night. Yes, it was good to see you, and I wanted to talk to you, but when you started on the broken heart thing, I freaked out because I don't love you, at least not like that."

"And I don't love you."

"Friends?" She held out her hand.

"Friends to the end." He grinned and took her outstretched hand in his and sealed it with a firm shake.

"Now, can we enjoy our dessert instead of dancing around each other, wondering about intentions?"

"Here, here!" He raised his glass in a toast. "To friends forever and ever."

"Forever and ever." She clinked her glass with his.

"Now that we have all that sorted out, I would like you to consider staying out at my house for the duration of your stay-in-place order."

"I couldn't impose on you like that, and I'm hoping we can sort all this silliness out by the time we have to leave Bree's house on Monday morning, but thank you. If we end up having to stay another day to wrap things up, then Paige and I will be fine at the B&B for a night."

"The offer remains open in case your stay is extended even longer, and don't worry, it's a huge house. Plus, there's only me and two live-in servants rattling around in it all day and sometimes at night too." He gave her a saucy wink.

She raised her brows with his reaction, hoping she hadn't been duped into thinking this was aboveboard when he really did have ulterior motives for the invitation.

"I sometimes write until dawn. Besides, it will give you the chance to see where the writing bug hit me."

Addie sat back and considered his offer. "Paige could come too, couldn't she, and Pippi?"

"Certainly." He sat back in his chair and laced his fingers together. "Have you ever seen Maisie's house?"

She shook her head.

"Then it's high time you do. You'll see instantly what led me to the gothic horror genre." A devious smile crossed his face.

Chapter 14

"**G**reat news, Paige," Addie called, entering the front hall. "Oh, hello, sweetie, I can't believe you're still up." She scooped Pippi up in her arms, snuggling her under her chin, and strolled into the living room. "Hi, Marc, I didn't expect to see you here so late."

"Hi." He glanced up from the easel he'd been writing on. "I hope you don't mind, but Paige and I got on a roll of suspects over dinner, and we came back here to write them out before we forget who's who."

"What's the good news?" asked Paige, glancing at Addie's hand.

"Nothing really, it can wait." She kissed Pippi's head, ruffled her fur, and set her back on the floor where she immediately went to her bed and laid her head on Baxter.

"I have a pot of Cozy Comfort tea steeping. Come into

the kitchen and help me bring it and the cups out," said Paige, gesturing with her head.

"Okay." Addie followed her into the kitchen.

Paige twirled around and grabbed Addie's hand. "Really? He didn't propose again tonight?"

"I wasn't out with Simon."

"You weren't? Where have you been?"

"I met Tony for dinner at the hotel."

"The hotel." She whistled. "Lucky you. I think as long as I've been coming here, I've never gotten past the lobby."

"It is something else, isn't it?" Addie fished around in her handbag and withdrew a brochure. "I picked this up on my way out. I had no idea it was designed by the same architect that designed some of the more fashionable hotels in Miami in the 1920s."

Paige glanced at the brochure. "Yeah, it's part of what drew all the rich here from Boston and—"

"Hollywood," interrupted Addie. "The walls are a who's who of the golden age of film. When you were talking about Pen Hollow's heyday, I had no idea what you meant."

"Is the food as scrumptious as I hear it is?" She placed a tray set with the teapot, three cups, and the creamer in Addie's hands.

Addie couldn't help her involuntary eye roll. "I thought I was helping you with this. Being a pack horse was never the deal."

"I have the honey pot." Paige giggled, holding the Winnie the Pooh jar in the air. "Can I guess that this great news you came through the door bellowing about has something to with Tony?"

"Yes, and if we're still forced to stay on the peninsula

after Monday when Bree gets back, he's invited us to stay at Maisie Radcliff's house with him."

Paige eyed her leerily. "Do you think that's a good idea after the way he carried on last night?"

"Yes," Addie said, heading for the door. "We got it all straightened out, and we're just friends."

"Yeah right. I saw him and how he reacted to you."

"No, really, he said kissing me was like kissing his sister if he had one. At first, I wasn't sure about accepting the invite, but the more I thought about it, the more I realized what better way to get more information about Luella, the library, and the changes Tony had seen in her these last few years."

"I thought he lived in England?"

"He does, but when he left school, he came to live with his grandmother. Apparently, Luella and she go way back. Maybe he has some information we can use to help figure out what in Luella's past got her killed."

"I brought the honey too, Marc," said Paige, crossing the living room. "I wasn't sure what you took in your tea." Paige set it on the side of the tray that Addie deposited on the coffee table.

Addie glanced at the board and smiled. "It appears you two were busy this evening. Let's see what you have." She started reading and nodded. "Yes, I agree. *Patricia* and *Bea* should stay as the top two suspects since we know there was bad blood between Patricia and Luella and Bea was going to lose her job, too."

"That was my thinking," said Paige, "because it might have been a revenge killing for Luella selling the bookmobile."

"Really?" Marc scratched his head. "We couldn't find any proof that either of them was alone with Luella during the timeline when the poison would have had to have been administered."

"By whose account? Theirs?" scoffed Paige.

"You're right." Addie perched on the edge of the sofa, studying what her friends had added. "If Luella ate early like everyone says she did, it's not to say one of them couldn't have slipped upstairs from the sale for a few minutes and doctored her plate while she was distracted. It was a hectic time up there before the dinner, and the volunteers only said that Patricia and Bea were downstairs when the dinner started, but mentioned nothing about the half hour or so before then. That's when Luella would have filled her plate."

"That's true." Marc scanned the board. "We'll have to talk to the volunteers again and find out exactly where they remember seeing Bea and Patricia in the half hour prior to the dinner."

"Or," added Addie, "if they recall seeing Luella's plate sitting around unattended while she ran off to do something else."

"Yes." Marc stared thoughtfully at the clues. "Witnesses often recall the smaller details after the initial shock has worn off. It won't hurt to talk to them again."

"I can do that tomorrow," said Paige, pouring her tea. "Valerie and Laurel are going back to the sale, so I can tag along, and it won't look suspicious."

"Perfect," said Addie, going to the board and tapping her finger on the next line. "Next we have *Turner* and his wife, *Wanda*."

"Yeah, after Paige told me about the affair, we decided they both should be on the list."

"What would the motive be?" Addie studied their names.

"Revenge, jealousy, payback, blackmail, to name a few." Marc shrugged. "Who knows, but they both warrant looking into."

"I agree," said Addie. "The only problem I have with those motives is the affair happened a while ago. Wanda found out, so it wouldn't be something like Luella blackmailing Turner. The wife already knew."

"Maybe," said Paige from the sofa, "the affair didn't end when she thought it had, and Wanda found out they were still seeing each other."

"Possible," said Addie, writing Luella's name beside Wanda's. "I'll try to look into that one tomorrow."

"Be careful." Marc sat upright in the chair. "If Turner finds out you're snooping around his wife—"

Addie glanced over her shoulder at him and screwed up her face. "Give me some credit, will you?" She shook her head and returned to the names on the board. "Now, who is this *Randy Carlyle*?"

"Oh," said Paige, setting down her teacup. "He was apparently Luella's business partner at the pharmacy."

"Yes," said Marc, coming to Addie's side. "I did some digging after you told me she previously ran the local pharmacy. It turns out that when she decided to enter politics, she pulled out of their business deal lock, stock, and barrel, leaving Randy up to his eyeballs in debt."

"Revenge?" asked Addie.

"Maybe, or maybe something else. Why would he wait two years to kill her if that was the reason? There has to be something else."

"I agree. Do you want to check that out, Marc?" She hovered the piece of chalk over Randy's name.

"Yeah, I wouldn't mind, especially since we're dealing

with poison. Who better than a trained pharmacist to know how to concoct a deadly solution and administer it."

"You're right, that one probably needs a police hand." Addie blinked and blinked again. "You can't be serious with Tony's name on here." She looked from Marc to Paige.

"Well, he does seem to be at the bottom of the library losing its funding and subsequently having to close, and also losing the bookmobile because of it," said Paige sheepishly.

"Exactly. He sounds like a better victim to me than a murder suspect, don't you think?" She glared at them. "Why would he put a stop to his grandmother's bequest and then turn around and kill the very woman who had the most to lose when he did, especially if she was skimming money off the top like Tony suspects? What possible motive did you think of when you wrote down his name?"

Marc glanced from a flush-faced Paige to a hot-faced Addie. "It was just a name that came up today when I was talking to the volunteers."

"Of course it did. They blame him for them losing their library. If you're going with that line of thinking, he should be the murder victim, not Luella."

"Okay," said Paige, grabbing a tissue from the box on the table. "I'll take it off. You might be right." She erased Tony's name. "Better?"

"Yes, for now, unless something else shows up in Luella's past that links the two of them. Hopefully, I can find out soon."

"Then leave it on." Marc plucked the stick of chalk out of Addie's hand and wrote *TONY*. "At least until we find out more about Luella and her links to the people in the community."

"Going by that, we need to write down pretty much everyone who lives in Pen Hollow," cried Addie, glaring at the capitalizing of Tony's name.

"And until we can figure out the motive, no one is cleared, right? We're going to take the opposite approach to Sheriff Turner. He doesn't want to include anyone, and we're going to start investigating everyone."

Addie looked at the board and blew out a frustrated breath. "I guess that means we won't be going home tomorrow, Paige."

Marc glanced at his watch. "Yes, and on that note, it's nearly midnight. By the looks of it"—he waved his hand toward the board and grabbed his jacket from the back of the chair—"we're all going to have to get an early start in the morning if we're going to cover all this ground."

Addie showed Marc out, returned to the living room, flopped into the chair still warm from Marc's body, and snuggled down. "If I drift off, just throw a blanket over me," she mumbled to Paige and waited for an answer that didn't come.

Addie sat upright and glanced over at the sofa. She smiled and tiptoed behind the sofa, removed a throw blanket from the back, and draped it over her snoring friend. Addie scooped Pippi up, grabbed Baxter, and trotted up the stairs to Chelsea's pink-and-white princess, wannabe-rock-star bedroom.

Chapter 15

"What the . . . It's seven in the morning!" Addie flung the front door open, wiping sleep from her eyes, and gasped. "Catherine? Felix? What are you doing here?" Was she dreaming or were Catherine and her new boyfriend really standing on the front steps?

"We decided that since you have been placed on peninsula lockdown, you might need a change of clothes and a few toiletries." Catherine held out Addie's suitcase, and Felix held out Paige's colorful Snoopy one.

Addie blinked and tried to focus. "That is so nice of both of you, thank—" She stared, not believing what she was seeing when they parted. "Serena, what are you doing here?"

"It's kind of a long story," said Catherine rather guiltily.

"Then you'd better come in and sit down. Start from the beginning because I'm dying to hear this one," said Addie, standing back so they could enter.

Catherine stepped into the front hallway. "It seems that Serena had the key to your house and—"

"They weren't getting it until they promised to let me tag along for the day," said Serena following her in.

Addie shook her head and glanced at her friend's bulging tummy. "I know a couple of people who aren't going to be happy you're here."

"Who?" Serena held her belly as she made a beeline for the chair.

"Your brother, for one—you know how he worries— and Simon. He'll be furious that you're defying Doctor Dowdy's orders and traveling right now. What did Zach say about it?"

There was silence.

"He doesn't know you're here, does he?"

Catherine shook her head and glanced at Serena. "I think not, and we tried to tell her this was foolish but"— she shrugged—"she's a natural redhead, that's for certain."

Addie pushed the footstool closer to Serena. "At least keep your feet up. Look how swollen your ankles and feet are just from the short drive here."

Serena groaned and heaved one leg then the other up onto the tufted stool. "Happy now?"

Paige's blond head popped out of the kitchen. "I was in the yard with Pippi and couldn't believe the voices I heard from in here. Hi, everyone." She waved.

"We brought you a suitcase," called Catherine. "Your mom packed it, so I have no idea what's in there, but it's probably better than the two outfits you brought for an overnight stay."

Felix stroked his chin and read over the information written on the two easel blackboards. "It looks like you two have made some headway in figuring out this mess you've gotten yourselves into."

"Not really," said Addie, joining him at the easel. "We still can't find a motive because what we've come up with so far doesn't fit with the crime."

"Hmm, well, maybe after I have another coffee, you can fill me in, and perhaps a set of fresh eyes on this might help."

"Yes, coffee is exactly what I need." Addie stopped beside Serena's chair. "You, my friend, will have tea."

"Maybe I want coffee today."

"Only if Simon okays it, but don't hold your breath." Addie spun and sauntered into the kitchen.

"Addie." Catherine followed her. "I know this isn't a good time"—she kept her voice low and glanced at the kitchen door—"but I need your advice."

Addie paused filling up the coffee carafe with water and set it on the counter. "Sure, what's going on?"

Catherine twisted her fingers together in front of her and winced. "Jonathan called me yesterday."

"Jonathan Hemingway? David's father, your ex?"

"Yes, well, except it sounds like he doesn't know he's my ex."

"What do you mean?"

"I mean he's coming to Greyborne Harbor next week, and he chatted on like we were still an item."

"Have you heard from him since he canceled out on Thanksgiving dinner and was a no-show through Christmas?"

She shook her head. "Not a word until yesterday. What am I going to do? I mean, I'm with Felix now."

"Does Felix know Jonathan phoned?"

She shook her head.

"Then you have to tell him. If you really care for Felix like I think you do, there shouldn't be any secrets, right?"

"Right, but what do I say?" She swiped the back of her hand over her forehead. "I've never been in a position like this, never in my whole life. Goodness, think of my age. Two men? I can't go through what you did with Marc and Simon. I couldn't handle it."

"I didn't handle it very well either, if you recall, and no, you don't have to. Just tell Jonathan you've moved on, that it was nice spending time with him, but since he hadn't been in touch for so long, you thought he was no longer interested, and, well, 'Heeeere's Felix Vanguard,'" she said, mimicking Ed McMahon, the announcer on the *Tonight Show Starring Johnny Carson* television show.

"I just don't know." She wrung her hands. "I seem to recall there's a restroom down here by the back entrance."

"Yes," Paige pointed, "just down there."

"Thanks, I need to splash some water on my face and think about this. I've been so stressed since he called."

Addie squeezed her arm as she passed her. "You'll figure it out. Trust your instincts but be honest with both of them."

"Thank you," said Catherine as she headed for the back entrance.

Addie glanced at Paige, who was dancing a little jig beside her. "What's up with you? You're grinning like your mom's cat Cleo does when she catches a mouse."

"I'm busting to tell you what Valerie just told me."

"What?"

"Guess where Sheriff Turner's wife Wanda works?"

"Are we playing twenty questions?"

"No, just guess."

"I don't know . . . . the police station."

"No, the pharmacy that Luella used to own with Randy."

"Really?"

"Yes, he hired her as a pharmacy assistant when Luella left him high and dry, which, mind you, wasn't long after the whole affair thing came out."

"So, she works with one of the other suspects on our board? I'd better get dressed and head over to the drug store to have a nice *casual* chat with her." Addie glanced at the clock. "What time do they open?"

"Don't bother. She doesn't work Sundays. I already asked Valerie, but at ten Wanda will be at the community center. Apparently, with Luella gone, they need to elect a new chairperson for the gardening committee."

"Wow, they're not wasting any time. Her body's barely cold."

"I know. Like Valerie said, not many people are broken up about her death. It's getting into prime gardening season, and the state's Communities in Bloom competition for towns with a population under two thousand is coming up the end of August."

"That's kind of sad though, don't you think?"

"Yes, but the fact is, according to Valerie, Wanda wants the chair position badly."

"Bad enough to kill the woman her husband had an affair with?"

Paige shrugged.

"What are the two of you talking about?" asked Catherine, sauntering back into the kitchen.

"Paige can fill you in while I run upstairs and get dressed." Addie tugged the belt around her robe tighter.

Pippi barked, and Addie poked her head out into the living room.

"It's just someone at the door. I'll get it," called Felix.

A moment later, Simon, looking more rested than he had the previous evening, strolled into the living room and stopped short when he spotted Serena sprawled out in the oversized chair. His brow creased, and he tugged at his earlobe. "Serena, I'm surprised to see you here. Does Doctor Dowdy know you took a little road trip today?"

Serena glanced up at him and twisted the wedding ring on her finger. "Not . . . really."

He glanced at her feet raised up on the footstool and scanned her tummy and face. "Would you mind if I did a quick blood pressure check?"

"Why?"

"No reason in particular." He relaxed his stance and took on a nonchalant demeanor, but Addie could see the concern in his eyes. "I would just feel better knowing the exertion hasn't taxed the little one too much."

"Come on, Simon." Serena huffed. "I'm having a baby, something women have been doing since the beginning of mankind. The way everyone is carrying on, you'd think I was sick or something."

"As a doctor, it would make me feel better. How about it?"

"If it stops everyone from worrying about me, go ahead."

"Thank you. I'll just grab my medical bag from the car and be right back." He disappeared again but not before giving Addie an uneasy smile.

Addie's tummy tightened as she glanced at her puffy-cheeked friend.

"I'm not sure why everyone is making such a big deal about this," cried Serena, jerking her thumb toward her tummy. "It's a baby, for goodness' sake. The drive here was all of fifteen minutes. If I lived in a big city, I'd be at least that far away from the nearest hospital anyway if I went into labor, right?" She huffed and slunk back in the chair.

"That's true, but I think it's just that there isn't a real hospital here, only a clinic. If things started to move along quickly, we couldn't get back to Greyborne Harbor in time, that's all." Addie fought to keep her tone soothing and not let the expression in Simon's eyes reflect in her words.

"Well," said Felix, rising from the sofa, "I think I'll go into the kitchen and see if I can move that coffee along quicker."

"Good idea. I'll be there in a second," said Addie, taking a seat on the edge of the footstool. "Look, hon, it's not that we don't want you here. It's just that perhaps this isn't the best time for you to—"

"Not the best time?" Serena stared at her in disbelief, her eyes wide. "It was one thing to miss out on the book sale, but then to find out that my two best friends are suspects in a murder investigation and that my brother has taken time off work to help investigate it! Tell me there is any better time to be here to see what I can do to help."

Simon, who had paused in the doorway listening,

cleared his throat, strolled over to the chair, and set his black medical bag on the floor. "Just so I feel better about your being here, let's have a quick check, shall we?" He pulled a blood pressure cuff and stethoscope from his bag. "After that we can decide just how much of an active participant you can safely be in helping to sort out this mess, okay?"

"Okay," Serena agreed reluctantly and raised her arm so he could secure the blood pressure cuff.

Addie reassuringly squeezed Serena's toes and rose to her feet. "I'm going to go get that tea for you. Simon, would you like coffee?"

He nodded as he guided the ear tips of the stethoscope into place.

The aroma of fresh brewed coffee tickled at Addie's nose when she poked her head into the kitchen. Paige, Catherine, and Felix sat at the kitchen island, each sipping a steaming cup. "Finally," she said, crossing over to the coffeemaker Paige had found boxed up in the bottom of the pantry. "Simon wants one too, but I think I'll hold off taking his out there until he's done assessing Serena." She closed her eyes and let the heady aroma work its magic in wakening her still sleep-shod mind before she took the first heavenly sip. "Umm, whoever made this, I thank you from the bottom of my heart." She slid onto the fourth counter stool and gazed from one of her friends to the other. "What's up?"

"Paige was just filling us in on what's been going on," said Catherine, setting her mug on the counter.

"Yes, and I must say, it's all very weird," added Felix.

"Weird doesn't describe it," said Addie, taking another

sip. "How Sheriff Turner could even have us on his suspect list in the first place is beyond me."

Catherine shifted on her stool to look at Addie. "It sounds to me that his whole reasoning is because you're outsiders and he can't believe anyone from the peninsula could do such a thing, is that right?"

Paige nodded. "That's what he says."

"Even though there is no proof and no witnesses that can place us anywhere in the vicinity of the food at the time the poison could have been added to something Luella ate."

"Plus, the fact that we never met the woman before Friday when we got to the sale." Paige set her cup down with a thud.

"I knew Luella," said Catherine, her cheeks blushing. "To be honest, it doesn't surprise me that someone wanted her dead."

"Was she really that difficult to get along with?" Addie eyed her friend over the rim of her cup.

"She never used to be, but a few years ago she changed. I really noticed it last year when the Greyborne Harbor Garden Society met with the Pen Hollow group to discuss the annual Communities in Bloom competition. It was her way or the highway. She chose the greenhouses to deal with, and she picked the theme. We had no say in any of the matters."

"You worked with them?" asked Felix. "But wouldn't you be in competition with them?"

"Because Greyborne Harbor is much larger than Pen Hollow, we are in different categories. We're deemed sister towns because of our proximity to each other. For example, Greyborne Harbor and Salem could never be sister towns because we compete in the same category."

"I see," said Felix, taking another sip.

"Since we were never in direct competition with each other over the years—actually since your aunt Anita was chair in Greyborne Harbor—it became possible for us to work together on themes and with things like ordering plants and seeds from the greenhouses in bulk. It helped both associations."

"I guess I have a lot to learn about how all these small-town communities work," added Felix with a grin. "It's not so amicable in the big city."

"*Amicable* isn't the word I'd use when describing our interactions with Luella once she became mayor and still held on to her seat as chairperson for the garden club." Catherine swirled the remains of her coffee in her cup and shrugged. "Like I said, it doesn't surprise me that someone wanted her dead."

Addie cupped her hand in her chin and glanced from Catherine to Paige. "There's a lot of motives, but everyone is focusing on the library closing or the bookmobile being sold, because that seems most logical, right?"

"Yes," said Paige, "but I think we're finding out the more we know about the victim, the more motives there are."

"Yes, and my gut still tells me it has nothing to do with the library or her past affair with Turner. What if the motivation behind her murder is something so seemingly insignificant in the big picture that everyone is missing it?"

"I don't know about that," said Felix, his back stiffening as he turned to look at Addie. "It sounds pretty cut-

and-dried to me. We have the affair, and then the wife finding out. Now we discover that same wife is working for the business partner whom this Luella person left in a financial lurch. It's a good place to start looking."

"I agree, those are all good motives to consider, but what *if* it has something to do with her being the tyrant of the garden club?"

"I guess there have been stranger motives," said Felix, staring into his cup. "What you're saying is—"

"I got it." Paige snapped her fingers. "I bet the killer will be at the garden club meeting this afternoon."

Catherine choked on her last mouthful of coffee. "They're having a meeting today?" She grabbed a paper napkin from the holder on the counter and wiped her chin. "But Luella just died two days ago. That seems a bit . . ."

"Disrespectful?" added Felix.

"It sounded a bit too soon to me, too," said Addie, "when Paige told me what the neighbor, Valerie, said this morning."

"Valerie Price?" asked Catherine.

Paige nodded. "Do you know her?"

"Yes, we're great gardening club friends, have been for years. I know most of the ladies in the Pen Hollow club." Catherine shifted on her stool and gazed at Paige. "Was Valerie in favor of holding this meeting today before they've even had Luella's funeral? That doesn't sound like the Valerie I know, especially after all she's been through recently."

"I don't think so," said Paige. "She seemed more put out about having to go today than anything."

"It might be perfect timing for us though," said Addie with a devious grin.

"How so?" asked Catherine. "The poor woman hasn't even been laid to rest and already they're vying for her seat as chairwoman? Despite my personal feelings for Luella, it's still horrible, if you ask me."

"Yes, it is," agreed Addie, "but since the gardening club is holding a meeting today and we need to investigate all our theories, who knows what we might learn? It just might be the perfect opportunity for us to see who's pushing so badly for the new election that they're holding so soon after her death, and that chairperson seat could be the motive for her killing that we haven't been considering."

"What was the poison Simon found in the autopsy again?" asked Felix.

"Aconitine, why?"

"If I recall from my years in the service as a military investigator, aconitine is a plant derivative, isn't it?" He glanced at Addie, a knowing glint in his eyes.

"Yes, it is." Addie grinned over the rim of her cup. "And what better source to find it than through the gardening club!"

"I can be the excuse for us to attend the meeting," said Catherine thoughtfully. "As the Greyborne Harbor representative, I can go and offer condolences for their loss and tell them our club will help with their new president's transition during these difficult times."

"Yes, and I can talk to Wanda to see how her garden grows." Addie gave Catherine a sly wink.

"What about me?" asked Paige, tossing a tea bag into the teapot.

"Aren't you going back to the book sale to talk to Patricia and Bea?" asked Addie. "We still have to keep open the option of motive, until we find one hard fact that leads us in the right direction."

"The book sale sounds more up my alley," said Felix. "If you don't mind my tagging along, perhaps we can make a stop by the sheriff's office, too? I'd like to meet this Turner character and find out why he's really so bent on you two being suspects."

"Do you think he'll talk to you?" asked Addie.

"I'm just hoping my service background and the years I spent in private security might open his door to me. Because I have a hunch it's more like he's trying to protect the real killer, and from what I've heard, it could be closer to home than we all realize."

"You mean his wife, Wanda?" Addie stared curiously at him. "She's already on our list."

He nodded. "And this Patricia, what's her connection to him?"

They looked at each other and shrugged.

"I think there is one," Felix added, "and that might help with the motive too. At least, his motive for keeping such a narrow focus on this whole investigation."

"Serena is asking about her tea," said Simon, sailing through the door and making a quick beeline for the coffeepot.

"I'm just waiting for the water to boil," replied Paige.

"Are you finished in there?" asked Addie.

He nodded and gave her a glancing kiss on the cheek, then brought his cup to his lips and took a sip. "Ah, that's better. They only had tea or instant coffee at the B&B this morning and, well, nothing beats the real thing to kick-start the day. Now, for something I wanted to do over half an hour ago when I arrived." He set his cup down, tilted Addie's chin upward with his forefinger, and placed a long, lingering kiss on her lips. "Good morning."

Searing heat rushed up from under the collar of her bathrobe and burned across her cheeks as she glanced sheepishly at her friends. "Good morning."

"I would love to stay and chat with you all, but I have to get back to the lab and finish testing samples."

"I thought you were done last night?"

"I was, but until I find the source, I have to test and retest everything. Swabs from the bus, from Luella's car, pretty much everything she touched later Friday afternoon."

Felix rested his elbows on the counter and made a steeple of his fingers. "In your testing, is there any way you can tell if the aconitine found in her system came from a natural source such as a solution made directly from the monkshood plant, or if it was from a synthetic source?"

"I can see what other trace elements there are. If it came from a natural source there should be something else. Why, what are you thinking?"

"Addie had a theory about the garden club, and it seems one school of thought"—Felix's gaze flitted from one to the other around the island—"is the motive might have something to do with that club and not the library at all."

"At this point, anything's a possibility," said Simon, chugging down his coffee. "I gotta run. By the way, I have relegated Serena to manning the blackboard updates as her contribution to the investigation, so phone her with any updates." He lowered his voice. "She needs to feel a vital part of this, whatever it is. I don't want her feeling neglected, on the off chance she'll get frustrated and start getting herself out there and joining you."

"Is there anything to worry about with her?"

"Not specifically. I am going to call Doctor Dowdy, though, as soon as I leave. I do have a question for him."

"Which is what?"

He kissed Addie again and smiled. "I'll tell you when I'm certain. I'll call later with an update on the samples."

Chapter 16

"Now that Paige and I are showered and dressed, get your game faces on. Everyone remembers where they're going today, right?" Addie asked, grabbing her satchel from the end of the sofa.

"Yes," said Catherine. "You and I are off to the garden club meeting."

"And Paige and I are heading over to the book sale at the library to see if we can find those missing first editions and speak with this Patricia woman." Felix retrieved his car keys from his blazer pocket.

"And I'm stuck here manning the phones and updating the board," said Serena, sounding none too pleased.

"Your job is the most important," said Addie reassuringly as she scratched Pippi behind the ear. "Plus, Pippi needs company for the day since Valerie will be at the meeting and then the library sale too."

"Where's Marc?" asked Serena as the group headed out the door.

"He said last night he was going to talk to Turner about allowing Paige and me to go home, but I haven't heard anything on it today. Maybe shoot him a text and let him know you're here and what you're doing. I'm sure he'll stop by. Call if you need anything," yelled Addie, closing the door.

The warm midmorning sun mingled with the aroma of spring flowers, and the briny scent off the ocean made Addie wish the day could be spent exploring the peninsula and not figuring out who had a motive to commit murder. But then again, days like this had become commonplace for her since moving to this part of the state. *It must be something in the air*, she mused as she wiggled into the driver's seat of the Wrangler and waited for Catherine to fasten her seat belt.

Addie glanced over at Catherine as she steered the SUV down the hill to Sea Spray Drive. "Have you decided what you're going to do about the Jonathan-and-Felix situation?"

"Yes. I'm going to take your advice and be honest with them both. Felix has been the best thing that's happened to me in a long, long time. He shows up when he says he will, I don't have to wait weeks or *months* to see him, and worry that something might come up with his work to delay him *again*. And . . ."

"And what?"

"He's going to start a business in Greyborne Harbor, so I know for sure he'll be staying put."

"That's wonderful! What kind of business?"

"He hasn't told anyone, but since it looks like it's going to be a go . . . He's been working on getting his private investigator's license," Catherine said, pride evident in her voice.

"Good for him. That certainly fits in with what he used to do in Navy Intelligence and as a security specialist at the Smithsonian and with Zach's dad, Oliver."

"Yes, but enough about me. It sounds like you've gotten yourself in another pickle, haven't you?"

Addie slowed down to read the road sign and gave a quick side glance at Catherine. "What are you talking about? Being a suspect?" She read the crossroad sign, shook her head, and drove on.

"Not the suspect part. That seems to come naturally to you," she said with a soft laugh. "Marc showing up to rescue you, and now this Tony fellow from your past . . . What in the world has Simon said about all this?"

"First of all, Marc didn't just show up. He drove here *with* Simon because he's known Sheriff Turner for years and—Is that Marc talking to Turner in front of the sheriff's office?"

"It looks like him."

Addie slowed down and went to tap the horn to honk and wave, but by the fierce glare in Turner's bulging eyes as he leaned forward and shook his finger in Marc's face, she had second thoughts. "Yikes, neither of them looks any too happy."

"I think we'd better drive on before Turner pulls you over on some concocted driving violation."

"I think you're right." Addie hit the accelerator. As she passed by, she glanced over at the two men and shivered at the sight of Marc's crimson face. "I'd love to be a fly to hear what's going on there."

"Turner's probably not happy about Marc's involvement since this is out of his jurisdiction. I imagine he's telling him to back off and stay out of his investigation."

"Probably, but Marc's worried that even without evidence, Turner will keep Paige and me at the top of his suspect list. I'm pretty sure he won't back off even if it's just to make sure Turner follows the book."

"I've known Jack Turner for years, and let me tell you, a little disagreement on the sidewalk is nothing compared to what he's capable of if he feels his authority is being questioned. He's run this peninsula as a one-man show for over thirty years and isn't going to accept the likes of Marc Chandler, an outsider, looking over his shoulder."

"What's his deal with outsiders anyway? Doesn't the economy of the town and the entire peninsula, including the amusement park, depend on them? You'd think he'd have more of an open attitude toward tourists and visitors."

"You'd think so since his paycheck and the various departments' operating budgets on the peninsula are based on the summer influx of people coming for their holidays. But I think what's really driving him is he wants more than anything to be able to retire with a stellar reputation and thinks if he can deter some of the unsavory outside elements from setting up shop here, he can save the peninsula from the volatile social events happening elsewhere in the country that might jeopardize that."

"So he thinks Paige and I are unsavory elements?"

"Who knows what that man thinks? We could try to

psychoanalyze him until we're blue in the face and still be no further ahead, but . . ." Catherine fixed her gaze on Addie, causing her to shift uncomfortably as she checked the next street sign. "What I really want to talk about is this Tony fellow."

"How did you hear about him anyway?" asked Addie, slowing down as they approached the next corner.

"When you were in the shower, Paige mentioned you ran into your old high school sweetheart last night who also just *happened* to be in town for the book sale."

"No, it's not quite like that." Addie went on to explain about Tony and his grandmother and her endowment to the library and how and why he pulled it.

"And this is *the* Anthony Radcliff, the author?"

"Yes, much to my shock." Addie laughed and glanced up at the street sign. "I think this is the street where Paige said to turn." She flipped on her signal light to make the right turn, drove up half a block, and turned right into the parking lot of the community hall.

"It's funny. I've never met Tony, and I've known Maisie Radcliff for years. She was a good friend of your aunt too. Actually, that's how I first met her."

"Then you'd know about the inscription in the book Paige and I found when we were looking at the bookmobile and trying to decide to buy it or not."

"A purchase I'm sure you regret now."

"I don't know. Turner won't let me see the bus to assess the damage. I don't even know if it can be repaired so we can salvage something out of this whole weekend. We had made so many plans on how we'd operate a traveling bookstore." Addie hung her head. "But what was I saying?" She got out and joined Catherine on the sidewalk leading to the community center's large oak doors. "Yes, the inscription," Addie said, trying to picture the words in her mind that had struck at her heart so deeply. "*'To my dearest friend Maisie and your beloved new baby grandson Anthony. May this bring you both great reading enjoyment for many years to come. All my love with a hint of tear-filled envy in your newfound happiness, your loyal friend, Anita.'* Would that have been Aunt Anita who signed it?"

"Most likely. Maisie and your aunt knew each other since they attended Garland College in Boston when they were teenagers."

"You're kidding?"

"No, they were best friends. Anita used to spend a lot of time in Pen Hollow during the day. Maisie's childhood sweetheart was Arnold Radcliff, so even before those two got married, your aunt and Maisie were constantly on the peninsula, partying during the season."

"*My* aunt was a party animal?" Addie hooted. "Somehow after reading many of her journals, I just can't see that."

"Then you haven't read the ones from her youth, have you?" Catherine said with a teasing wink. She flung open the hall door and stepped into the boot room. "Just a word of warning before we go into the hall. I've met Wanda Turner many times during our joint meetings, and to be honest, she can be a little prickly. So, I'll introduce you and then you can ask whatever questions you have in mind. But remember, she is Sheriff Turner's wife and fiercely protective of him."

"Enough that she might have wanted a rival for his af-fections dead?"

"Possibly, but I think she's too smart to have done the deed herself. My guess is she would have planted the seed in Randy Carlyle's mind because he had his own is-sues with Luella. All Wanda would have to do is stand back and see what transpired from there."

"Good things to know. Thanks, and since you know these people," whispered Addie, "I'll just take your lead on this and hang back as the supportive friend here to console you and everyone else in their mutual grief over the passing of Luella."

Hoots of laughter echoed from the great room off to their right, and Catherine glanced at Addie. "Grief?"

"I guess everyone grieves in their own way." Addie gulped and poked her head inside the door and gazed around the large room filled with chairs set out in theater style. The seats were filled with happy, smiling faces. There was not one teary-eyed person in the room. Addie's tummy quaked with a sense of misgiving over their deci-sion to attend today. "Maybe this isn't a good idea. It doesn't appear there will be much consoling going on, so we won't have an excuse to be here."

Catherine shored herself up and threw back her shoul-ders. "Nonsense, I'm here as a representative of their sis-ter town to offer my support in their transition in any way I can, remember?" She gave Addie a crooked smile and sauntered into the hall. Her silvery hair, bobbing and shim-mering under the rays of sunbeams streaming in through the windows, gave her a guardian angel glow.

She paused momentarily before strolling over to Valerie seated in the first row. "Valerie, my dear." Catherine took Valerie's hand in hers. "I came as soon as I heard the news about Luella. How are you all holding up during this trying time?" Catherine leaned over and kissed Valerie's cheek.

"Oh, Catherine." Valerie, clearly touched, patted her free hand on her chest. "How kind of you." She rose to her feet and took Catherine's hands in hers. "To be honest, old friend"—she leaned closer and dropped her voice— "this has turned into a nightmare."

"I can only imagine. Her loss must have hit everyone hard. Luella was such a vital force in the community." Catherine smiled in condolence.

"Tornado is more like it. Now we're trying to deal with the aftermath left in her wake."

Catherine's head jerked back. "Oh dear, is there a problem?"

"You bet." Valerie motioned with her head toward a staunch, unapproachable-appearing woman with bobbed auburn hair. Despite being across the room next to a table laid out with a coffee urn and snacks, she seemed to dominate the room. "Wanda Turner has decided she will be the next chairperson of the club and has scared off every other person who even thought about running against her. This little meeting, I'm afraid, is only for show so the minutes can reflect her victory and make the position official."

Addie glanced over at the stern-faced woman who appeared to be assessing the crowd. She locked gazes with Addie. An uneasy feeling swam in the pit of her stomach. Where had she seen Wanda before? Addie scanned through her memory files but came up empty. Perhaps if she talked to her, the woman's voice would trigger something.

Wanda set her coffee cup on the table and clapped her hands. "If I could have everyone's attention!" she called out.

Not only had she seen Wanda Turner somewhere, but she had spoken to her. *But where?* She needed more to flip the switch on that memory and waited like the rest of the room, which had gone deathly quiet, and focused on Wanda, waiting to hear what else she had to say.

"I see we have been blessed by the presence of Catherine Lewis, whom many of you know is the chairperson of our sister town of Greyborne Harbor in the Communities in Bloom competition." Wanda appeared very much in charge of the audience. "Please, join me in welcoming her to our *closed-door* meeting." Her words slithered off her tongue as though she spit them out under protest.

The group stirred in their seats. By the looks on their faces, they weren't sure, given the tone of Wanda's voice, if they should applaud Catherine's presence or throw stones at her. Addie shifted her weight from one foot to the other, now quite certain that their coming here might not have been a great move, especially when she glanced at Wanda and detected a small, smug smile. Then it hit her. She'd seen that snarky little smile before, and she recalled where else she had seen Wanda Turner. At least, she was ninety-eight percent sure, but she'd need more to make a positive identification. But by what Wanda had just said, it seemed she and Catherine might soon be escorted out of the building.

Dauntless Catherine, of course, held her head high and glided across the floor like royalty. She seized Wanda's hands in hers, locked gazes with the stunned woman, and smiled demurely. "Your community has suffered a great loss, and I would like to do whatever I can to assist you through the transition during what must be the most difficult of times."

Wanda's face paled, and she appeared speechless. The gardening club members collectively held their breaths.

"Yes . . . yes." Wanda stuttered and struggled to find her voice. "It is a most difficult time, thank you." Looking more confident, she straightened her shoulders and gazed out over the room. With a more confident voice, she announced, "Yes, and we all knew Luella well and know that she would have wanted this club, like all the others she chaired, to carry on as usual in her absence. Am I right?" The members sat still. An eerie silence settled in the hall. "I said, am I right? We must carry on."

"Here, here! In honor of Luella," cried a gangly woman in the back row.

"Yes, to Luella's memory," the group murmured.

Thank you, Catherine. Addie made her way over to Catherine and Wanda before she lost the opening and reached her hand out in introduction. "Hello, I'm Addie Greyborne, and I just want to say how sorry I am. I know this has hit the community hard."

The woman pulled her head back and studied Addie. "You're the one who bought our bookmobile, aren't you?"

"Yes, I am. My friend and I came for the book sale and had the pleasure of meeting Luella before it got underway, and she mentioned that it was for sale. We liked what we saw and so—" Addie shrugged, aware the woman's eyes shot her lance-like blows with every word she muttered. Addie dropped her gaze. "Well, it's a tragedy what happened later."

"For whom?" Wanda's voice lowered and took on a waspy hiss. "For Luella, or for you and your precious bus, the one you stole out from under this community?" She folded her long, slender arms over her inflated chest and stared down her nose. "Tell me, Miss Greyborne, did you give Luella the poison before you convinced her to sell you Patricia's bus, or was it after, in the hope that she would die before your payment went through? If that was the case, I'd say it was a pretty dumb move on your part since your plan probably didn't include her smashing the bus into a stone wall and making it undrivable."

"Wanda!" cried Valerie, joining them. "That's enough. These are our guests."

"Yes, out-of-towners who seem to have had a good reason and ample opportunity to feed our *dearly* beloved Luella a deadly cocktail, don't you think?"

Addie was uncomfortably aware that all eyes in the room were on them, but she planted her feet and stared Wanda in the eye. This woman was either parroting her husband or the one feeding him the theory to take the heat off the real killer.

"I know you." Addie gasped. "Aren't you the woman I saw on the stairs just prior to the potluck dinner starting? Yes, I'm certain it was you. Paige and I were heading down to the book sale for one final look before the dinner commenced, and you were on your way up to the meeting room. You stopped and asked us if we'd seen Luella upstairs. I remember clearly now. I told you she was in her office, and you said, and I quote, 'The poor dear must be starved. I bet she hasn't eaten a thing all day. I hope

Gretchen has started to put the food out so *I* can make up a plate for her.' " Addie pierced the woman with her own lancing gaze. "As you are obviously aware, it was something she ate that night that killed her, right?" Addie stood back as Wanda's bubble popped.

"I . . . I have no idea what you're talking about. I was downstairs at the book sale the whole afternoon helping Patricia on the desk, just ask her."

"I could be wrong, of course, but it was definitely someone who looked *a lot* like you." Addie studied her for a moment. "Yes, a lot like you." She shrugged. "But, perhaps, I'm mistaken."

Chapter 17

Addie and Catherine charged through the community hall doors and staggered out onto the sidewalk.

"Whew!" choked Catherine, brushing stray hairs from her eyes. "I'm surprised Wanda didn't have us lynched on the spot after that."

"What goes around comes around. I couldn't just stand there and let her accuse me of poisoning Luella in front of everyone, could I?"

"You do know she will run directly to her husband now and tell him how you embarrassed her in front of the gardening club."

"Can it get any worse? He's already decided exactly what Wanda said, and if I'm not mistaken, she's the one who's been feeding him that garbage to cover for the real killer."

"You're probably right," said Catherine, "but did you actually *see* her on the stairs looking for Luella, or was that just something you said in retaliation? You never mentioned this incident before."

Addie fumbled to insert the key into the door of the Wrangler. "I didn't say anything because at the time a woman on the stairs looking for Luella seemed so insignificant. It was opening day of the sale, and everyone was running around looking for her. All the volunteers were struggling to get organized because they weren't prepared for such a large turnout. But as soon as I saw her and heard her speak, I remembered what took place that day in the stairwell. She just shot to the top of my suspect list."

Catherine slid into the passenger's seat and smoothed the creases from her silver-blue, flowered blouse and stared straight ahead. "You do realize that now Wanda will not work with the Greyborne Harbor gardening club."

Addie tilted her head to the side and glanced at Catherine. "Did you really think she was going to anyway, after the vinegary greeting she gave you?"

Catherine let out a laugh, snorted, covered her mouth, and snorted again. "No, I knew before we went that if she became the next chairperson, there would no longer be a sister town for us to bulk-order with."

"Then it's their loss because Greyborne Harbor has quadruple the membership and that alone gives you more buying power than they have." Addie shook her head. "Not a loss as far as I can see," she muttered as she pulled out of the parking lot and headed back to Sea Spray Drive.

When Addie turned right onto Bree's street, she swerved

to the right to avoid the sheriff's department cruiser coming directly toward them. It slowed down and moved
over slightly to allow her to pass. Addie glanced over and
locked eyes with the driver. Her fingers tightened around
the steering wheel. "News travels fast here, doesn't it?"

"Judging by the look in his eyes, I'd say Wanda wasted
no time telling Jack Turner about your little run-in."

Addie parked in front of Bree's and hopped out. "I just
hope he wasn't here hassling Serena. That's the last thing
she needs right now." She dashed up the sidewalk to the
door and flung it open. "Serena? I saw Sheriff Turner
leaving, is everything—" Addie stopped in the living
room doorway. "Marc, you're here?"

His eyes narrowed as he rose from the sofa. Addie
couldn't miss the telltale tic of his jaw.

"What happened?" His breaths quickened. "Are you
okay?"

"Yeah, I'll be fine."

"Sit down."

"No, I'm fine."

"It wasn't a request. Sit down."

Addie swallowed hard. It had been a long time since
Marc had used his authoritarian voice on her. And just
when it looked like they had moved on and were having
such a nice working relationship. She eyed the sofa and
glanced back at him. He stepped over in front of the
easels. She slunk down onto the soft cushiony surface
and held her breath. When he was in this mode, he had a
way of making her feel like she was back in school and
had been sent to the principal's office.

"What did you do today?" His voice wobbled as
though he were struggling to keep it even. He glanced at

Catherine still lingering in the doorway. "Were you there when she"—he jerked his thumb in Addie's direction—"saw fit to accuse Turner's wife of murder in a roomful of people?"

Catherine shored herself up and graciously strode to Addie's side and placed a protective hand on her shoulder. "As a matter of fact, I was, and Addie was not out of line. That horrible woman accused her of poisoning Luella. Addie was in the right to turn the tables and cast doubt on the woman herself, considering what took place not long before Luella died."

Addie glanced over at Serena still propped up in the chair, her feet on the footstool and Pippi curled up on what little lap her extended belly had left. She hoped for another supportive gesture but was met instead by a glint of amusement in Serena's eyes. Was this because she too had been a recent victim of Marc's wrath about her making the trip today? Was she pleased the heat was off her and now directed toward someone else?

Addie was never more tempted to stick her tongue out at her best friend, but remembered she was supposed to be a grown woman. But as always, Marc Chandler's RoboCop-attitude made her revert to being a silly little girl again. She crossed her arms and slid back in her seat to await the tongue-lashing she knew would follow. Best to get it over with, then she could get back to work on the suspect board.

Marc drew in a long breath. His jaw relaxed, and he met Addie's gaze. "I'm sure at the time whatever you said to Wanda Turner was indeed called for, but your little outburst in public has undermined all the headway I finally made with the sheriff."

Addie shot forward in her seat. "What do you mean?"

Marc sat down on the edge of Serena's stool and rubbed his hands together. "I spent a contentious morning with Jack, going over every bit of evidence and every witness statement, pointing out that nothing pointed to you or Paige as possible suspects. He finally relented and said that as long as you returned to Greyborne Harbor and made yourselves available for questioning should anything concrete turn up, he would allow you to leave the peninsula."

"That's fantastic. I better call Paige and let her know." Addie excitedly fished her phone out of her bag.

"Not so fast." Marc held up his hands. "It seems since your"—he cleared his throat—"*conversation* with his wife, he's had a change of heart."

Addie's heart plummeted to the pit of her stomach. When would she ever learn to keep her mouth shut and that not every bone needed to be unearthed?

"He now insists you're still his two best suspects. He said you spent time alone with Luella at the municipal yard and were the last people she was seen talking to before the accident. He admits he doesn't have the evidence yet to arrest you, but he's not giving up and is sure that something will turn up."

"But look at the facts and the witness statements. What's he basing this hunch on? Because that's all it is."

"He said his thirty years as a cop tells him you two did it. He doesn't know how or why exactly, but he won't let it go."

"So, we're stuck here?"

"At least until he exhausts all his options."

"Or his wife stops whispering in his ear. I'm starting to

wonder who really is in charge of this investigation. I'll tell you, she must really have something on him to make him jump through her hoops like this."

"He did have the affair with Luella and got caught," said Catherine, walking over to the easel and reading what was written. "I'm sure that has a lot to do with him wanting to appease her now."

"Yeah," said Addie, joining Catherine. "And playing on his guilt gives her the perfect cover to commit a murder and get away with it, doesn't it?"

"This is not even believable," said Serena, moving Pippi from her lap to beside her. "Where in the real world can someone like Turner get away with this? No evidence, no witnesses, and no official charges, but he still can dictate where Addie and Paige can go and not go? It doesn't make sense."

"No," said Marc, "it doesn't, but it is an ongoing murder investigation, and as the official law enforcement representative here on the peninsula, he can lock down the area until the case is solved."

"There are a lot of things that happen in life we can just shake our heads at because they seem too unbelievable to be truly happening, and this is one of those moments, I guess." Catherine sighed.

"Yes," grumbled Serena. "This is definitely one of those too-bizarre-to-be-real, scratch-your-head-in-amazement moments."

Laughter echoed through room when the front door opened, and in walked a grinning Paige, Felix appeared as though he'd just eaten a canary, and behind them, a beaming Simon.

"What's up with you guys?" asked Addie, sensing the shift in the mood of the room.

"Sherlock Holmes would be proud of us today." Felix laughed, made a direct line to Catherine, and kissed her cheek.

"Do tell," Catherine said, her cheeks flushing. "We need some good news right about now."

"Why the long look on your faces? What's happened?" Simon came to Addie's side, wrapped her in his arms and softly kissed her. "Are you okay?"

"*Okay* is not the word I'd use," mumbled Serena.

"No, it seems I went and put my foot in some real doo-doo today and made our situation worse." Her gaze darted from Simon and set on Paige. "I'm sorry, but it appears we're stuck here for a while longer. I know Bree and her family come back tomorrow, but we'll figure something out."

"The B&B is nice and clean and reasonably priced," said Simon reassuringly. "Let's make some coffee, and you can tell me what happened because *we* did make some headway today."

"Then good news first. What did you find out?" Addie asked, locking her hopeful gaze with his.

"Did you find the source of the poison?" asked Marc, excited anticipation in his voice.

"No, sadly," said Simon letting his hands slip from around Addie, "and I've finished all the tests, swabbed everything in the library, the bus, Luella's car, and came up empty. I still don't have a clue about the source, but we did find out that—"

"Patricia is Jack Turner's sister-in-law!" squealed Paige, grinning. "We were right about him accusing us because the killer might be too close to home."

"Yes," said Felix, "and as I far as I can see, she had means, motive, *and* opportunity."

Chapter 18

"I'm not so sure about that," said Addie, scanning the clues on the board and feeling deflated by what Paige and Felix had just revealed. "All we know is Patricia might have had a motive to kill Luella, but if we can't find the source of the poison, or figure out by what means it was administered, then we can't connect it all and prove to the DA it was her, right?" She glanced at Marc.

"Right." He thrust his hands in his jeans pockets and studied the easels. "Unfortunately, we have a long list of motives and suspects and not one clue that points conclusively to anyone specific." He tapped *means* and *opportunity* on the board. "I don't see where we have this with anyone."

"Maybe you're right," said Felix, rubbing the back of his neck. "But I see you have Wanda's name circled on here. What makes her a top suspect?"

"There was a confrontation today between Addie and the sheriff's wife, which brought to light an incident that places her at the top of the list."

"Interesting," said Felix, "but after what we learned today, I still think Patricia and/or Bea might also be vying for that position. It seems the first editions you and Paige discovered *hidden* in the shelves of the bookmobile and which Luella took back to the library . . . well . . ."

"Yes?"

"Patricia says Luella only *told* her they had been found and denied seeing them in Luella's possession after she went back to the library on Friday. But later, I happened to overhear her telling Bea that by the time this is all over with, they should be able to make enough money to offer to buy back the bus from Addie because now that it was a write-off, they could pick it up for a song and a dance. They appeared to be celebrating Addie's misfortune and the damage the crash caused."

"But I still I don't have any idea yet if the bus is even repairable. Turner wouldn't let me see it."

"I have a feeling the damage might not be as bad as he led you to believe, and that's why he won't."

"He's hoping I'll just write it off and walk away so Patricia can offer me some spare change and take it back?"

"Yeah," added Paige. "When Felix overheard that, we guessed with the money she's going to make from selling those first editions she must have taken from Luella's office after the accident. That she'd be able to offer you a dime for every dollar you paid and still have plenty left-over to use to cover the maintenance and restocking costs to keep the bookmobile operating."

"You know"—Addie gazed at Simon—"maybe it won't be such a bad thing that Paige and I are forced to remain on the peninsula for a while, because, aside from some bogus suspicion that we're murder suspects, it sounds like there might be a bit of a con game going on here. I don't like people thinking they can play me for a fool."

Serena shrieked in pain.

"What's wrong?" cried Addie, rushing to her side and gaped at her friend's flushed cheeks. "You don't look well, maybe I should call Zach to come and get you?"

"Don't you dare!" Serena snapped. "He doesn't know I'm here, and if you call him, he'll be furious with me and a menace on the highway. Besides . . . it's . . . it's nothing. Just a few twinges," she said, panting and holding her tummy.

"Twinges or pressure?" asked Simon as he grabbed his medical bag from the front hall.

"It's nothing, really. I've been having them off and on all day. Doctor Dowdy called them Braxton-Hicks contractions."

"How far apart are they?"

"Oh, I don't know, but really they're nothing," she said, waving Simon off.

"I would feel better if you'd let me examine you."

"It's just as Dowdy said, my body is preparing for delivery."

"True, but I'd like to be certain. Do you think you can make it into the den?"

Serena tried to maneuver off the chair and grabbed her tummy, crying out again. "Maybe in a minute."

Simon fixed his gaze on Addie, concern clearly on his face. "I think I'm going to have a quick look and then get her back to Greyborne Harbor."

"That sounds like the best thing." Addie studied her

friend's face and saw the discomfort in her eyes. "Why don't we all go in the kitchen and get that coffee so these two can have some privacy," said Addie, keeping her voice light.

Catherine searched Serena's contorted face. "I think since you're in such capable hands and don't need us hanging over you too, that Felix and I will head back now. It's going to be dinnertime soon, and I have pork roast defrosting. If Simon is driving Serena back, Marc, will you be coming with us then?"

"No." He studied his sister and then looked intently at Simon. "Unless this is the real thing?"

Simon gave a slight shrug of his shoulders.

"Okay, then until I hear differently, I think I'll stay in town a few more days. I don't like the turn this case has taken, and I want to try to get to the bottom of what's going on because I agree that there's more here than meets the eye."

Simon nodded his agreement. "Addie, are you okay with me taking Serena home and Marc staying?"

"Yes." Addie said. "An extra set of eyes is always welcome, but once you get Serena settled at home or in the hospital, you'll come back, right?"

"To be honest my duties as county coroner here are done. I've tested everything there is, and the only thing left is to go through the results again to see if I've missed something. That I can do from my lab in Greyborne Harbor, but don't worry, I'm only a phone call and a fifteen-minute drive away if you need me."

"I understand." She hung her head, disappointed that he was going to leave her, but on the other hand, relieved that he was still going to be working on clearing them. Even if it was from a distance—an ever growing distance between them, given his cool physical responses to her over the last couple of days. That realization instantly brought on an attack of queasiness that rolled over in the pit of her stomach. Was all this craziness making him second-guess their relationship and their unspoken commitment to each other?

"Marc, you'll keep an eye on Addie . . ." Simon's Adam's apple quivered. "I mean things here, while I go back and work through the results again, won't you?"

"Yeah, for sure, you know I will."

Simon's jawline visibly tensed with the apparent eagerness evident in Marc's prompt reply.

"You know what I mean," added Marc quickly. "Since I've already booked off work this week, I might as well stay and see if we can wrap this case up sooner rather than later and get Addie *and* Paige both back home where they belong."

"Okay." Simon nodded, appearing less troubled by his explanation. "Serena, I'm going to help you lie down. I want to have a quick peek at what's going on down there. Are you okay with that?"

She nodded.

"That's our cue to leave." Catherine grabbed Felix's hand. "Addie," she called as the door closed, "I'll call you later."

"Bye," Addie hollered as she ushered Paige and Marc toward the kitchen.

A few moments later Simon came into the kitchen, his face grave. "I'm just going to give Doctor Dowdy a quick call," he said solemnly and made his way through the kitchen to the back porch.

Marc looked at Addie, concern etched on his face. "Not sure I like the look of that." He dashed into the living room, and Addie went to the door, trying to hear what Serena was saying to him. It was no use. She tiptoed through the kitchen and into the adjoining dining room and hid around the corner where the acoustics made her eavesdropping much easier. There was something Simon wasn't telling them. Addie mentally crossed her fingers that Serena would be straight with her brother, and she could find out what he was concerned about.

"Don't worry, Marc. Simon said it's looking closer, but everything is still intact, so I won't be having the baby today."

"Serena, if anything happens to you . . ."

"Nothing is going to happen. He's taking me home, and everything will be fine. He is a doctor, and who better to have as my chauffeur?"

"None of this would have happened if you'd stayed home like you were supposed to," said Marc, his voice taking on a stern fatherly tone.

"I don't think me being here is the question. Why are you here?"

"What do you mean?"

"I mean, why did you come with Simon? This is his jurisdiction, but it's not yours."

"I came because I know Turner and how he runs things here, and I wanted to be sure he followed procedures. That's all."

"I'm not buying that. I think you came because Simon told you Addie was a suspect and . . ."

"And what?"

"And you're still in love with her, even after all that's happened, right?"

"That was a long time ago."

"Do you see her as the one that got away? Because I

think you do. She's with Simon and has been for a long while. They're even talking about getting married, so stay away from her. She's moved on."

Silence fell over the room, and Addie held her breath. Was what Serena said true? She did know her brother, and Addie thought she did too, but had she been wrong? Did Marc still have feelings beyond friendship for her? Is that what Simon sensed too? Could that have been why he clearly became uncomfortable about asking Marc to stay and keep an eye on things, or . . . was it a test he was putting her and Marc through before he did actually make a commitment to her?

Addie rubbed her temples. All this overthinking about Simon's lack of physical contact lately was getting the best of her, and she had to stop it. Simon and she loved each other. He'd been busy and preoccupied with trying to prove her innocence. What more proof than that did she need about how he felt about her? The cuddles and kisses would come later when this was all over, of that she was—hopefully—certain, but to be sure, she crossed her fingers.

"Serena, I have no idea where you got that from. I moved on too. Remember Ryley?"

"Yeah, your rebound girlfriend, the one you hooked up with after Addie broke your heart and turned down your marriage proposal."

"Not true. She wasn't a rebound relationship. It just didn't work out between us because of professional differences."

"Professional differences?" Serena snorted. "That's what you want to call it. Think about it, Marc. How could it ever have worked out with Ryley when you were more focused on making Addie's life miserable and treating her like she was the enemy because she didn't love you back the way you wanted her to?"

"That's not true."

"Isn't it? You were a jerk and treated Addie horribly after you got back. Why? Admit it, Marc, you behaved like a child and wanted to punish her for breaking your heart, but in turn you broke Ryley's and she left. So don't mess with what Addie has going on now. She loves Simon—"

"Does she?"

"Of course, she does, and you hanging on to false hope is going to get you into trouble and then she won't even want to be friends with you anymore. Do you want that?"

Simon strode into the living room. "Do you know where Addie is?"

Marc jerked with the sound of his voice and looked up at him. "I thought she was in the kitchen."

"No, not there," said Simon.

Addie pulled back and grabbed a large tray from the top of the buffet and darted back into the kitchen. "I found one, Paige."

Paige looked blankly at her.

Simon poked his head around the door and glanced at them.

"You know, the larger tray we wanted because we're going to put food out." Addie shot her a just-follow-me look.

"Right, for the food," Paige said, turning back to the carafe of coffee she had placed on the small tray.

"Food sounds perfect, but I just spoke to Doctor Dowdy, and he wants Serena to meet him at the hospital in Greyborne Harbor."

"Simon." Addie set the tray on the island. "You're scaring me. What's wrong?"

"Nothing." He took her hands in his. "I swear there's just something I noticed earlier, and he wants to check to see if I'm right."

"What is it?"

"I can't say until we know. He's going to do an ultrasound, then we'll know."

"Is something wrong with the baby?" Addie's heart filled with terror.

"No, and don't say anything to her. I don't want her thinking that either. Everything's fine, just something Doctor Dowdy might need to know before the delivery, that's all."

Addie's mind raced. Of course, she had no firsthand experience with these things, but from what she knew, the fertilized egg grew into a baby, and after nine months or so, in Serena's case if her dates were right, more like eight, then the baby came out. What besides that would Doctor Dowdy need to know?

Addie stood on her tiptoes and kissed Simon on the lips, held his face in her hands, and stared him in the eye. "You're sure it's not labor? I really don't want to miss the birth."

"It looks like it's just as she said, Braxton-Hicks, but I think it's best to get her back because there are signs it might be soon. Let's hope the three of you can sort this mess out fast and get you home. Remember, I'm still working on it. I just won't be here, but I'm not far if you need anything."

She kissed him again. "We still have my birthday to celebrate, so I'm going to hold you to that."

He grinned and headed back into the living room. With Marc's assistance, Simon settled Serena into the front seat of the Tesla.

Marc started down the street, waved and called back to Addie and Paige on the step, "I'm going to head back to the B&B. I'll call you guys tomorrow unless something comes up tonight."

When Simon got in the car, he blew Addie a kiss and gave her one of his dimple-cheeked smiles that radiated from his eyes. A smile that telegraphed to her that everything was okay between them, and her earlier suspicions that he was testing her and Marc were simply the result of her overthinking, and completely unfounded. He really did trust her and love her.

Chapter 19

"There," said Addie, flipping the dishwasher closed. "All done. The floors mopped, dishes washed and put away, main floor vacuumed, and I cleaned up after Pippi in the yard. If you're done upstairs, I think we can go."

"Yup," said Paige. "I changed the bed linens as soon as we got up, the garbage is taken out, and the bathrooms are cleaned. So don't you dare use one again this morning before we leave." She chuckled as she stood back and surveyed the kitchen. "I think it looks better than when we arrived."

"I put those flowers from Valerie's garden in a vase on the coffee table with a thank-you note letting Bree and Darren know how much we appreciated them letting us stay here."

"Yeah," said Paige. "I saw them. She'll like that, as

she's always going on about Valerie's flower gardens and her green thumb. She'll like having a touch of that in the house when she comes home." Paige took another look around and peeked into the dining room. "Okay, I think we can be off. What time was Tony expecting us?"

"He said he'd be there all morning so to just come when we're ready."

"And you're sure he doesn't mind us staying with him? I mean, we could go to the B&B."

"No, when he heard we were stuck in town he insisted, and thought it would be a good time for us to catch up."

"Okay, as long as we're not putting him out and he doesn't mind me and Pippi tagging along."

"He's the one that suggested we all stay with him, so stop worrying."

"What did Simon say when you told him we were going to stay at Tony's and not the B&B, or was he relieved you wouldn't be under the same roof as Marc?" Paige asked with a soft chuckle.

"When I explained it was the best way of getting more information about Luella, the library, and her relationship with Maisie because that seems to be important to all of this, he understood."

"All right then, as long as it hasn't caused problems." Paige looked at her skeptically.

"Besides, knowing you were there too really eased his mind. I think, or so he said."

"Alrighty then, we should be off. You have the directions, right?"

"Yup, on my phone." Addie patted her skirt pocket.

"I'll drive, and you can navigate." Paige grinned and took the keys from Addie's fingers. "Besides, there's a shortcut we can take to the bay side of the peninsula, and I don't want to spend the rest of the day being lost in the woods," she said with a laugh and headed toward the front door.

"This is nice through here," said Addie, her gaze taking in the sights. "It's a lot lusher than I would have expected, and I can see now why you made the remark about getting lost in the woods."

"It's the route we could have taken when we arrived, but I wanted to give you an idea of the layout of the entire peninsula and not scare you off on your first day with stories of the ghosts that supposedly live in these woodlands."

"Gimme a break." Addie couldn't help her involuntary eye roll.

"I'm serious. Back in the early 1950s, a young man was found murdered, and his body was put up on a scarecrow stand. They say his ghost still haunts these woods today."

"I know, Marc told us. But I think you should have been the gothic horror writer, not Tony." Addie laughed as they came to Bayside Drive.

"Now where?" asked Paige, coming to a stop at the intersection.

Addie glanced at her phone. "It says turn right on Windgate Road."

"That's just up here," said Paige, turning left and heading toward the Coast Highway intersection. She flipped on her signal light and made a sharp right. "Now where?"

"He says follow the road down the hill, ignore the

other gated houses, and go directly through the wrought-iron gates at the bottom of the hill. He'll leave them open."

"You're kidding? He lives in *the* Windgate House?"

"I guess so, why?"

"Why, it's only the largest and oldest home of the Boston rich from back in the day. They were the first to build here and that set off the building boom of these mansions you see on either side of the road." She waved her hand as she navigated the twisting road downward toward the bay they could see poking through the trees in front of them. "Apparently, it's modeled after an estate the original owner had back in England."

"Maybe that's why Tony relocated to England. He felt at home over there, but he did say it was his great-grandfather that built it, so why wouldn't it be called the Radcliff House?"

"They probably had a house in Boston called that. Remember, this would have been their holiday getaway house," said Paige, slowing to go through the fretwork-pattern, wrought-iron gates either side of the drive.

Addie gasped and Paige slammed on the brakes. "What's wrong?"

"Look." Addie's hand shook as she pointed to the house that had become visible through the thinning trees. Before them was a stunning, three-story, early Georgian mansion. "It's massive. Some summer home." Addie's heart raced as they pulled around the circular drive and stopped in front of an immense arched wooden door flanked on either side by a set of pillars. "I had no idea houses like this existed on the peninsula."

"Like I said before, this house is a good example of

what it was like here in its heyday. It's really amazing to think that for these people this is what they called a summer cottage," Paige said with a little laugh.

Addie cuddled Pippi close to her as she stood on the herringbone brick driveway and whistled. The roofline of the house towered into the sky, and three massive dormer windows above the circular balcony winked in the sunlight. "I wonder who has to get up there and clean those?"

"I'm sure if you live in a house like this," said Paige, setting her suitcase down beside them, "you'd have *people* for that."

Addie stepped up onto the half-circle entrance and raised the antique door knocker. Its heavy weight thumped against the plate, and she stood back, preparing for an enthusiastic Tony to answer the call. Instead, her heart plummeted when a dour-faced woman, dressed head to toe in a uniform of black dress, stockings, and shoes, opened the door and pinned Addie with a steely gaze.

"May I help you?" The woman showed no indication that she knew of their expected arrival.

Pippi wiggled in Addie's arms. Her tiny ears shot back, and a low growl escaped her throat. Horror filled Addie, and she glanced apologetically at the woman she supposed was the housekeeper. However, by the way she glowered at the little dog, Addie knew that if the woman herself were another dog, then she and Pippi would be in an all-out dog fight right about now, and neither one would give up the fight and roll over.

The woman's gaze, filled with obvious disdain, flitted from Pippi and locked on Addie. "I take it you're Miss Greyborne?" Her disapproval was made clearer by the tone of her voice.

"Yes." Addie cleared her throat. "Yes, I am, and this is

my friend, Paige Stringer, and this little girl is Pippi." She lifted her elbow as she introduced the growling dog.

"I see. Won't you come in? Mr. Radcliff is down on the dock on a business call. I'll show you into the parlor. Follow me."

Addie grabbed her bag and she and Paige followed the woman through the door. Addie chuckled to herself. When the woman walked it appeared as though she were floating on air, but when they stepped through the vast entranceway, Addie forgot completely that they had been ordered to follow her and stopped short, taking in the spectacle in front of them.

The main hallway was a large room, and directly in front of them was a double-wide staircase that led up to a landing where two single staircases branched off. One led to the right and one to the left.

At a glower over the housekeeper's shoulder, Addie hurried to catch up while her gaze continued to dart from one feature of the entrance hall to another. The carved handrail on the staircase took her breath away, especially when she traced it with her eyes and saw that it extended around the entire perimeter of the floor above them. She paused and gazed back in the direction of the main doors, following her sight line upward. A reverence seeped through her at the sight of French doors flanked by stained-glass windows that extended upward.

"Wow," she whispered to Paige as they picked up their pace and followed the woman through a double-wide doorway. "If this was a holiday home, can you imagine what the house in Boston looked like?"

The housekeeper stood, hands folded in front of her, beside a round Charles X rosewood table. "Tea?"

"Yes, that will be lovely," said Addie, scanning the antique furnishings in the small room. A portrait over the fireplace caught her eye, and she wondered if that was a painting of Maisie and her husband when they were younger. Judging by the white dress, it might have been a wedding portrait. "This is a lovely room. Someone went to a lot of trouble to make it so homey and comfy," said Addie, her gaze settling on the woman in black.

"This was the mistress's drawing room." The woman's stern mask slipped away for just a second, and Addie could have sworn her dark marble-like eyes teared over. Then the look was gone and so was the woman.

Addie caught Paige's bewildered look. "Weird. She just sort of disappeared, didn't she? I blinked, and she was gone, just like that."

"Doesn't she remind you of someone?"

"Nobody I know." Addie placed Pippi on the floor. She trotted to where the woman had been standing and growled. "Pretty sure I've never met her before. I'd remember Pippi reacting like that," said Addie, pouring tea from the Sadler vintage teapot into a matching cup and raising it her lips.

"Do you really want to drink that?"

Addie gazed down curiously at the tea she was about to drink. "Why not?"

"Because she reminds me of Mrs. Danvers."

"Mrs. Danvers?" Addie tilted her head, and then it hit her who Paige meant. "You don't mean Daphne du Maurier's fictional character in *Rebecca*?"

"Yes, and don't you find their mannerisms eerily similar?"

"Now that you mention it." Addie studied her cup of tea and set it down, untouched, on the tray.

"Addie! So good to see you." Tony rushed over to her

side and kissed her cheek. "Paige, you look as delightful as ever." He grinned and rubbed his hands together. "I see Mrs. Bannerman, the housekeeper, has brought tea, but I suspect after what the two of you have been through this weekend, something a wee bit stronger is in order? Shall we go to the study where I have a lovely selection of brandy and liqueurs?"

Addie glanced at Paige—who still, judging by her pale complexion, appeared overwhelmed by their surroundings—and shook her head. "Actually, it is a little early in the day. Perhaps later, after dinner. But I would kill for a cup of coffee right about now. How about you, Paige?"

"Yes, coffee would be perfect."

"Then coffee it is." Tony reached for a bell cord beside the fireplace and gave it a tug.

Addie didn't hear anything, but a moment later, Mrs. Bannerman appeared in the doorway.

"You rang, sir?"

"Yes, my guests and I will take coffee in the library shortly." He winked at Addie. "But first I'll give them a short tour of the house so they can get their bearings."

"Very good, sir." The housekeeper nodded her head and left as silently as she had entered.

"I'll leave the library for last as that is one room I'm certain will captivate your interest, Addie." He grinned and ushered her and Paige toward the door.

"Wait, I have to take Pippi." Addie spotted her curled up on an antique Marseille French Provincial sofa by the front window. Her little ears perked, and her lips drew back as she stared in the direction Mrs. Bannerman had gone.

"I assume she's house-trained."

"Of course."

"Then leave her. You can collect her once we're done before we go to the library for our coffee."

Addie hesitated, but Pippi appeared to have relaxed now that the threat she sensed from the formidable woman had passed. Her head rested on her front paws, and her eyes fluttered closed. Soft snoring sounds rumbled from her little body.

"Well, she does look happy for the moment." Addie mentally crossed her fingers the housekeeper wouldn't come back in while they were gone. A lawsuit for a biting dog was all she'd need now. "Okay, I'll leave her. But just so you know, she really hasn't taken to your housekeeper, and I won't be responsible for what happens should they cross paths and I'm not here."

Tony threw his head back in a belly laugh.

"Glad you think me getting sued for a vicious dog is funny. I don't." Addie started toward Pippi. The last thing she was going to do is leave her friend here now.

"That's not what I meant," chuckled Tony. "I'm fairly certain that Mrs. Bannerman, who used to be my nanny, wouldn't tolerate that and would have Pippi straightened out before we got back."

Addie's eyes flew open, and she spun around toward Tony. "Would she hurt Pippi?"

"Never. She'd only show her who's boss and that she won't put up with any insolence. Come on, they'll be just fine. Now, I think we'll start upstairs so you can see where your rooms are. This room here on the main floor is the winter parlor." He gestured to the room they had just left. "There, across the foyer, is the grand parlor used for entertaining. There is also a formal dining room farther down the hall. But judging by the dust motes, I don't think it's been opened for years. There's also the study up here on the right." He pointed to a closed oak door. "And, of course, off it is the library. To the rear of the house is a large kitchen and pantry and access to the conservatory. Now upstairs"—he began ascending the stairs—"is the grand ballroom." He stopped and turned. "See how the ceiling is lower over the entranceway where the second-level gallery floor is; but then when you see it from this angle, the grand ballroom entrance and the stained-glass windows actually extend up to the roofline, meeting the domed skylight of the foyer ceiling?"

Addie tilted her head and strained to follow where he pointed above them and nodded when her gaze rested on a stained-glass dome on the high ceiling. "It's beautiful," she whispered.

"Yes," echoed Paige.

"But a grand ballroom, really? Did people actually host elaborate parties back in the old days? I thought that was only in the movies?" said Addie.

"Believe it or not, yes. There was a time when they were common with the gentry and that room was used regularly, but society norms changed and people had to adapt. When I was in middle school my grandfather and -mother turned it into a game room, something more practical for the generations to follow."

Addie was momentarily transported back to the hey-day of the house and visions of what life here must have been like at the end of the nineteenth century. Her hand caressed the warm mahogany railing, and she wondered about the history of other people who might have done the same over the years.

When they reached the small landing at the top of the double-wide staircase where it branched off into two sets of stairs, Tony paused and gestured to the right. "These steps lead to the guest wing, and those to the left are to the residents' apartments. As you can see, the gallery banister encircles this entire upper floor. So, if you get mixed up, it's no problem. Just follow the landing around until you're headed in the right direction. Now"—he bowed low at the waist—"if you follow me, I'll show you where Mrs. Bannerman has placed your belongings."

Addie wasn't certain if it was the opulence of the house or Tony's suddenly very British mannerisms, but for a split second, she felt like she was visiting royalty and couldn't wipe the grin off her face. She wasn't usually impressed by such gestures, but somehow this felt vaguely familiar, and she racked her brain, trying to figure out how and when.

Tony led them down a long hallway and, much to her relief, she and Paige had side-by-side rooms. When she stuck her head into her guest bedroom, her breath caught at the back of her throat.

It was as though she had stepped back in time and was living the life of that old world. The welcoming four-poster bed and the ornate furnishings gave her the illusion that nothing had been touched since the last person who slept in this room had put them in place. Everything, including the silver hairbrush and hand mirror on the dressing table, was placed exactly as she imagined it would have been back then. She looked at Paige, who was grinning from ear to ear after she had inspected her own room.

"Now," Tony said, rubbing his hands together, "I'll let you explore the main floor at your leisure and"—he glanced at his watch—"I have a quick call to make to my agent, and then I'll meet you in the library for that coffee that the cook, Mrs. Ramsay, has hopefully arranged for us."

"I noticed from the outside that on the wings there appear to be three stories. What's up on the third?" Addie asked as they made their way downstairs.

"That is the servants' quarters," he replied.

"Servants' quarters, really? How many do you have on staff?"

"These days it's only Mrs. Bannerman; the cook, Mrs. Ramsay; and George, Mrs. Ramsay's husband, who works as the gardener. He used to be the butler, but as my grandparents aged and my parents were traveling so much with their careers and came less and less, the live-in servants were let go. At one time, there was a butler, a footman, upstairs and downstairs maids, and a large kitchen staff. Now, there's only a maid service that comes in daily to clean—under the direction of Mrs. Bannerman, of course—but gone are the days when they live in."

"I see," said Addie, pausing at the bottom of the stairs to take in the great hallway, trying to envision what it must have been like with servants bustling about.

"It sounds a lot like *Downton Abbey* life, doesn't it?" whispered Paige, obviously trying not to giggle. "Come on," she said, grabbing Addie's hand. "We have a few minutes to explore, and I don't know about you, but I'm dying to see the rest of the rooms."

Addie glanced at the closed door to the winter parlor and an uneasy twinge tugged at her, but Paige was showing no hesitation as she dragged Addie across the foyer to the main parlor and threw open the door.

"Wow." Paige gasped as she stood transfixed in the doorway. Her blue eyes sparkled as her gaze darted around the room. "Picture this without all the dustcovers, and I bet it looks like something out of Buckingham Palace."

Addie's uneasiness grew when tiny prickles formed at the back of her neck. She glanced over her shoulder into the hallway, expecting to see Tony or Mrs. Bannerman, but there was no one. There had only been one other time in her life she had this exact same feeling, and she searched for an apparition's telltale sign of wisps of smoke. Seeing none, she scanned the hallway for portraits, something else she knew from experience that often had very *real* eyes behind the painted ones. Only portraits of landscapes and flower arrangements hung on the ornate walls.

The lack of all these things known to induce these sensations in her should have appeased the prickling sensations, but her apprehension that something was wrong grew. She dashed across the hall and flung the winter parlor door open. "Pippi, I'm here. Mommy didn't forget about you."

The edgy sensation in the pit of her stomach rose and clutched at her chest. She was completely alone in the room.

Chapter 20

"Pippi, Pippi, come here girl," cried Addie, racing into the hall. She clicked her tongue. "Come on, let's go, here girl."

"Addie," called Paige from the far side of the foyer. "You have to come see this dining room. I swear the table can seat fifty people."

"Have you seen Pippi?" Addie asked, rushing toward her.

"No, isn't she in the parlor?"

"No, she's gone." Addie's gaze darted around the entranceway. "I don't understand. The door was closed. How did she get out, and why isn't she coming when I call?" Her words burned in her throat. "What could have happened to her?"

"Now, now, she has to be here somewhere. Don't

worry. I'm sure she just crawled under something cozy. Let's go take another look."

"See." Addie waved her hand. "I told you she's not here."

"You're sure the door was closed when you came in?"

"Yes, I'm positive."

"Coffee is served in the study," Mrs. Bannerman announced.

Addie spun around, and by the housekeeper's feet—sitting like a marble statue—was Pippi.

"Where have you been?" Addie rushed to her and scooped her into her arms and kissed the back of her head. "I was so worried." Addie fought to keep her tears from flowing and fixed her gaze on the housekeeper. "Did you take her?"

Mrs. Bannerman, unflinching, returned Addie's steady gaze. "I went in to remove the tea tray, and she followed me out."

"I see." Addie, without breaking her gaze on the woman, snuggled Pippi. "Traitor," she whispered in Pippi's ear.

"Coffee?"

"Thank you," Addie said, following the woman down the hallway to a door on their right.

"Master Radcliff will be along shortly."

"Thank you," said Paige, grabbing Addie's elbow and steering her through the doorway. Addie glanced back but the woman in black was gone.

"I told you. Just like Mrs. Danvers," she whispered.

"Yeah, if Mrs. Danvers had witchy powers over animals. I just can't believe Pippi followed her out. She can't stand the scent of the woman."

"Well, you saw her sitting like a guard dog at her feet."

Addie glanced behind her to make certain the ethereal

Mrs. Bannerman hadn't retaken her human form, and lowered her voice. "I know, and it was weird, don't you think?"

"Just keep an eye on Pippi. If she starts acting strange, we know she really has been bewitched." Paige chuckled and poured two cups of coffee and handed one to Addie.

"Don't say that." Addie took the cup and brought it to her lips and hesitated. "I wonder who made this." She glanced into the cup and set it down on the corner of the desk. "As it is, I won't sleep a wink tonight anyway. Something is really off with that woman, and I don't trust her."

"I think the problem," said Paige, "is we've both read too many of the types of books Tony writes, and given we both have overactive imaginations, we tend to see things that aren't really there."

"Like those books?" Addie's hand rattled the cup beside her as she flung it out and pointed to a small bookcase under the bay window.

Paige looked at what Addie was pointing to. "Are those the missing books from Luella's office?"

Addie set Pippi down and grabbed the top book. "Yes. Look, it's *A Child's Garden of Verses* with the inscription by Anita in it."

"So, Tony stole the books, not Patricia?"

"This changes everything, doesn't it?"

"Yeah, and I'm thinking you might not know your old friend as well as you thought you did."

Addie looked at her and swallowed hard. "I think you might be right."

"I see the years haven't dulled those eagle-eyes of yours." Tony slipped the book from Addie's hand.

"You went into Luella's office that night and took these off her desk?"

"They're mine. Why would I leave them there?"

"But she said your grandmother donated them to the library."

"Perhaps, but I already told you my grandmother suffered from dementia in her final year. She had no idea what she was doing. I believe that vile woman took advantage of her, and at my expense."

"What do you mean?"

"This book"—he waved it in her face—"was the one perfect memory I have of my lonely childhood. My parents would dump me off every summer here while they traveled the world, disappearing for months on their archeological digs, searching for their precious relics. This book is the one thing my grandmother and I shared, *together*." He laid the book on the top of the bookcase. He took the first edition of Wilkie Collins's *The Woman in White* from her hand. "And this book is one of the books that helped inspire my writing career."

"It must have been a great relief when they were discovered stashed away on the bookmobile."

"You have no idea. So, as you can see, all I did was take back what legally belonged to me since I already fought my grandmother's endowment to the library in court and won. It is against the law to take advantage of someone with diminished mental capacities, and that's exactly what Luella had done." He dropped the books on the top shelf of the case with a thud.

"I never knew all that about your parents—you know, leaving every summer." Addie glanced at Paige, who had picked up Pippi and backed toward the door, the fight-or-flight look in her eyes.

"If everything is okay in here . . . ?"

Addie nodded.

"Then I think I'll take Pippi into the library and let you two catch up." Paige left but didn't stray too far from the door.

Probably ready to use her fight instincts if Tony makes any threatening moves. After all, he did just admit to theft.

"When we were in school, you never mentioned being sent here for the summers. I always figured when you went away at the end of the year, you were off on a family vacation."

"If only. No, you see, Addie, as you know, my father was an archeology professor and bound to the classroom for the academic year. However, as soon as summer break started, he and my mother, his faithful assistant, were off for the entire summer to some distant dig site, except that last year when I disappeared from school just before the end of the year. He'd taken a six-month sabbatical because the summer before they'd discovered some leads on an ancient artifact and wanted to get back into the field before someone else beat them to it. That was the year he found a ruby-encrusted cross, the same artifact that ultimately led to their murders and my coming to live here full-time."

"I had no idea."

"No one did. The police officially reported the cause of death as an automobile accident, but by every indication, it was murder. That information going public would have created an international incident, so it was kept hush-hush . . ." He pulled a green cloth-covered book from the shelf. "Actually, it was this book by Wilkie Collins, *The Moonstone*, that inspired my first novel,

Crimson Cross—you know, a tale about a cursed artifact, since some believed at the time that's what killed my parents."

"A curse?"

"Sometimes the truth is stranger than fiction, isn't it?"

"Yes, yes it is." Addie eyed the book. "You know I read that when it came out, but I had no idea you were *the* Anthony Radcliff that wrote it."

"Yes, it was based on me piecing together clues of their last dig."

"So, your first book was based on fact?"

"More or less. I pieced together what I could from my father's letters and photos of the cross they had discovered, and wrote a fictitious account of what might have happened. You know, the curse lying over the cross, which led to the deaths of the archeologist that discovered it and everyone else who encountered it after. I guess it was my way as an eighteen-year-old to make sure their killers met with a karmic justice or something. Anyway, I poured my heart and soul into that book; and when it was completed, a friend of my grandmother's visiting from London asked to read it. I never thought much about it until he asked if he could show it to a publisher friend of his in England."

"And the rest is history. It became a best seller and BBC movie."

"Right, crazy, isn't it? How a young man's cathartic scribbling launched a career."

"But that's the amazing thing, isn't it? After the *Crimson Cross*, you went on to write another *New York Times* best seller.

"Yeah, *The Jaded Secret*."

"Well, you clearly have the talent, or your writing career wouldn't have continued to include five *New York Times* best sellers and two other movie deals."

He nodded.

"I just can't believe that I never put two and two together and realized that Anthony Radcliff was my Tony."

"Your Tony?"

"You know what I mean." Addie hoped the heat rising on her cheeks was only because the room had become uncomfortably warm and not a reflection of the way her insides burned in that moment as she took the copy of *The Moonstone* from his hand. "This is what inspired you to start writing?" She flipped the cover open, curious about the publication date.

Her breath caught.

My dearest Maisie,
As soon as I saw this in a bookstore in London, I knew your grandson would love it since it was an adventure story that might bring him closer to his parents.
All my love, Anita

"This is the second book I've seen inscribed by a woman named Anita." She locked her gaze on Tony's. "Do you know if she was Anita Greyborne?"

"I'm not really certain. I asked once who the friend Anita was, and my grandmother said she was a dear friend she had met at college and they had remained very close. As a matter of fact, when I was young, a woman named Anita came to visit my grandmother regularly. But I never knew her last name."

Addie found this revelation most intriguing and knew

that at some point she'd investigate it further. However, Luella's murderer was out there, and she had to stay focused on the case so she and Paige could go home.

"Excuse me," said Paige, popping her head through the door. "Mrs. Bannerman just informed me that dinner is laid out now in the conservatory."

"The conservatory?" said Addie. "Now that is something different."

"I'm sure on your rounds today you noticed the dining room hasn't been used in years. My grandparents dined at the tea table in the winter parlor, and after my grandfather passed, I'd take meals with my grandmother there. When I came back, and then after she passed"—he gestured at the study desk—"I ate here, working through most normal meal hours. Shall we go? Mrs. Ramsay doesn't like to be kept waiting."

If Mrs. Ramsay was anything like Mrs. Bannerman, then Addie wasn't keen to get on her bad side, and they followed Tony out into the main hallway. A shiver raced up her spine, and she glanced around, sensing eyes were on them. A shadowy movement from the dining room doorway across the great hall caught her eye, but when she blinked and looked again, it was gone.

Uneasiness crept over Addie. Her spidey senses told her that something here was dangerously real—not ghostly real, because she didn't believe in all that, but something was wrong with this whole picture. It made her even more convinced that their decision to stay here might lead them to Luella's killer.

She took a quick look at the back of Tony's head as she trotted along behind him, trying to keep up with his long strides across the grand hallway. As much as she didn't want to believe it—and she didn't like where her thoughts were leading—he had admitted to taking the books from Luella's office Friday night. And that was the tug-of-war that her head and her heart were playing. She knew him, at least she did at one time, and couldn't wrap her head around the fact he might be a killer. However . . . she glanced back at the dining room door. That still left three other loyal members of this household who might have seen fit to punish Luella for what they perceived as her taking advantage of Maisie's declining health and mental status.

"Tony, since you write gothic horror, did you ever read Daphne du Maurier's novel, *Rebecca*?"

"Certainly, that's a staple read of every gothic novelist. Why?"

"Do you ever find a certain similarity between her housekeeper, Mrs. Danvers, and your Mrs. Bannerman?"

He laughed and shook his head. "I think you should have been the writer between the two of us. Mrs. Bannerman has been with this household for over thirty-five years and was totally devoted to my grandmother."

"See, just the way Mrs. Danvers was devoted to the first Mrs. de Winter."

"Are you suggesting she's afraid that you might become another Mrs. Radcliff and take over the running of the estate from her?"

Addie gasped and stared at Tony. "No, not in the least." Addie took a fleeting look over her shoulder and shivered. "But does she know that?"

"I'm quite certain it's clear to everyone here that you are a friend and no threat to her position as the head housekeeper or to me, so relax and enjoy your stay."

Despite Tony not seeing what both Addie and Paige had sensed earlier about the housekeeper, Addie couldn't shake the feeling that every move they made was being watched. Tony paused in front of a wall of windows that ran the length of the back of the house and pressed a button. With a swoosh, the glass door slid open, and an intoxicatingly heady scent wafted over them.

"Tony, this is amazing," cried Paige, her gaze flicking from one end of the conservatory to the other. "Judging by the height of the ceiling, I'd say this is an authentic Georgian orangery, isn't it?"

"Very good." Tony beamed. "I see someone has been reading up on their architectural history."

"Georgian, Victorian, Edwardian, any one of those periods is something I've always dreamed of having in my own home someday." Paige's smile widened. She thrust Pippi into Addie's arms and excitedly pointed out to Addie the elaborate detailing in the high-arched window panels and the overhead cast-metal cresting and frame. "I always wanted one with the copper frame like you see in the movies."

"I just can't believe the size of this room," Addie said, shifting Pippi, who wanted nothing more than to get down and explore the pathways of trees and plants in this *indoor* park. "It runs the entire length of the house. How do you ever manage to keep up with the plant care?"

"That falls into Mrs. Bannerman's area of expertise, not mine. She and my grandmother spent hours and hours in here over the years. As a matter of fact, I heard Mrs. B. was so knowledgeable about all the plants growing in the conservatory that she was asked to give talks at some of the local gardening club meetings."

"You're kidding? She knows that much about all these," Addie waved her free hand around the conservatory, "that she gave talks to a gardening club?"

"Oh yes. But it was before I came back so I'm not sure what she specifically talked to a so-called group of plant experts about. However, I did hear her and Mrs. Ramsay talking one day in the kitchen garden"—he pointed to the far end of the conservatory—"she said it was scary that so many people who call themselves gardeners and have small children and pets in the home, didn't know that some flowers and plants they grew were not only beautiful, but were also deadly and couldn't tell the difference in them before it was too late." He shrugged. "And if anyone would know the differences she would. So perhaps she thought it a good idea to educate the club members."

Addie nodded her understanding and snuggled Pippi closer as she glanced over at the space he'd gestured to off the kitchen where there was a well-laid-out area of raised planters all marked with sticks, which she assumed were markers naming the various herbs. She scanned the area she stood in front of that contained a central group of orange and lemon trees, with beds of flowers, greenery, and variety of tropical plants planted throughout the bases of the grove.

"And what's this to the right with the sign that says DO NOT TOUCH?" Addie stepped closer and squinted to read the labels.

"Ah, that was my grandmother's pride a joy. She was a big Agatha Christie fan, and whenever she read one of her books that dealt with a poisoning, my grandmother would seek out the plant that the poison was extracted from." He stood in front of the garden cordoned off with a chained border fence. "This was her poison garden, *all* highly toxic and deadly, or so I'm led to believe by our resident expert." He laughed.

Addie bent down and peered at the plant names. "Yes,

some of these I recognize from a set of botanical prints I have of the actual plants in Agatha Christie's poison garden at her summer home in Torquay. That's nicotiana, a plant that contains high levels of nicotine and is extremely toxic." She pointed to a plant that to the untrained eye might have looked a lot like a delphinium, with its beautiful spires of purple flowers, and glanced up at Paige. "Isn't that monkshood, one of the most common plants that produce aconitine, a poison that can kill within hours?"

Paige's eyes widened, and they both looked at Tony. Addie was hoping for confirmation or, at least, some acknowledgment of the plant growing in his greenhouse, but they only got a shrug.

"You tell me. I don't use poison much in my books. They deal mostly with curses and necromancy. To be honest, I can't tell a tulip from a daffodil."

Addie studied the plant for a moment and forced a laugh as she took a seat at the antique wrought-iron table. "This conservatory truly is amazing. I imagine it was well-used when your grandparents lived here."

"Yes, but I'd say even more so with my great-grandparents when orangeries were all the rage of the blue-blood Boston families, and entertaining a few hundred people every weekend was considered normal." He laughed and took a seat that had been laid out with silver-covered serving dishes. Addie's mouth salivated with each dish uncovered. "Are these lovely herb garnished vegetables from the kitchen garden in here?" she asked between mouthfuls and then glanced uneasily at the sign that said Do Not Touch.

"Some, but most are from the outdoor garden over there, toward the woods away from the beach."

"Master Radcliff. Cook has asked me to tell you she has taken the liberty of preparing a chocolate fondue for dessert. She hopes this is to your guests' liking."

Addie turned and studied Mrs. Bannerman, who as per usual had appeared suddenly and quietly and stood motionless in the conservatory doorway. Her hands were neatly folded in front of her, which Addie realized was her usual stance when addressing Tony.

Tony's face lit up. "If it's not"—he glanced at Addie apologetically—"it certainly is to mine. Provided, of course, she has included some ripe cherries for dipping?"

"Of course, she does know what your favorites are, sir."

"She hasn't failed me yet. Tell her thank you. We'd be delighted to gorge ourselves on the after-dinner feast."

Addie's mouth salivated at the thought of the chocolaty goo she'd soon be dipping fruit into, but then she recalled that she and Simon often shared the same treat, and a tiny twinge tugged at her heart. Yes, she'd have to get this whole mess figured out and soon. How very much she missed Simon.

"If you're not partial to cherries dipped in mounds of gooey chocolate, don't worry. I'm sure Cook has included slices of other fruits and breads, a little something for everyone."

Addie gave Tony a smile of approval, but as she toyed with the last of the beef Wellington on her plate, her smile faded.

"Is something wrong with your meal?" asked Tony, studying her over the rim of his wineglass.

"Not at all, it was delicious, thank you," she said, laying her fork on the plate. "It's just funny how little things about a person who died can creep back into your mind later."

"What do you mean?" Paige tossed her napkin on her cleaned plate and took a sip of her wine.

"It's stupid because I didn't know Luella at all, but I just remembered that she also loved chocolate-covered cherries." Addie's mind flashed to Luella asking her to take the peppermint chocolate so she could have the cherry one underneath. "A silly thing to remember, I know." She pushed her plate away. "But it just popped into my head." Addie swirled her wineglass and glanced over at Maisie's poison garden. "Did anyone else know that Luella preferred the chocolate-covered cherries?"

"I'm sure the whole town did," said Tony.

"It was common knowledge?"

"I guess, if people knew Luella well."

"How did you discover her preference?"

"It was last Christmas, soon after I arrived. I found out there was a town council Christmas party and I, as my grandmother's representative, was expected to attend since she was too ill to go."

"You used to hate those kinds of parties, if I remember correctly." Addie chuckled.

"I still do," Tony said, setting his glass on the table. "I can't stand having to make small talk with virtual strangers, but I was still in the process of trying to figure out what was going on with her finances and exactly what money she had bequeathed and to whom. So, I thought what better place to start? At the party, I snapped up a chocolate-covered cherry, and Wanda Turner, the sheriff's wife, told me if Luella saw me with it, I'd have to arm wrestle her for it. Of course, Luella, who happened to be standing nearby, overheard, and we argued, good-naturedly, over the last one in a box." He locked his gaze on Addie. "Why do you ask?"

"No reason." She shifted in her seat and glanced over at the poison garden. "I just had a thought."

Addie knew she had to talk to Simon. If her hunch was right, she'd have to find out who took the chocolates to the potluck. That was the only plausible explanation since everything else had come up negative.

Chapter 21

"Come in here," Addie whispered, pushing Paige into her bedroom.

"What's going on? You couldn't get out of there fast enough. Tony looked a little stunned when you grabbed me and said we should turn in for the night and left him sitting there alone in the conservatory. What the heck happened?"

Addie checked both ways up the hall before she quietly closed the door. "Did you hear what he said about the chocolates?"

"Yeah, so?" Paige climbed onto Addie's bed, crossed her legs, and hugged a pillow to her body. "What are you thinking?"

"I'm thinking," said Addie, joining her on the bed, "that everything from the potluck that Simon tested came up negative, right?"

"Right, so why are you suddenly focusing on the chocolates? Simon said he didn't find anything in them."

"But did he test *all* the chocolates or just do a random sampling?"

"You think someone injected just a few of them with poison?"

"Yes. Remember I ate one and didn't die. Logically, after hearing what Tony said about the chocolate-covered cherries, it makes sense that they would have been the contaminated chocolates." Addie locked her gaze on her friend. "Don't you see? If it was well-known that Luella preferred the cherry ones, those would have been the ones containing the aconitine."

"Thanks to your eagle eye and the prints you have of some of the plants in Agatha Christie's poison garden, we now know there's monkshood growing in Tony's conservatory."

"Keeping Mrs. Bannerman on the list."

"Not Tony?" asked Paige.

"You heard him. He doesn't know a tulip from a daffodil, and he said Mrs. Bannerman worked in the conservatory with Maisie for years and helped her set up that garden."

"I wonder if she went to the potluck dinner."

"Maybe she made up Tony's dish and dropped off his contribution for him. I can't see him carting around a Tupperware dish, can you?"

"No, I can't." Paige said shaking her head.

"But the fact remains all the food was tested and came up negative, so it had to have been in the chocolates." Addie flopped back on the bed and stared at the ceiling. "I have to talk to Simon because my guess is he didn't test all of them." Addie sat up and scanned the spacious bedroom. "We need a crime board. All these pieces are starting to come together, and I have to see how they fit."

"We can't have one here. Remember Mrs. Bannerman? She seems to have eyes everywhere."

"I know." Addie thought for a moment. "But we could have one in Marc's room at the B&B."

"Knowing him, he might have started one already."

"You're right, and he needs to know about this, because if my hunch about the chocolate-covered cherries is right, we can find out who took the chocolates to the dinner—"

"Then we have our killer."

"Exactly!" Addie leapt off the bed and grabbed her phone. Her thumbs flew over the small keyboard. "Just give me a minute to see what Simon says. I hope he's not working tonight."

When you tested the chocolates from the potluck, did you test the chocolate-covered cherry ones?

. . .

I don't remember exactly the flavors I tested. I did a random sampling, looking for any evidence of the aconitine, why?

. . .

Because I have a theory. Are there any cherry ones left?

. . .

I don't recall, but that's pretty specific. Why would only the cherry ones be poisoned?

. . .

Because those were Luella's favorite, and more than one person knew that.

. . .

Interesting. Okay, I can be back in Pen Hollow in the

morning. Heading into an emergency surgery now. Chat soon! XXXXX

Paige rose to her feet and tossed the pillow aside. "The problem is I wouldn't be surprised if every person we had on our suspect list knew about her love of cherry chocolates. Little things like that are common knowledge in a small town."

"I know, so we have to figure out who has the know-how and the equipment needed to make a poisonous solution from a plant base and then inject it into a chocolate." Addie scrolled through her phone. "I might not have the board, but I did take a photo before we erased the ones we used at Bree's house and . . ." She tapped the screen. "That's it, Wanda and Randy. They both work in a pharmacy and both had motive."

"How do we find out if one of them took the chocolates to the dinner?"

Lost in thought, Addie tapped her phone against her palm. She snapped her fingers. "Gretchen! She was the kitchen volunteer and most likely saw who brought what. First thing tomorrow we have to track her down and see if she remembers who dropped them off for the dinner."

"Are you sure you don't want me to come in with you?" asked Addie, pulling up in front of the library.

"No," said Paige, opening the passenger's door. "I've built a good rapport with most of the volunteers because of my connection to Bree, and I think I'll be able to find out what we need to know easier on my own."

"Are you afraid I'll come on too strong?" asked Addie with a nervous giggle.

"Kind of." She winced. "You know the whole dog with the bone thing."

"I'll behave, honest. I know how important it is to Bree."

"I know you do, and I appreciate that, but I still think it's better I speak with Gretchen alone. Go tell Marc over at the B&B our hunch about the cherry chocolates."

"You're right. I keep forgetting how good at this whole sleuthing business you've become. I have to learn to let some of it go."

"We just both have our areas of expertise, so let me use mine, and we'll cut the workload in half and maybe get home sooner."

"You're right." Addie waved her arms in surrender. "Do you want me to pick you up a coffee when I grab one for me and Marc?"

"That's okay," said Paige, starting to close the door. "I'll get one on my walk over to the B&B. I have to go past the coffee shop anyway."

Addie glanced over her shoulder. "Maybe I should wait and drive you to the B&B. The morning fog's getting really heavy now, and you'll be soaked by the time you get there."

"It's only two blocks, and with a stop halfway in the coffee shop. I'll be fine." She waved her arms. "Now, shoo, go tell Marc what we found out, and I'll see you soon."

With mixed emotions, Addie watched Paige climb the stairs to the library. She wasn't certain why she was so hesitant about this. Maybe it was the thickening fog. Everything felt so closed in, but a sense of foreboding niggled at the base of Addie's skull. Still a little unsure about counting on her friend with such an important undertaking, she reminded herself that Paige had presented a good case, one she couldn't argue with.

Her sister was a well-respected member of this tight-knit community that clearly didn't take well to outsiders, and Paige, because of Bree—and the fact she'd spent so much time here with Emma—had already made inroads where Addie certainly hadn't. Yes, Paige was a big girl now and had proven on more than one occasion she was capable of handling herself. Addie had to learn to let go and to remember that Paige wanted this to be over as much as she did so they could get home.

Paige would be fine, as demonstrated when Paige had called Valerie, clearly waking the poor woman from a deep sleep. Paige had still managed to find out that Gretchen, along with most of the other library volunteers, would be at the library packing up what was left after the sale. They would also be sorting out the office, since the police had released it as a crime scene.

Fingers crossed that Paige could find out who dropped off the chocolates. Marc could then take the information to Sheriff Turner, who could make an arrest, and *bam*, she and Paige would be free to leave—unless, of course, the killer was Wanda Turner. Addie cringed. If the killer turned out to be Wanda, that most definitely would lead to a whole new set of problems. But, she had to stop thinking worst-case scenarios. In this case, the facts would be facts, and the sheriff wouldn't be able to deny them when they were presented, right?

Or would he?

Addie had a sinking feeling as she flipped her turn signal on and pulled out into the traffic on Sea Spray Drive.

* * *

"Addie," cried Marc, flinging his room door open. "When you said you were coming bearing fresh coffee and not the instant stuff they have here, I could have kissed you!"

Addie's eyes flew open, recalling his conversation yesterday with Serena, and she suddenly thought twice about entering his room. She didn't want him to get the wrong impression about her visit.

"Come in, come in." He stepped back, allowing her entry, but obviously sensed her hesitancy because he added quickly, "You know what I meant, figure of speech, that's all."

He took the paper takeout cup from her hand and smiled weakly. "Pardon the mess." He waved his hand toward the unmade bed and the table covered in file folders. "I've been going over my notes, trying to figure out what's what."

He turned his back to her, and she wondered if it was to try to hide the tell-all twitch, he would surely have in his jaw showing his embarrassment over what he'd said about kissing her when she arrived with the coffee. After all this time, it kind of felt good to know she could still make him squirm . . . even just a little. It would help in giving her the upper hand when she presented her theories and stop him from discarding her too quickly. A wave of relief surged through her and she stepped inside.

"I'm surprised you don't have a makeshift crime board started. I know you don't like mine, but it is something you use at the office, isn't it?"

"Sometimes," he said, clearing a stack of papers from the only other chair in the room and gesturing for her to take a seat. "Police have a lot of other resources at our disposal that *amateurs* don't have."

Even though he followed his statement with a crooked smile it did nothing to camouflage the dig he took at her with his words.

"Besides," he added, "this is a small town, and people get curious about strangers, and I didn't want Mrs. Granger, the B&B operator, to see a list of her friends and neighbors on a board. Wouldn't help for people to start putting two and two together about what I'm up to."

"Yes, we have the same problem at Tony's. His housekeeper has eyes everywhere it seems, and we don't want to raise suspicions or have someone tip off the killer before we can build a solid case either."

His laptop pinged, and he pressed the touchpad, bringing it to life. "Simon's at the lab. He says he's going to recheck the chocolates." He glanced up at her.

"He's in Pen Hollow already?" She tugged her phone out of her cropped jeans pocket and scanned it. Nothing from Simon recently. "Did you tell him I was meeting with you this morning?"

"Yes. After you sent me the text saying you had some information, I mentioned you were dropping by. Why?"

Addie shook her head and lowered her phone to her side. "No reason."

Inwardly, she fumed. Was Simon not telling her he was already back in town his way of punishing her? Was he upset that she had been staying at Tony's like Paige had inferred or was it because she hadn't let him know she was going to meet with Marc this morning? Really, could he be that petty and jealous? She wished he'd remember that it had been over sixteen years since she'd last seen Tony and two years since she and Marc dated, and that by now he should trust her not to fall back into the arms of another man at the drop of a hat. Especially, when all of them only happened to be in the same town at the same time and drawn into this case, one way or another—whether they liked it or not—him included. She shoved her phone back into her bag.

"Addie, are you okay?"

She straightened in her chair. "Yeah, just thinking about something."

"Wanna tell me about the chocolates? Is that what was so urgent this morning?"

Addie drew in a deep breath and steadied her churning emotions regarding Simon's odd behavior this week—after all, he had let her birthday pass with little fanfare, something that still ate at her. She sat back and stroked the smooth wooden arms of the captain's chair she sat in. It wasn't *her* chair, but sitting here with Marc as she told him about the chocolates and the poisonous plants felt like her early days in Greyborne Harbor.

Soon, she had put all her qualms about Simon's behavior out of her mind and focused on the case. When she finished, she wiped her damp palms on the knees of her jeans and waited for a rebuke or a reason why her theory wasn't plausible.

Instead, Marc steepled his fingers and placed them under his chin. "What makes you think the aconitine was a plant derivative, not a synthetic form?"

"It makes sense. If someone purchases synthetic aconitine, the sale is traceable. If it's extracted from a plant in a homemade lab, then it's virtually untraceable."

"Meaning our list of original suspects just got a little shorter, didn't it?"

"Yes, because it would have to be someone with a collection of or knowledge of exotic and tropical plants. Wanda Turner is the new president of the garden club, and Randy Carlyle is a pharmacist who has the equipment and the know-how to perform a solution extraction like that."

"Okay, actually that makes a lot of sense and something worth looking into. Let me get Lieutenant Jerry Fowley, back in Greyborne Harbor, working on this and see what he can find out about those two." Marc's fingers flew over the keyboard of his laptop. "There, I've asked him to run a background check on both Randy and Wanda and to keep it hush-hush for now."

"Good, the less people who know we're suspecting Sheriff Turner's wife the better, but maybe have him run a background check on Mrs. Bannerman, Tony's housekeeper, too. She apparently looks after the conservatory at the Radcliff estate, where there is an Agatha Christie poison garden."

"Like the one you told me she had in England?"

Addie nodded.

"Maybe Mrs. Bannerman and your friend Tony should move to the top of the list."

"Tony doesn't know a thing about exotic or poisonous plants. It's Mrs. Bannerman who tends them."

"Or so he says." Marc shot Addie a side glance as he continued typing. "And remember what your father use to say about—"

"I know, anyone is capable of murder. I just don't think in this case it's Tony," Addie said, mounting all the conviction she could as her mind played out all the possible scenarios.

Chapter 22

"Mrs. Bannerman needs to be on it for sure. She's been with the Radcliffs for over thirty-five years and was there when Maisie passed. Perhaps she knew Luella was taking advantage of the poor woman in her final years, and was out for revenge."

"Hmm." Marc stroked his chin. "If that's the case, it's an easier theory to sell Turner on than the theory involving his wife."

"True enough, but do we have to sell him on anything beforehand? Couldn't we flush out the killer and then present Turner with a nice, neat package all wrapped and ready to go?"

"That is an ethical question. He's been relatively open to my tagging along and sharing files with me as long as I have gone along with his line of investigation—"

"Yes, but his line of investigation is narrowed in on me

and Paige. You can't be serious about going along with that."

"No, but he doesn't know that. I'm just afraid if he discovers I've started my own side investigation, especially one involving his wife, that line of communication between us will slam shut, and he could file a complaint with Mayor Bryant about me for interfering outside my jurisdiction."

"Speaking of Mayor Bryant, did you find out anything regarding that land developer he introduced Luella to, the one who is making a bid on the library property? Did you find out if it was on the up-and-up or if there was something crooked about it?"

"Nothing concrete yet, but if it was a shady land deal, then it's also one of the gazillion motives we have for someone wanting Luella out of the way."

"We can't get overwhelmed with the motives," said Addie. "We have to start with the most probable and either prove or disprove them one at a time."

"Look at you thinking like a real police officer now, something I never thought I'd see." He grinned, and by the glint in his eyes, he offered her a genuine compliment and not one of his backhanded ones. He sat back, and his eyes held steadfast on Addie. "I know being the drummed-up suspect in all this is hard on you, but I get the feeling something else is bothering you? Wanna share?"

She dropped her gaze and shook her head.

"Addie, come on. We've known each other long enough now that I can tell something is wrong."

She looked up and met his gaze. "It's just that . . . No, never mind." She glanced away.

How could she tell Marc she was feeling like Simon was pulling away from her? Or the sick feeling in the pit of her stomach that said he was testing her love for him by throwing her and Marc together to work on this case, and was going to sit back and see what happened before he made the next move cementing their relationship?

No, that was crazy thinking. This whole ordeal had taken more out of her than she thought. She needed to stay logical, and logic told her Simon was being pulled in too many directions at the same time. After all, he had a demanding job in Greyborne Harbor and was going into surgery last night on top of working a full shift in the emergency department.

She pinched her toes together in her sandals to quiet her reeling mind and jerked when there was a knock on the door.

"Good morning." A grinning Simon sauntered through the door and placed a steaming cup of coffee on the table in front of Addie. "But I see you already have one of these." His face fell and he started to remove it.

Addie covered the lid with her hand. "You know me. I can't get enough in the morning, so leave it where it is."

"Marc, I brought one for you too." He held out the paper tray containing three more cups of coffee. "And one for Paige." He glanced around the room.

"She's still at the library, but I'm sure she'll appreciate it with this damp weather." Addie took a cup from the tray and set it on the table.

"Yes, I'm afraid I'm like Addie, can't get enough of this first thing in the morning," said Marc, taking a cup.

Simon glanced from the unmade bed covered with files to the file folders stacked on the table. "It appears you two have been busy this morning."

"I just got here," said Addie quickly, "and have only

just filled Marc in on my theory. I take it that since you're not at the lab, you found something."

Simon looked at her over the rim of his coffee cup and smiled. "As a matter of fact, your theory was right. There was one chocolate-covered cherry left, and it was filled with aconitine."

"I knew it. When Tony told us last night that those were her favorite chocolates, it all made sense after I recalled how she asked me to eat the top chocolate so she could have the cherry one without touching the whole dish."

Paige flung the door open and stared at Simon. "Didn't you see me when you left the coffee shop? I was in the parking lot waving my arms like a mad woman."

"No, sorry, I haven't slept much in the past twenty-four hours, and all I could think about was getting the coffee and telling Addie what I found out."

Paige peeled off her soaked jacket and flicked it, sending water droplets spraying across the room.

"Is it raining now, or has the fog gotten so heavy it's like rain?" Addie peered out the window.

"Rain, snow, fog, who knows, but the air is heavy with moisture, and look what it did to my natural curly hair. I look like a poodle." She finger-combed her mass of curls and sat down on the bed with a moan. "I hope one of those coffees is for me. When I saw you leave with the tray, I didn't bother to get one."

"I am truly sorry," said Simon with an apologetic smile. "I would have picked you up had I seen you."

"I know. I'm just feeling like this entire morning has been a catastrophe." She looked at Addie. "I came up empty in my mission."

"Gretchen wasn't there?"

"She was, but she has no idea who brought the chocolates. She said they just sort of appeared."

Simon snorted. "Okay then, if she doesn't know, then who else would?"

"Aside from the killer?" Marc said, toying with his coffee cup.

"Yeah, but that person isn't going to volunteer the information, are they?" Addie slumped back in the chair. "We have a dozen motives, double the number of suspects, and now finally the means, but how do we narrow down the other two?"

"Dumb luck," said Paige, cradling her hands around her coffee cup, "and what do you mean by, we now have the means?" She gazed at Addie over her cup lid. "Did you find the source?"

"Yes, Simon did, and we were right about the chocolate-covered cherries." Addie retrieved her phone from her bag and scrolled through the list of names she stored in Notes. "My money is still on Randy and Wanda. They have motive, means, and we just have to find out where the opportunity was." She glanced up. "That shouldn't be too hard, given they were both involved with the library committee."

"I think," said Marc, "that's going to take some good old-fashioned police work, which means we do need a crime board. There's just too much to mentally keep track of, and if we're all keeping track of different notes on our phones then something is going to fall by the wayside."

"What do you suggest?" asked Simon from where he leaned on the window ledge behind Addie.

"I don't know," said Marc. "We can't invade Bree's house again. This room is off-limits because Mrs. Grainger treats her guests' rooms as her own and thinks nothing of popping in to check on me when I'm going through files. I'm not sure if she's playing a good hostess or overly curious about what I'm doing and hoping to get a peek."

"She's probably working with Turner to make sure you stay in line," said Paige.

"The way this town appears, she's probably related to Turner," Addie scoffed. "But you're right, Marc. We are in the same position with Mrs. Bannerman. She's on our suspect list too, and even if it's not her who filled the cherries with poison, she might know who did and tip them off about the names and clues we have on a board."

"There is a little thing called technology?" said Simon, a hint of teasing sarcasm in his tone. "Dropbox, the cloud, file share, I'm sure you've heard of those?"

"Of course," said Addie, feigning offense. "It's not my preferred way, but I guess if that's what we have to use then we have to."

"Yeah," said Marc, his voice thoughtful. "We can do up a spreadsheet and share that so we're all on the same page, but . . ." He looked at Simon. "Are you heading home today or staying over?"

"I need to get back and sleep. Unfortunately, I have a shift in emergency tonight."

"You have to go back right away?" said Addie, trying to keep her tone even and not let on she was feeling trapped and alone here.

"Sadly, I do. When this case came across my desk, it was fairly cut-and-dried. A traffic accident and the presiding sheriff wanting blood samples for drugs and alcohol to see if that caused the accident. However, when poison was discovered, it opened up something much bigger and complicated by the fact you two were at the top of his suspect list." Simon looked at her apologetically. "Had I forecasted the ensuing chaos, I would have made arrangements with the hospital to change my shifts and reschedule surgeries, but when it all blew up, it was too late."

"I get it," said Addie. "None of us had any idea that there would be such a turn of events and that Paige and I would be held hostage by a biased sheriff."

Marc's laptop dinged. He tapped the touchpad and began reading. "Well now, this is interesting. Jerry ran those traces we talked about, Addie, and Mrs. Bannerman has no criminal record. Neither does Wanda Turner, but Randy Carlyle is in the FBI database."

"What for?"

"According to this, his pharmacy license was revoked in Texas back in 2001. It says he operated a compounding pharmacy and there were discrepancies when a shortage of controlled substances was discovered following an accountability audit. It could never be proved if it was because of poor record keeping, or if he or one of his staff was abusing drugs or selling them under the table. Either way, he lost his license to practice."

Chapter 23

"If he lost his license," said Addie, "how can he be a practicing pharmacist here in Pen Hollow?"

"Was he the actual pharmacist or a pharmacy assistant?" asked Simon, setting his empty cup on the table.

"Good question," said Marc, tossing it in the wastebasket. "Paige, do you know if the drug store is also a compounding pharmacy?"

"What's a compounding pharmacy?"

"It's a pharmacy that mixes and prepares a prescription from a doctor," said Simon.

"Isn't that what they all do?"

"No, most pharmacies dispense medication that comes directly from the drug manufacturer in predetermined delivery doses, like a cream, liquid, or pill form, and they just measure the prescribed amount and sell it to the customer. A compounding pharmacist is kind of like a baker or a cook and creates the medications, which involves mixing one or more active ingredients, each at a specified amount. It also helps with patients who have a difficult time swallowing pills as many medications can be made into a different delivery system than the pharmaceutical companies produce. As long as they have the raw ingredients and the patient is willing to pay for the service, a lot of drugs can be compounded for convenience and ease of administering. They are made for you at the pharmacy based on your doctor's prescription."

"I read," said Addie, "that they are good for people who also have allergies to some of the ingredients drug companies use as fillers in their medications. Pharmacists can make them without those, is that right?"

"I get it," said Paige. "And yes, they must have been a compounding pharmacy when Luella was there because Bree got her thyroid medication from them. When Luella left and went into politics, Bree had to go to Salem to get her prescriptions, which I never understood at the time, but I do remember she said they could make the kind she needed because of an allergy she had."

Addie clapped her hands excitedly. "That means they have the equipment needed to make their own solutions, which would also include the equipment needed to synthesize something from a plant, wouldn't it?" Addie looked up at Simon.

"Yes, and if Randy was a compounding pharmacist in Texas, he would definitely have the skill along with the equipment."

"Wait a minute," said Marc. "Paige just said that when

Luella left, Bree had to go to Salem to get her compounded prescription, so that means Randy wasn't compounding."

"Unless he is dispensing without a license," said Simon. "Luella might have had the license, and after she left, he thought it too risky to compound because that opens him up to a whole new set of state audits. Maybe he decided not to continue with that part of the drug store's services."

"What I don't get," said Paige, "is if he lost his license in Texas twenty years ago, how can he still be operating as a pharmacist?"

"It's easier than you'd think," said Marc, scrolling through his computer. "It's not uncommon for doctors, teachers, and probably pharmacists too, who had their licenses revoked to show up in another state and pick up where they left off."

"Yeah," added Simon, "the biggest problem is most of those areas aren't federally regulated. Meaning there isn't one convenient database where employers can run a check on them. It would have to be done by state, and then that only works if the person involved doesn't omit the state where the infraction occurred, on their résumé. In that case, of course, it wouldn't be checked."

"I wonder," said Addie, "if Luella knew about Randy when she went into business with him."

"Hard to say, and I'm pretty sure he won't be forthcoming with that information now . . . Crap!" Marc slammed his fist on the table.

Addie jumped when her coffee cup splashed over. "What?"

"Another email from Jerry. Apparently, Mayor Bryant

is on the warpath about me using my vacation time to investigate a murder in another jurisdiction without his authorization, and I'm to return to Greyborne Harbor immediately and explain myself."

"That means Turner has been speaking to him," said Simon.

"And," added Addie, "it also means we've touched a nerve somewhere too close to home, and Turner's getting nervous."

"Yeah, but I still have my files and notes, so I can work on these back in the office." He glanced over the laptop screen at Addie. "Where I can build a crime board."

"As long as Bryant isn't going to fire you over this."

"Yeah"—he shrugged one shoulder—"there's always that, I guess." Marc closed his laptop. "Can I catch a ride back with you, Simon?"

"Of course, as soon as you're ready we can leave."

Addie's stomach tightened, and she looked out the window. "It's still really foggy. Can't you wait and see if the sun's going to burn it off? That drive . . ."

Simon took her hand in his. "Don't worry, we'll be fine. It's looking pretty socked in, and I can't wait it out because I have a shift to work, but don't worry."

Marc packed his files into two cardboard boxes. "You know, Doc, since you haven't slept, you could let me drive that fancy sport coupe of yours," Marc said, his voice filled with the same hope that a teenager might have given the chance to race in the F1 finals.

Simon glanced at Addie. "Would that make you feel better?"

She glanced at Marc and then Simon. The knot in her

stomach, now a full-sized boulder, ricocheted off her insides, but arguing with the ghost of her father wouldn't get her anywhere. She simply nodded.

"Is this box ready to go?" Simon asked Marc, who was putting the lid on a second file box.

"Yeah, and this one too. I'll just pack my clothes, and we should be ready to go."

"Great, I'll take this box down, and you can bring the other one."

"I can take this one," said Addie, sliding it off the table and balancing it on her hip. "Then Marc can finish packing." She glanced at Pippi asleep in her carrier. "Paige, can you watch her? I'll be back up in a minute."

Addie placed the box in the back of Simon's car, and after he set his down, he leaned in and kissed her cheek. "I've wanted to do that all morning."

"I'd prefer something a little more intimate."

"Here, on the street? Whatever would Mrs. Grainger and the neighbors say?"

"Probably 'Look at that lovely couple and how much they care about each other.'" She cupped his face in her hands and placed a kiss on his lips. Under her hands, he flinched, and she pulled away. "You can't be serious. Since when are you so self-conscious about public displays of affection?"

"I'm not." He gave her a weak smile and lightly brushed his lips with hers.

"Simon, are we okay?"

"Yes, why wouldn't we be?"

"I don't know. I guess I'm feeling like you're pulling away."

"No, not in the least. I'm tired, and this case has me all

twisted up. The fact that Turner is so convinced you and/or Paige are behind it, without a shred of proof, really isn't sitting well with me."

"Is that the only thing not sitting well with you?"

"What else would it be?"

She glanced at Marc and Paige making their way down the stairs and heading toward the car park. "Look, I know, its mystifying to me too how this is heading, but we've always stuck together in times like this, but this time I feel . . ."

"What?"

"Why didn't you tell me you were in town this morning? I had to hear it from Marc."

"Because I just arrived. He messaged me that you were on your way over with some information, and I knew he'd let you know I was here."

"Is that the only reason?"

"Of course. There's no ulterior motive. I'm tired, and that's it. I was in surgery all night and haven't slept yet, but I wanted to get here and run the test on the chocolates as soon as I could, but now I really do have to get home to sleep before my shift tonight. Just bear with me." He laid his hand on her shoulder and gave it a light squeeze. "I'm trying to do three jobs at once. Forgive me if I'm not as attentive as you need me to be right now, but I'm doing the best I can."

Addie glanced through her lashes at Marc and Paige, standing off to the side of the car, making a good show of fawning over Pippi, clearly pretending none of this conversation was taking place within earshot of them. Now that was a sign of a true friend. She gave a weak smile of appreciation to Paige.

"Got everything cleared up with Mrs. Grainger?" asked Simon, holding his hand out for Marc's suitcase.

"Yeah, it's all good, I told her I might be back later in the week." He glanced at Addie. "Depending, of course, on what we can dig up between now and then that I can hopefully present to Turner."

"Did you tell her all that?" asked Addie, mortified.

Marc rolled his eyes. "What do you think?"

"Yeah, I guess not." Addie closed the back of the Tesla and looked at Simon. "Are you driving back on the coastal highway?"

"I hope not." Simon looked at Marc. "That takes too long, and I need sleep."

"We'll take Cliff Side Road."

A vise grip cinched Addie's heart. He was taking the same route her father had, and it was just as foggy as the police report said it was that day too. "No, Simon, please tell Marc to go the other way."

"We'll be fine. I'll call you when I get up later this afternoon. Love you." He scooped her into his arms and kissed her, then kissed her again and rested his forehead on hers. "See, I don't care who witnesses my public displays of affection." He winked and got into the passenger's side and rolled down the window.

Marc leaned over. "If you're going to do any snooping around today, remember to keep Wanda's name out of it, and be careful of Randy. He has a criminal record, and the fact that he's practicing without a license tells me there might be whole lot of other criminal activity we're not aware of."

"We'll be careful." Addie glanced at Paige. "Right?"

Paige chuckled "I know I will be as long as you leave

some of those buried bones hidden and try not to unearth them all at once."

"Pfft, me?" Addie laughed and waved as Marc and Simon pulled away.

"I'll wait in the car with Pippi because I've been in there a few times with Bree. If Randy recognizes me, it will be harder to convince him you're a naïve tourist."

"Yes, and hopefully I don't start digging too deep." She grinned teasingly at Paige and closed the door. Addie pulled the collar of her sweater tighter, but it was no good. The damp air seeped through right down to her skin. She couldn't wait to get back to Tony's to warm up in a delicious hot bath and get the chill out of her bones.

Addie stood in the doorway. The pharmacy was smaller than she expected, but it appeared serviceable. There was a small gift section, everyday sundries, and rows of over-the-counter medications. A rack of silver charms glimmered at the back by the pharmacy area. As she approached the rack, one, in particular, popped out at her. It was a filigree baby carriage, and perfect for Serena's charm bracelet. As she tugged it off the bracket, the one below it made her pause. It was two hands wrapped around a little dog and in the background was a heart. That would look good on her own bracelet. She snapped them up, paused, then grabbed a second one of the dog and heart, headed for the man wearing a white lab coat in the shielded pharmacy area, and laid her purchases on the counter.

"Good afternoon." She smiled when the balding middle-aged man turned and greeted her with a cheery smile of his own. "Besides these, I also need a prescription filled.

It's for a compounded thyroid medication, and I understand you do those here."

"Sorry, we haven't done compounds since the previous owner left."

"Really, I was under the impression you were a compounding pharmacist."

"No, that was all Luella Higgins, my former partner. It's not my area of expertise."

"What am I going to do now?" Addie feigned distress; at least, that's what she hoped it came off as and not that she was having a stroke. "You don't even have the equipment to do it? I'm really desperate. If I don't get this soon . . ."

"Sorry, the closest compounder is in Salem. I'd be happy to give you the drugstore's name."

"I must have misunderstood. I was told you were a compounder too."

"Yes, you must have misunderstood. That takes some specialized courses, and, sadly, I never had the inclination for it, but if I can look at your prescription, I can tell you a good dispensing alternative that I might have on hand."

"No, that's okay. Maybe when the fog lifts, I'll make a run to Salem. It's not far, is it?"

"Nah, half hour up Coast Highway is all. Will these be all?" he asked, ringing up her charms.

"Yes, and thank you." Addie scanned her bank card, turned to leave, and glanced at the pharmacy license behind the counter on the wall. It was still in Luella's name. "Say, you know you look familiar to me, and I've been trying to place you. Have you ever worked in Texas?"

"Texas?" The tips of his ears turned bright red.

"Yes," she said, "back in about 2001? My parents and I would visit my grandmother all the time, and I'm sure I remember seeing you before when we had to go and pick up her medications."

"Never been to Texas. You know what they say about everyone having a twin somewhere in the world." He appeared uncomfortable, but managed a half-hearted laugh. "I guess mine's in Texas."

"Yeah, and he's a pharmacist, too, so that makes it especially science-fiction-y, doesn't it?" she said with her own feeble attempt at a lighthearted laugh.

He glanced away, clearly uneasy about her questioning him, and she wondered if this might be a good time to make him squirm a bit more. "Say, you wouldn't mind explaining to me how the whole compounding thing works, would you? It's just that I know nothing about it and find the whole concept of pharmacists creating their own mixtures like they used to back in the old days fascinating. I run an antique business and am totally in love with anything old-school."

"Sorry, I can't help you." Not even bothering to look at her, he went about sorting some tiny white pills from a bottle.

Addie judged by the look on his face he was either going to toss her out onto the street or call the police, neither of which appealed to her. "Never mind, it was just a thought, but I can see you're busy." She ducked out the door and scurried back to the Wrangler.

She hadn't gotten the answers she hoped for, but at least she'd verified that the compounding had ended when Luella left. However, if she took the equipment with her, did that mean whoever tampered with the chocolates used Luella's apparatus, or did someone else in town have the wherewithal to carry out the aconitine extraction from plant to poisonous solution?

She would have to ask Marc to check Wanda's school and previous employment records. After all, if she was working as a pharmacy assistant, she would have a strong background in sciences. That only made sense to Addie.

Chapter 24

Even after a long, soaking bath and a light dinner with only Paige as her dining companion, because as Mrs. Bannerman had relayed from Tony, he was in the writing zone and wouldn't be joining them for dinner, she still couldn't get more than a half hour of sleep here and there through the night. Her mind wouldn't turn off, and she kept replaying the events leading up to her and Paige being forced to remain on the peninsula and the smatterings of evidence they had turned up in Luella's murder. She needed her crime board to make sense of it all, because right now, there weren't even puzzle pieces she could fit together. It was a jumbled mess of fuzzy kaleidoscope images.

She checked the time on the bedside clock. Nearly five a.m. Done with wrestling the elusive sleep monster, she flipped back the covers, threw her robe on, shoved her toes into her slippers, and scooped an excited Pippi into her arms.

"Ready for an early breakfast?" she whispered, tiptoeing out into the hallway as Pippi wiggled and stretched in her arms. Addie was certain she was confused about having to be carried everywhere in the huge house that should have been, by rights, her indoor playground. Unsure of Mrs. Bannerman's true reaction to the dog, Addie felt it was in everyone's best interests to restrain her exuberant friend.

The squeak of a door caused Addie to pause. Then she heard the sound again and peered over the gallery banister to the hall below, where she could make out the dim glow of a light. *Probably the study*.

"Should we go say good morning to Tony and see if he's ready for coffee?" she whispered in Pippi's ear.

When she peeked through the study doorway, her notion of having coffee with him evaporated. His head was lying on his arms, and he was snoring softly. *Strange*. Sensing eyes on her, she glanced around the great hall and glimpsed a shadowy movement by the grand parlor doorway, but then it, and the sensation, disappeared.

Addie shivered, snuggled Pippi tight to her chest, and crept across the hall toward the kitchen. "Okay, where do you think Mrs. Ramsay put your bag of kibble?" Addie asked as she opened one cupboard after another to no avail.

Pippi squirmed and yipped, and her little head turned toward the doorway leading off the kitchen. Addie flipped the light switch and laughed. "The pantry, of course. Smarty-pants, trust you to smell your food from a room away." She set Pippi down with instructions to stay and opened a cupboard at the end of the room. Pippi yipped again and thumped her little tail on the floor as Addie retrieved her bag of food and poured a cup into the small bowl. She set it down in front of her ravenous friend, who to any bystander would have thought the poor little creature hadn't eaten in days when in fact it had only been hours.

Addie chuckled as she took a seat on the top of a two-step ladder, which was probably there so that Mrs. Ramsay could reach the upper cabinets, due to her short stature. Addie surveyed the long, narrow room. A peg rack ran along the far end of the counter and bunches of herbs tied neatly with string hung upside down. Below the drying herbs was a large marble mortar and pestle. Behind it, arranged alphabetically, was a rack of small spice jars probably containing herbs from the kitchen garden. Curiosity getting the best of her, she continued surveying the sparkling clean and precisely arranged butler's pantry.

Beside her was a blue plastic bin with a recycling logo on the front of it. She smiled. At least the people in this house dripping with opulence made some attempt to keep up with the times and not follow old traditions of throwing everything into the landfill for future generations to deal with. The corner of a red box in the bin caught her eye. There was something familiar about it, but instead of popping up with a clear answer, it played right into one of the images that had tormented her through the night.

Addie gingerly plucked the large, square, red box from the recycling and stared at the gold-and-black ST on the top. That's why the peppermint chocolate she ate on Friday night tasted familiar. It was from Sweet Treats in Greyborne Harbor.

"May I be of assistance in helping you find something, Miss Greyborne?"

Addie whirled around and came face-to-face with Mrs. Bannerman, appearing as a stealth-like entity in the doorway. "Good morning," Addie said as lightly as she could muster once she placed her racing heart back in her chest where it belonged.

Even at this early hour, Mrs. Bannerman appeared as she always did: attired, of course, in her usual black knee-length dress, black stockings, and black shoes. Her hair was neatly pinned up, not one strand out of place.

Does this woman ever sleep?

Addie touched her bedhead with her free hand, and a wave of self-consciousness swept through her. "No, I was only getting Pippi her breakfast."

Mrs. Bannerman glanced down and the look on her face told Addie that she regarded her friend more like a furry pest than anything else.

She locked her unyielding gaze on Addie. "I see you found the food and something else, didn't you?"

Addie glanced down at the empty box in her hand and nodded.

"I can take that. As you can see, with the foil, it shouldn't have been placed in the recycling box but in the black garbage bin by the gate."

Addie peered over at the mortar and pestle, then at the neatly arranged herbs. An image of the sign in the poison garden flooded her mind. "It's okay. As soon as Pippi finishes her breakfast, I'll be taking her for out for a morning walk, so it's not a problem for me to put it in the bin."

"Really?" Her sharply arched, penciled eyebrows shot up to her hairline. "It is part of my job," she said, taking a step toward Addie, "and I wouldn't want to bother you with it." She held out her slender hand.

"No, it's fine really." Addie backed away and thudded

into a tall cupboard. A door above her flew open, and a sack of rice slipped out, spilling over her and the floor.

"Now, see what you've done," Mrs. Bannerman snapped. "Cook will never tolerate this, ever. I expect this to be cleaned up before she comes down to prepare breakfast, and don't think that Master Radcliff won't be informed about you sticking your nose where it doesn't belong." Mrs. Bannerman spun on her heel and disappeared.

"Oh dear, Pippi. It looks like we have a mess to clean up, don't we? Too bad dogs can't eat raw rice. It would make this so much easier." She laughed as she searched out a broom and dustpan. Her mind worked overtime trying to gauge the housekeeper's reaction to the empty box of chocolates.

After she had cleaned up the spilled bag of rice and surveyed the floor for any remaining grains, she put the broom and dustpan back into the cupboard where she'd found them. She flipped off the overhead light in the pantry and started through the kitchen when Tony came through the doorway, his hair looking worse than hers did.

"Addie," he said, wiping sleep from his eyes, "what's this I hear about you ransacking the kitchen and stealing from me?"

"What?" She glanced at Mrs. Bannerman standing behind him. A smug little smile touched the corners of her lips. "I was feeding Pippi her breakfast and bumped a cupboard. A bag of rice spilled out and"—she shot the housekeeper a dagger-filled glare—"that was the extent of my ransacking."

"Is this true?"

"Yes, of course, and as far as stealing, I'm not sure what it is I was supposed to have taken other than this."

She held out the empty red-foiled box. "It was in the recycling, but I know it was meant for the garbage bin, and that's exactly where I intend to take it when Pippi and I go for a walk."

He turned toward Mrs. Bannerman. "Thank you, that will be all."

She harrumphed and swiftly turned, vanishing out into the hallway.

"I don't know about you, but I need a coffee. Want one?" he asked, reaching for the carafe and filling it with water without waiting for Addie to answer.

"Yes, please, and then you can tell me about the chocolates."

"What chocolates?" He appeared to still be trying to wake up and not comprehending what she was saying.

"These chocolates." She shook the box in her hand. "The ones your housekeeper seemed to think that I was stealing, but as you can see, it's empty."

"Oh, those."

"Yes, these. I had one at the dinner on Friday, and I know they were from this chocolate shop in Greyborne Harbor. Did you take them to the potluck?"

"Why, yes, yes I did, but don't tell anyone."

Addie's hand tightened around the box. "Why wouldn't you want me to tell anyone?"

He ran his hand through his hair. "Because I don't want them to know I cheated and didn't take a homemade dish. That Gretchen woman thinks I took a flan and was most appreciative. It wouldn't bode well now if she found out I took credit for someone else's dish, would it?"

"Probably not, but how in the world did that happen?"

"I was heading upstairs, when an elderly woman with a cane stopped and asked if I was going to the potluck.

When I told her yes, she asked if I could drop off her contribution as she didn't think she could manage the stairs carrying it. I told her about the service elevator in the back corner of the library. She thanked me, but said that going down to the lower level to get to it with the cane and juggling the dish was just as difficult for her."

"When you dropped it off in the kitchen, you never thought to tell anyone that it wasn't your dish?"

"No, but in truth, I never said it was mine. I just let Gretchen assume and never corrected her. I felt embarrassed when I saw the food everyone else brought and all I had was two dishes of chocolates."

"I see." Addie glanced down at Pippi waiting patiently at her feet for her morning walk. She backed away from Tony, not sure what to believe anymore. "Well, I'll have to pass on that coffee. My friend here is reminding me she hasn't relieved herself yet, so I'd better get her outside."

"Okay, I'll leave the pot on the warmer and you can have a cup when you're done."

"Thanks." Addie bolted out of the kitchen, flew upstairs, threw on some clothes, and made a dash outside. When she smelled the scent of the crisp briny morning air, she could finally clear her head and think. Was Tony the killer? Had she been wrong and he did have a motive for wanting Luella dead, revenge perhaps? Then she recalled Mrs. Bannerman's reaction to seeing Addie with the box. Or was the tampering done by someone else, someone who knew about the poison plants in the conservatory and poor Tony was only her stooge in the whole thing?

Regardless, she had to tell Marc what she'd learned. Her thumbs flew across the keypad, but when she went to press Send, she hesitated. Tony was one of her dearest and oldest friends. Really? What was she thinking? Fingers crossed Marc would read between the lines and see that she was simply reporting the facts. She reread what she had written until she was certain that she had stressed what she knew about Mrs. Bannerman and her odd reaction to Addie having the box and that Tony didn't seem at all fazed about it, which in her mind meant he wasn't the guilty party here.

Then that familiar crawling sensation snaked up her neck and inched across her scalp. She turned and glanced back at the house. The prickliness on her neck increased. Let Marc figure it out because if Tony was innocent— like her gut told her—then Mrs. Bannerman might not be. She pressed Send. Out of the corner of her eye she spotted movement in the window behind her, confirming what she suspected.

A wave of panic surged through her. *Paige!* She was still sleeping and vulnerable, and by defying Mrs. Bannerman Addie had just played one of her cards.

Addie tugged Pippi's lead, darted through the door, and raced up the stairs, taking them two at a time. She flung open Paige's bedroom door and froze. The bed was empty.

Chapter 25

To Addie's relief there was the sound of running water. She knocked on the attached bathroom door. "Paige, it's Addie. Is everything okay?"

Paige opened the door. Her eyes were half-closed with sleep, and her tousled blond curls fell over her face. She gave Addie a curious look. "I'll be out in a sec," she mumbled around the toothbrush in her mouth.

Addie closed the door, patted her hand over her chest to steady the arrhythmic fluttering in her heart. Pippi jumped up on the bed and nestled into a pillow, yawned, and closed her eyes. As much as she enjoyed having her breakfast at this early hour, she clearly wasn't ready to start the day.

Addie smiled, sat on the bed, and ruffled Pippi's head. "I know the feeling, girl. Get your nap in now because I suspect this is going to be a very long day."

Paige came out of the bathroom and tossed the towel she'd been using on the dresser. "What's got you in such a state this early in the morning?"

"I'm sorry I burst in on you, but"—Addie wrung her hands in her lap—"I did something, and I think Mrs. Bannerman knows it, and I was afraid she'd take it out on you."

Paige sank onto the side of the bed. "Wanna know why I'm up at"—she glanced at the bedside clock—"six thirty in the freaking morning?"

Uneasiness sat at the base of Addie's spine and began snaking upward.

"I was woken by a sound that I swear was the door squeaking. I thought maybe it was you, but when I looked, no one was there."

Addie swallowed hard and proceeded to tell Paige about the empty box of chocolates she'd discovered in the kitchen and Mrs. Bannerman's peculiar reaction.

"What did Marc say?"

"I haven't heard back yet. I think he was still off this week, so he's probably not up. But I think until he can give us some advice on what we should do next, we better stay clear of her. And, for goodness' sake, don't eat or drink anything she prepares or serves us."

Paige looked at her thoughtfully. "And you're sure it's her, not Tony, who would have doctored the chocolates."

"I don't know what to think, but it makes more sense, and he didn't care that I found the empty box of chocolates except to keep his secret about not taking a home-made dish to the potluck. Plus, you heard him the other night. He doesn't know one poisonous plant from another and . . . and no! I just can't believe he's capable of murder.

Her, on the other hand, she wasn't pleased that I found it."
Addie shrugged. "It's the only lead we have so far and it's
one that makes sense. I think she wanted revenge on
Luella for scamming that poor old woman. Tony did say
she was loyal to her. How much more loyal can she get
than by killing the person who wronged someone she
cared about?"

Paige slipped back into the bathroom to dress, and
Addie tapped her phone screen, bringing up the photos
she'd taken of the two blackboards they had used at
Bree's house. "Yes, Pippi, I think we're on the right track
now with Mrs. Bannerman."

Pippi's ears perked, and she stared at Addie.

"I know, girl, this has been a tough one. Too many suspects and too many motives, but like your Grandpa Greyborne used to say, 'Motive always matters. Until you
discover which motive leads to the actual murder, you
can't determine which of the suspects is the one, but
when in doubt, always bank on love because it's far more
a motive than hate.'"

"What was that about banking on love?" asked Paige
from the bathroom doorway.

"It's something my dad used to say when he was
working as a New York City police detective. If you're
not finding the answers to the questions, you're not asking the right questions. So far, we've been focusing on
who was mad enough with Luella to kill her, and came up
with a list of people who might have wanted revenge, but
we didn't focus on someone who was protecting someone
they loved dearly." She stood up and shoved her phone in
the back pocket of her capris. "Yes, killing Luella was a

form of revenge, but it was for hurting the person they loved, so the revenge wasn't for themselves. Does that make sense?"

"Yeah," Paige said, retrieving her own phone out of her purse and scrolling down the screen. "But how do we disregard everyone else we have on our suspect list? There's Wanda, whose husband had an affair with Luella. There's Randy, who was put in—from what we were told—near financial ruin after being in business with her. And don't forget about Patricia and Bea. They both lost their jobs because of Luella closing the library and selling the bookmobile out from under them. Then there's that land developer and Mayor Bryant. That's one clue we haven't had much luck in turning up any information on." Paige flopped down on the bed. Her hand mechanically stroked Pippi, who inched across the bed and nestled her head on Paige's lap. "I think now we have to focus on the facts and not speculation. First, Luella was poisoned."

"Yes," said Addie.

"And the source was the chocolate-covered cherries at the potluck."

Addie reluctantly nodded.

"And Tony admitted to you that he took them to the dinner, so . . ."

"I know," said Addie. The sounds of vehicles on the driveway below drew her to the partially open window. "I can't believe it." She tugged her phone out and glanced at it. No messages. She glared at the commotion below her.

"What?" Paige rushed to her side.

"Marc, Simon, *and* Sheriff Turner, plus half a dozen other deputies just showed up."

"I guess Marc *was* up when you sent the text."

"Oh boy, we've got to get down there. I have to explain to Marc why I think it was Mrs. Bannerman and not Tony, even though he took the chocolates."

"Are you sure you want to do that? Marc does know how to run an investigation and perform a suspect interview. He'll figure it out, but if you tell him what to do, well . . . you know that won't go over well."

"It's not him I'm worried about. It's Sheriff Turner and his dogged determination to pin this on an outsider. Tony lives in England now. How much more of an outsider could he be?"

She scooped Pippi off the bed, cradled her to her chest, and dashed out the door into the gallery, but by the time she got there, she saw over the railing that Mrs. Bannerman had beat her to it and was leading the entourage down the hallway toward the library.

Turner said something to Simon and instructed two of the deputies to go with him, and they headed toward the conservatory. The other deputies disappeared, dispersing in groups, two in different directions. Two of them went up the stairs to the galley and continued on to the servants' rooms on the third floor.

Addie was certain she was going to be sick. Simon knew his stuff and would find the monkshood in Maisie's poison garden for sure, and that would seal Tony's fate in Turner's eyes. When she told Marc what she had discovered, she had no intentions of launching a police raid on Tony's home—only for Marc to investigate and get to the bottom of the chocolate mystery.

Addie clutched Pippi and charged down the stairs, Paige close on her heels.

"What are you going to do?" Paige whispered hoarsely, fighting to catch her breath.

"I don't know," snapped Addie, "but I caused this, and now I have to fix it." She came to a stuttering stop as Marc entered the library and turned to close the door. His eyes fixed on hers. He dropped his hand, leaving the door open a crack, and followed Turner into the adjoining study, leaving Addie and Paige in the hallway.

Addie glanced at Paige and then at the partially open door. Was this Marc's way of saying you can't be part of this, but help yourself to some information? Did he know what was going on or had this spiraled out of his control too? Both women leaned in closer to the door opening. Addie's ears perked as she strained to hear what was going on inside.

"Are you Anthony Radcliff of Yorkshire, England?" Sheriff Turner's voice boomed through the door crack.

"Yes, may I help you, Sheriff?"

"It's our understanding that you took the chocolates to the potluck."

"Yes, is that against some archaic law you have here in the colonies?"

Addie could hear the smirk in Tony's voice.

"Just answer the questions, Mr. Radcliff," Turner snapped.

"Yes, I took some chocolates that I had at the house."

"Where did you get them?"

"I don't know."

"You took a box of chocolates to a community dinner, but you have no idea where you bought them?"

"That's correct."

"What, they just magically appeared?"

"In a way, yes, they did."

"Are you messing with me, sir?"

"Not in the least. I'm assuming they were left by someone who attended the open house I had after Gran's funeral last December."

"But you don't know who brought them?"

"No, I have no idea. There were so many people coming and going that day to pay their respects that I never saw who left them."

"But that was six months ago, and you still had them?"

"Yes, we ate the fruit baskets, of course, and Mrs. Bannerman, my housekeeper, put the flowers around the house to try to cheer the place up, but I wasn't in the mood for chocolates at the time. I had just buried my grandmother, who was like a mother to me. They must have gotten put away in the pantry."

"Then how did they end up on the table at the library dinner?"

"When it came time for the potluck, I remembered I had forgotten to tell the cook, Mrs. Ramsay, to make something. I scrounged through the pantry to find something I could take, saw the unopened box, and thought, what the heck. So, I threw them in a couple of dishes and took them as my contribution."

"Not much of a dinner contribution, was it?"

"Probably not, but I didn't want to go to the dinner anyway."

"Why did you?"

"Because I had heard Luella had arranged for a television news crew to be there, and I wanted to hear what she had to say about the library closure, in case I had to get my lawyer involved."

"It sounds like you had a grudge with Luella Higgins. If that's how you felt, why even bother taking the chocolates?"

"I don't know, call it a gesture of goodwill. I knew the town already blamed me for the library closing, and I didn't want them to hate me even more by showing up empty-handed to their stupid dinner. I have a reputation, and my publisher's public relations department is having a hard enough time keeping this whole mess out of the news. I can see the headlines now. BESTSELLING AUTHOR CLOSES DOWN COMMUNITY LIBRARY. How do you think that's going to go over in a press release? My book sales would plummet."

"Okay, talk us through what you did when you got to the dinner."

"I put the dishes on the table and was going to find a chair in the back corner to wait until the on-air interview, and that's when I saw Addie."

"You're referring to Addie Greyborne of Greyborne Harbor, Massachusetts?"

"Yes, we're old friends and went to high school together . . ."

"Addie, what are you doing out here?" Simon whispered in her ear.

Addie's hand few to her mouth to stifle the shriek she was about to unleash. "Simon, you scared the bejesus out of me."

Simon glanced momentarily at the deputy behind him, looked at Addie and set his gaze firm. "If you'll kindly step back, Miss Greyborne, and allow us to pass."

Addie did as she was asked and the two men slid into

the room. Simon hung back a second and motioned as though closing the door, but to Addie's relief his hand dropped, and he followed the deputy into the study.

"*Miss* Greyborne." Paige giggled. "That's a first." Her warm breath wafted across Addie's neck, but it was quickly replaced by that familiar clammy, crawling sensation. Addie spun around. Mrs. Bannerman stood staunchly in the doorway of the conservatory.

The library door flew open, and Addie and Paige reeled back as Tony, his hands behind his back in handcuffs, was escorted out of the room by two deputies flanking either side of him.

Sheriff Turner followed behind, paused, and leveled his bulbous eyes on Addie. "Miss Greyborne, Miss Stringer, you are both free to leave the peninsula now." He, and Marc close by his side, marched down the hallway where they were met by the deputies that Addie assumed had searched the house.

"What's going on over there?" asked Simon over her shoulder.

"You tell me. What did you say to Turner to cause this?" She waved her hand toward Tony and his two deputy escorts by the door.

"I verified what you told Marc about the monkshood plant in the conservatory. With the know-how, aconitine could be easily extracted from it in the same deadly concentration that killed Luella."

"Did you happen to also mention that I suspected Mrs. Bannerman because of her knowledge of deadly plants and not Tony, who can't tell a tulip from a daffodil?" Addie glanced back at the entourage still in the foyer. Marc was right there in the mix, listening to what the deputies were telling Sheriff Turner. He steadied his gaze on Addie, and his jaw ticked.

"Wait!" bellowed Turner to the two deputies escorting Tony outside. "Uncuff him. He's free to go . . . for now. But stay in town." He turned and glared at Addie. "You two, stay put too. I'm not done with any of you!" He stomped outside, a gaggle of deputies falling in behind him.

"What just happened?" Addie glanced from Marc to Simon.

Simon shrugged. "Beats me." He stalked off toward Marc.

"Oh crap," hissed Addie.

"What?" Paige said, turning to look in the direction Addie was.

"Look at Mrs. Bannerman's face."

"Yikes, if looks could kill," she whispered.

The housekeeper's eyes were ablaze with hatred as they narrowed on Addie. "I think we'd better call Mrs. Grainger at the B&B. I don't know about you, but I doubt I'll be able to sleep a wink tonight."

Addie clutched Pippi tight and scurried over to Marc and Simon. "What just happened?"

"The sheriff considers the case closed."

"Just like that," she snapped, staring at Tony wobbling toward the front parlor.

"Yes. Simon identified the monkshood plants in the conservatory, and his lab results confirm the chocolate-covered cherries were tampered with, and Tony confessed to taking the chocolates to the dinner."

"And," added Simon, "remember Tony had the strong-est motive for wanting Luella dead."

"You can't be serious. I'd say it was the other way around. He held the purse strings, and she was the one fu-rious with him for pulling Maisie's bequest to the library, causing its closure. Why would he want to kill her? And you"—Addie turned and pinned Marc with a look—"I only told you about the empty chocolate box so you'd in-vestigate it, not so you'd show up here with a posse and arrest an innocent man." She planted her hands on her hips. Her body vibrated with rage. "And you"—she glared at Simon—"I can't even . . ." She spun on her heel and dashed into the parlor.

"Wait, Addie," Simon called, "there's more."

But Addie didn't want to hear anything else he said. "Tony, wait," she cried, setting Pippi on the floor, and raced toward him where he sat, head in hands, in a wing-back chair beside the fireplace. "I'm so sorry. I told Marc about the empty box of chocolates. I never thought he'd tell Turner and that it would lead to this."

Tony stared up at her, his cognac-brown eyes empty and dull. "I don't understand. Do you really think me ca-pable of murder?"

"No, and I told Marc that, but . . ."

"But what?" He rose to his feet. "That Mrs. Banner-man was? How dare you come into my home and make these wild accusations about me and someone who is a beloved member of this family." He pointed his finger at her face. "I thought we were friends, and for you to even think—"

"We are friends, honestly. I don't know how this happened. Turner is so willing to believe that an outsider committed this murder that he won't even look at other suspects."

"You mean like Mrs. Bannerman?"

"Yes, her and everyone else on the suspect list who had a motive to kill Luella. Don't you see, Tony"—she placed her hand on his arm—"he wants it to be me, Paige, or even you because we aren't part of this little tight-knit community, and he's not looking at the people right under his nose who could have done it."

Tony raked his hand through his brown-sugar-colored hair. "That makes sense because I told him exactly how I came to be in possession of the chocolates, and he didn't even care."

"Well"—she swallowed—"whatever you told him, it must have helped because he ended up not arresting you."

"No, I overheard what they were saying. I was only let go now because they didn't find any evidence of the equipment needed to make the poison that killed Luella."

"Okay, why don't we sit down, take a deep breath, and you can tell me the whole story about how you came to be in possession of the chocolates."

"With all respect, Addie, I don't want to talk about it anymore. I've been through this with the police already."

"I know, but maybe if you tell me the whole story and picture what happened, something you forgot before might come back to you and give us a clue we can work with."

"Fine." Tony dropped back into the chair. "All right." He rubbed his temples. "It's like I explained to the sheriff and your two friends. It was during the memorial tea and open house I held after my grandmother's funeral. I saw the box on the hall table after a large group arrived. Later, after everyone left, I went to get one of the chocolates, but the box was gone."

"Did you ask Mrs. Bannerman about them?"

"No, I never thought anything about them again. It had been a long day, and I had just buried the woman who was like a mother to me."

"So how did you end up bringing them to the dinner?"

"On Friday I realized I had forgotten to tell Mrs. Ramsay to make a dish for me to take, and I didn't want to show up empty-handed and give the locals any more fuel for their gossip machine. If you haven't figured out by now, they hate me for what I did about the library funding. Anyway, I searched the kitchen for something I could take. Mrs. Ramsay always has some dessert treats in the fridge or biscuits stashed away, but that day there was nothing I could pass off as my own. Then I came across the box of chocolates at the back of one of the bottom cupboards in the panty. I thought why not, they looked untouched, so I dumped them into a couple of crystal bowls, and that was it. I went off to the dinner to try to repair some of my damaged reputation and make sure Luella wasn't going to make things worse for me with her television interview."

"So, if you didn't inject the concentration of aconitine into the chocolate-covered cherries, and you're sure Mrs. Bannerman didn't—"

"How could she have? Think about it. She had no way of knowing beforehand that I would take them to the dinner. You think she poisoned them just in case I found them in the cupboard and decided to kill Luella someday?"

"Good point. That means someone at the dinner tampered with them before they were put out on the table and everyone came upstairs."

"We have to find out who had access to them between the time I dropped them off in the kitchen and the dinner started."

"Yes, but between Paige and Marc and Sherriff Turner, everyone involved with the preparations has been accounted for and claims they know nothing about who even brought the chocolates."

"Then one of them is lying."

"Yes. But who?"

Chapter 26

"**P**aige, we have to go back and talk to everyone we have on our suspect list."

"Do you really think we can slip one of them up and have them come right out and admit to injecting poison into a couple of chocolates?"

"No." Addie slumped on the bed as Paige closed her suitcase. "But I don't know what else to do. This has me so confused because we've hit a dead end on every lead. Nothing, zilch, nada."

"Maybe if we could find out who brought the chocolates here in the first place?"

"You mean to Maisie's memorial tea?"

"Yeah."

"But that was six months ago. How would it help us now?"

Paige perched on the side of the bed, her fingers tracing the Snoopy character on her bag. "You're right, and giving chocolates as a gift isn't against the law, so it wouldn't prove anything."

"See, another dead end. It doesn't mean anything because it doesn't matter who brought the chocolates in December. It's about who had access to them Friday before the potluck and just happened to be carrying around a syringe filled with a lethal concentration of aconitine."

Addie's phone vibrated a text alert. She tugged it out of her pocket. "Serena. She wants an update and says if I'm not there when the baby is born, she'll never talk to me again." Addie dropped the phone on the bed. "Do you think she hates me for being stuck here when she's going through what she is, and I'm not there for her?"

"Serena hate you? Never, you two are like sisters, maybe even closer, judging by my own experience with having blood-related sisters. She's just scared. She knows her life is changing, and she's having a hard time with that."

"I know but . . ."

"No buts. We have to get this solved so you can get back to holding her hand through this, and I can get back to my own little bundle of joy." Paige swiped at a tear edging down her cheek. "Let's focus. What were some of the things your father used to do when a case stumped him?"

"Hmm . . . he used to talk to himself while going over the clues. He often said, 'If you can't find the answer, you're asking the wrong questions.'"

"Good, we can start there."

Addie propped herself on one elbow. "Another one was, 'Many things are possible, but what is probable?'"

Paige's thumbs tapped across her phone keypad. "Let's

not lose sight of those and find someplace where we can reconstruct a crime board."

"Look at you going all PI on me." Addie laughed, climbed off the bed and grabbed her suitcase, and the doggie bed and carrier beside the door. "Yeah, we might have to invade Bree's house. You heard what Marc said about Mrs. Grainger at the B&B." Addie opened the door and paused. "I just had a thought. Turner hasn't mentioned anything about the bookmobile, has he?"

"Not lately that I recall."

"Then it's time to call him and find out if he's done with it yet. After all, he released the library as a crime scene, and I am the owner and have a right to see what condition it's in and remove it from the police impound lot."

"Yes, but how does that help us with the crime board situation?"

"I am the owner, remember."

Paige looked curiously at her. "Right, I get it, we could set it up in the bookmobile."

"Bingo!" Addie laughed as they headed down the gallery to the stairs and then the main floor.

Addie opened the back of the Wrangler and shoved a box of books against the back seat. "There, these should fit now." She maneuvered their luggage in between the boxes of books and the legs of the table they were taking back to Greyborne Harbor from their library sale purchases.

"Do you want to talk about it?"

"About what? Why we bought so much and barely have room for us and Pippi now?"

"No, about the elephant in the room that you haven't mentioned since he left today on what, I should point out, wasn't the sweetest of partings."

"Nope, I'm still too furious with both of them to talk about it. What happened, happened." Addie's hand wavered on the tailgate of the SUV. "And I don't care to hear either of their excuses. All I know is how much embarrassment it caused Tony, when I only told Marc about the chocolates and asked him what he thought of Mrs. Bannerman as a suspect. Then for him to involve Simon." She slammed the tailgate.

Paige winced with the bang. "Speaking of Tony, how did he take us moving over to the B&B because we're leery of his housekeeper?"

"I didn't tell him that part. I only said it was hard on Pippi here, and she would be better in a fenced yard where she could go in and out whenever she needed."

"Can you do that at the B&B?" asked Paige, buckling her seat belt.

"I have no idea, but it was better than telling him that we're afraid Mrs. Bannerman would kill us in our sleep or poison us." Addie glanced at Paige. "Remember, she's still at the top of our suspect list."

"Yeah, but I think it's a draw between her, Wanda, and Patricia, don't you?"

It didn't take long to snake their way down the back road to the police station, but when Addie turned onto Sea Spray Drive, her foot hesitated over the accelerator. She peered over into the visitors' parking lot. "Well, it looks like Simon and Marc are still here."

"Should we go in and see what the plan is now?"

"Not a chance. I'm mad at them both, remember?" Addie stepped on the gas. When they came to the cross street that led to the pharmacy, she whispered, "If you can't find the answer, you're asking the wrong questions."

"What are you talking about?" Paige gripped the dashboard when Addie slammed on the brakes to make a left turn at the light.

"I asked the wrong question."

"To whom? About what?"

"To Randy, about Luella. Duh. The license behind the counter should have made me see it before." She pulled into the small parking lot beside the drug store. "I shouldn't be long. I just want to ask Randy one more question."

"Addie, wait. Tell me what's going on," Paige called through the open window, but Addie only waved her hand over her shoulder and scooted around the side of the building to the pharmacy entrance.

She stepped over the threshold of the drug store and shoved her sunglasses on top of her head. Once satisfied there were no other customers in the store, she made a beeline to the back pharmacy counter. "Good afternoon, Randy."

He looked up over the rim of his dark-framed glasses. "You again? I already told you I can't make your compounded prescription." He scowled and went back to counting out pills into a plastic tray.

"I just wanted to ask you about the time you worked in Texas."

"I told you that too. I've never been there."

"I have some very reliable sources that say otherwise."

"What sources?"

"People who have access to the FBI database." She

leaned on the counter, feeling a little smug when she saw how she had his full attention. "Tell me, did Luella know when she went into business with you that you had your license revoked?"

He didn't move; his fingers froze over the pills he'd been counting.

"That's okay, I can see you're busy. Maybe I'll ask Sheriff Turner to look into how the pharmacy license was issued, and to whom, since you already told me that Luella hasn't been involved in the business for a couple of years but on the wall you still have her certificate as the licensed pharmacist." She turned to leave.

"Wait," he called, pulling off his rubber gloves, tossing them aside and trudging over to the counter. "That was our deal. On paper we make it look like I ran the business side of it, and she would be the licensed pharmacist for state audit purposes. As long as I kept my mouth shut, she would too and let me continue to practice."

"And when she left?"

"She took all the equipment but left the paperwork as is. By doing that, it would appear to the state that she was still the pharmacist."

"But she wasn't actually involved in the business, was she? And I heard around town that she took all her money out and left you with a mound of bills. Is that true or only gossip?"

"It's true, but it was going to cost her a fortune to break our contract, and she told me if I ever tried to sue her or retaliate in anyway, she'd report me and tell everyone how I conned her and lied about my past charges. She told me point-blank that she'd swear she knew nothing about it and would make sure I did prison time for practicing without a license."

"She was blackmailing you."

He nodded.

"That's a pretty strong motive for murder, and given the means in this case, you, as a trained compounding pharmacist, would be well-equipped to pull it off, don't you think?"

"I haven't compounded for years. When I told you that Luella looked after those prescriptions, I wasn't lying. That's the truth."

Addie recalled Paige telling her that Bree had to go to Salem to have her prescriptions filled, so that probably was true.

"After Luella left the business, do you know if she ever did special orders as a favor to a friend or show anyone the finer art of compounding?"

"Not that I know of." He shrugged.

"No one ever came in and asked you or her to teach them how to extract a chemical from a plant source?"

"I don't know what you're getting at. After Luella left, what she did was her business. I was just happy not to have to deal with her on a daily basis."

"Then I should take that as a no to my question? No one asked you anything in the last two years about aconitine or monkshood?"

Randy's face paled, and pearls of perspiration glistened across his forehead. He shook his head. "Look, I have to get back to work. I have customers that will be coming in to get their prescriptions soon and . . . and . . . are you going to report me?"

Addie shrugged.

"If you want to know what equipment Luella had, here, take her house key and go look for yourself. As far as I know, when she went into politics she sold everything, but maybe she was giving compounding lessons on the side."

"Why do you have her house key?"

"My wife, Irene, is her sister."

"You're married to Luella's sister?"

"Yes, we met when I first came from Texas. Actually, Irene introduced me to Luella, and that's when we started the business."

"Your sister-in-law?" Addie nodded her head. "So much of what you told me makes more sense."

"Like what?"

"Why she would go into business with a criminally convicted pharmacist in the first place and why she allowed you to continue to operate under her license."

"Families, aye?"

"Yeah, families." Addie turned and toyed with the key in her hand as she studied Randy when he turned and went to the back counter of the pharmacy station. This gave her another thought.

She whipped her phone out of her pocket, typed out a text, reread it, and pressed Send.

"I'll drop the key off later," she called.

"Thanks. I don't know what you're hoping to find in her house, but good luck."

"Now, mind telling me what's going on?" Paige glared at Addie as she climbed in and clipped her seat belt on.

"I'm sorry. I don't mean to exclude you. It's just that without my crime board, I can't see the puzzle pieces and how they fit together. Right now, they are all going *pop, pop, pop* in my head like fireworks. I'm trying to work through them because I have a hunch."

"I get that. I'm like you. I need to see it in black and white and then make the links. The best thing we can do now is go pick up the bookmobile and make the board. We have all the information, and I know we'll both feel better when we can see what fits and what doesn't."

"We have one more stop to make first."

Addie could sense Paige's exasperated eye roll.

"I told you, I have a hunch, and my gut tells me this is where we're going to find the answer." Addie glanced down at her phone to check the address and pulled up in front of a large two-story Cape Cod.

"Who lives here?"

"Luella."

"We're going into a dead woman's house?" Paige gasped. "I don't think breaking and entering is something we should be considering."

"We aren't breaking in anywhere. We've been invited."

"By whom?"

"Her brother-in-law."

Paige did a double take. "When?"

"Randy Carlyle is married to Luella's sister and he answered a lot of questions." Addie unclipped her seat belt.

Paige folded her arms. "Well, I still have a few. Like what are we doing here? What are you hoping to find? I'm not budging until you tell me."

"Suit yourself, but if my hunch is right, Luella was showing someone, and recently too, how to extract aconitine from a monkshood plant."

"Why would she do that?"

"She might not have known what it was for or what the person had in mind. Remember, she was chairman of the gardening club. Maybe it started off as a simple question one of the members had, and through teaching the person about poisonous plants, she inadvertently showed them how the compounding process worked."

"And how is searching through her house going to tell us if she did that?"

"I'm hoping to find some of the equipment she used at the pharmacy, but you know what?" Addie snapped her fingers. "Here, I'm texting you a photo I took of Mrs. Bannerman. I didn't think she knew I took it, but as soon as I snapped it, she stared straight at me with those haunted, distant eyes of hers." Addie shivered. "Anyway, why don't you canvass the neighbors and see if anyone saw her around here in the last month or so, while I check out the house."

"Good idea. I also took a couple of photos of Patricia, Bea, and a few of the other volunteers when I was at the library. I was hoping we could make it a real crime board like the police use with the photos of the suspects and everything."

"Actually, that's a good idea. Because we're visual learners, it would really help, and it's a great help right now. Good thinking." She grinned at Paige as she closed the door.

"What about Pippi though?" Paige called and glanced at the small dog. "Although, if I take her with me, maybe I won't look so nosy or threatening if I'm out walking a dog when I start accosting the neighbors about the comings and goings in Luella's house."

"Good thinking." Addie laughed and made her way up to the door, fished the key from her front jeans pocket, and inserted it in the lock. When it clicked and the door opened freely, a feeling of foreboding washed over her, and she shuddered. "This can't be good karma," she whispered. "No, I really shouldn't be meddling in the life of a dead woman." But it was for the sake of the dead woman. *Right?* It was to try to figure out which of the names on her list injected cherries with a poisonous substance. Someone Luella had thought her friend, really wanted her dead and used her own knowledge of how to make that happen, against her.

Addie stood in the bedroom doorway. She thought she had felt uncomfortable about being on the front steps, but seeing a dress, stockings, and shoes laid out on the bed sent a chill rushing through her. Those were most likely the clothes Irene had selected for Luella to wear when her body would finally be released for burial. She backed out of the room, not even checking the attached bathroom.

So far nothing else in the house had turned up any evidence of compounding equipment. She might as well be grasping at straws. For all she knew about the science of extracting poisons, a twenty-dollar children's home-chemistry set could have done the trick. But as she hadn't unearthed even that contraption, she closed the front door, knowing she'd hit another dead end.

She started down the porch stairs and wondered how Paige had made out. She should have been back by now. Addie walked around the side of the house and spied a shed and a small greenhouse in the backyard. "Might as well." She shrugged and trotted to the outbuildings.

The shed was unlocked, and Addie peered in. Nothing out of the usual lawn-and-gardening equipment jumped out at her. Lawnmower, rakes, a couple of shovels, a garden hose, and other miscellaneous objects littered the space. She closed the door and headed into the greenhouse. She gasped. There on the potting counter was exactly what she had been thinking: a chemistry setup. A Bunsen burner, coils of glass tubing, glass flasks, and large glass syringes. Without touching anything, Addie examined the tip of the syringe. It was too large to have been used to inject poison into the chocolates but probably useful to draw solution out of a petri dish just like the ones in the corner.

Addie's phone vibrated a text alert. She jumped and fumbled her phone like a hot potato before she could read the message from Felix.

I went to Sweet Treats as you asked and spoke with Sally Harrison about the box of chocolates you sent a picture of. She said that they were a deluxe box she only offers during special holidays. I had her check her records for anyone who had purchased them within the past year, and one name on the list stood out. Luella Higgins bought a box this past December.

She typed a quick, *Thank you! I owe you a lunch.*

Nothing made sense. Luella had been poisoned by the very chocolates she took to Tony's six months ago. How did such a thing happen? Did the person who killed Luella also know she took the chocolates to the memorial tea? Were the two events even related? She was clearly missing the connection.

She shoved her phone in her pocket. Perhaps Paige had had more luck discovering who the fake friend was who milked Luella for her knowledge and then poisoned her with it. Addie turned toward the door and paused. She scanned the shelves of potted plants in the small green-house. Three spiked purple-flowered plants jumped out at her. One of which had a broken stalk, and threads of dried roots dangled over the side of the plant pot. She looked over at the chemistry setup on the potting table and it hit her. That was it. Why didn't she see it before?

Her gut told her who murdered Luella Higgins, and if she was right, Mrs. Bannerman held the key.

Chapter 27

Addie dashed out onto the street and spotted Paige and Pippi two houses down, speaking to a woman with a stroller.

"Paige, we have to go," she yelled.

"Be right there." Paige said something to the woman, tugged Pippi's leash, and ran toward her. "You aren't going to believe what I found out," puffed Paige. "That was Luella's next-door neighbor, and she told me that since Luella became mayor, her friends stopped coming around. Any visitors seemed to be members of the town council, and"—she dropped her voice—"Sheriff Turner, of course, and"—she squealed excitedly—"Randy Carlyle and his wife. Interesting, huh? I wonder what they were doing here all the time. With all that bad blood between them over the whole business thingy and financial ruin, you'd think they would have avoided her like the plague."

"So, Valerie was right," Addie said thoughtfully. "Luella did change after she became mayor, and if only those people were coming around . . . no Mrs. Bannerman?"

"No, no one I showed her picture to recognized her. I'd say if she ever does come to town, she keeps to herself." She grinned mischievously. "Or maybe she only comes at night when there's a full moon."

Addie laughed. "You might be right about that, but I think I figured out who killed Luella." Addie stared back at the house. "Yes, and if I'm right, we have to get to Tony's right now."

"Wait a minute. You found proof in there that it *was* Mrs. Bannerman, and you're going to confront her? No way! We saw Marc's car at the police station. You tell him and let him do the honors. You're not trained for this."

"But I am, trust me."

"No, I won't let you have another showdown with a killer. You got lucky before, but that fairy dust won't last forever."

"But you don't understand." Addie raced to the Wrangler. In her excitement, she fumbled the keys and dropped them on the road.

"I understand well enough, and it's obvious you're not thinking clearly," said Paige, picking up the keys. "Get in the other side. I'm driving, and we're going to the police station. As Marc is always telling you, leave it to the professionals. Those professionals have guns, we don't."

"But Paige—"

"No buts."

"Okay, but just a second." Addie stepped away from the Wrangler. "I want to make a quick call first."

They pulled up in front of the station. Paige hadn't even come to a full stop at the curb when Addie jumped out, stumbled, and caught herself before she did a face-plant on the sidewalk.

She raced up the steps and burst through the door. "I need to see Chief Chandler and Sheriff Turner, now!"

The deputy raised a quizzical brow. "You're that woman from Greyborne Harbor, right?"

"It doesn't matter. I need to speak to the sheriff."

"He's in a meeting now—"

Addie skittered around the counter, pushed open the gate into the main squad room, and marched toward the office.

"Wait, you can't go in there!"

She flung the door open. Marc and Simon spun around in their chairs. Turner leapt to his feet. "What's the meaning of this?"

"I know who killed Luella Higgins," she cried. "And you have to get out to Tony Radcliff's house immediately and talk to Mrs. Bannerman."

"Miss Greyborne, we've been over this already. Mrs. Bannerman is *not* the killer."

"Maybe not, but she can prove who the real killer is, and I think if you talk to Randy Carlyle, he can corroborate it."

The blue vein in Turner's temple bulged. "You want to implicate Randy Carlyle, an esteemed member of this community for over twenty years, in this murder too?" He slammed his hand on the desk. "It was bad enough when you pointed the finger at my wife, Wanda. Now this!" He scoffed. "Are there no limits to your misdirection in this case?" He shook his finger. "*You*, Miss Grey-borne, are the guilty party here, and I know it."

"But I can prove what I'm saying. Please . . ." She glanced at Marc and Simon. "Hear me out and then you decide."

Marc rose to his feet. "She has a point, Jack. The least we can do is hear what she has to say, because everything we've come up with has led to a dead end."

"Addie has some experience in matters like this," added Simon, coming to her side. "The DA, Jeff Wilson, has even hired her under contract on a few occasions."

Turner's eyes blazed like torches. "And that goes directly to my point. She's a sneaky one, knows the law." He snorted. "Has the two of you eating out of her hand like puppy dogs. Well, my money is still on her as the only guilty party in this whole investigation."

"But, but . . ." Addie sputtered.

Simon gave her hand a reassuring squeeze. "What does it hurt to hear what she has to say?"

She glanced at Simon and mouthed, "Thank you."

Turner dropped down in his chair. "Fine, impress me with your great detective skills, Miss Greyborne." He sat back and folded his arms over his barrel chest.

Marc gave her a nod, boosting her confidence. She drew in a deep breath. "From the beginning, this was a puzzling murder. We had a victim who over the past few years had made several enemies for one reason or another. We had a poisoning, but we couldn't determine how, or in what, if it was in any of the food she ate prior to her death since the food samples all came up negative in testing. When the source of the poison was discovered, the question came down to, who took the chocolates to the dinner?"

Sheriff Turner's attention appeared to be preoccupied with the length of his pens and pencils in the pencil holder on his desk. She cleared her throat. He raised his eyebrows, looked slightly sheepish, and laid his hands on the desk.

"When it was determined that Tony Radcliff had taken the chocolates as his contribution to the potluck, it was also made clear he knew nothing about poison, and I can attest to the fact that chemistry was never his strongest subject. The focus was on his housekeeper, Mrs. Bannerman."

She drew in a deep unsteady breath and forged on. "Of course, it only made sense. She was a loyal employee of the Radcliffs for over thirty-five years. She worked tirelessly in Maisie Radcliff's greenhouse. She had a good knowledge of poisonous plants in the Agatha Christie garden. The question was, did she also have the knowledge to extract the aconitine from the monkshood plants?"

"But there was no evidence in the Radcliff house connecting her to the production of the poison." Turner leaned forward in his seat. "Look, Miss Greyborne, as far as I can see, you're just talking in circles right now." He sat back. "I thank you for your interest in the case that—if I might remind you—you are still the number one—"

"Jack!" snapped Marc. "Let her finish."

"Thank you." She smiled weakly at him and shored herself up. "Since Luella was also the chairman of the gardening club"—she glanced at Turner—"a group I believe your wife is now chairperson of—"

"Don't you—"

"Luella's knowledge of plants combined with her expertise as a chemist and pharmacist gave her a very desirable skill base for someone who might want to take advantage of their association with her and use her own expertise against her to commit a murder. Her murder, to be exact."

"Wait," said Simon, "are you saying Luella trained the person who ultimately killed her?"

"She had the know-how and the equipment to conduct that kind of chemical extraction, and my feeling was someone on our suspect list also saw the advantage in her skill set."

"But," said Paige from the doorway where she stood cradling Pippi to her chest, "I'm confused because I told you I spoke with all her neighbors today, and they didn't recall seeing Mrs. Bannerman at all, or anyone else on our suspect list. Well, except Randy coming and going from Luella's house over the past few months, but he has the skills to make the poison, so he wouldn't have needed Luella's help."

"No, he wouldn't have." Addie fought the excitement bubbling up inside her. The name of the person sat on the tip of her tongue. It took every ounce of willpower within her to bite her tongue because she knew she was going to have to present the strongest case possible before Turner would ever consider her suspicions.

"Let's take a step back for a moment," said Addie. "When Tony and Mrs. Bannerman were ultimately ruled out due to the lack of evidence linking them directly to the murder, the next question became, who had access to the chocolates before the volunteers' dinner began? Patricia and Bea, our two top suspects, have the strongest motive. They harbored some serious ill will because of Luella's actions. Not only did they lose their jobs, they lost the bookmobile, dashing Patricia's dreams of being able to continue on as the librarian."

"But eyewitnesses placed them downstairs the entire time in question," said Marc.

"Exactly," said Addie. "The only other volunteers were the usual kitchen workers for the library events, and they were setting up tables and chairs. Gretchen was preparing the dishes in the kitchen and didn't see who dropped off the chocolates. Besides, there wasn't any reason to suspect any of them anyway."

"So where did this window of opportunity occur?" snarled Turner, sitting back and glaring at her with his pea-sized eyes.

"It didn't. At least, not that night."

"Are you saying the poison was in the chocolates before they showed up on the table at the dinner?" asked a clearly bewildered Marc.

"Yes."

"Then that takes us back to Mrs. Bannerman and Tony Radcliff, both of whom have been cleared," scoffed Turner.

"Not exactly."

"What did we miss?" asked Simon.

"Something we all missed. It wasn't until I searched Luella's house—"

Turner gripped the edge of his desk and shot to his feet. "You went into Luella's house and searched it? That is breaking and entering, and I'll have you charged."

"No, Sheriff. I was invited there and had a key. No breaking and entering occurred."

"Who gave you a key?"

"Luella's brother-in-law, Randy Carlyle."

"He's her brother-in-law?" asked Simon, confusion clouding his eyes. "But why didn't we know this before?"

"I only found out today, and I also discovered that Luella was blackmailing him."

"For what?" sputtered Turner.

"That I will tell you later, but right now, I also got the feeling when I was talking to him that there was something else. After a visit to her house, I figured out what it was. If you bring him in for questioning and he finds out his first crime has been publicly exposed, I'm pretty sure he'll freely talk about the second one."

"Darn you, woman." Turner slammed the desk. "You're talking in circles again. Spit it out. Who killed Luella Higgins?"

Addie contained her inward smile. This is exactly what she hoped for. In a minute, he wouldn't be able to deny what her gut told her was the truth. "You see, I also had a friend of ours, Felix Vanguard, verify something in Greyborne Harbor, and . . ."

"And what, Addie?" asked Marc. "What did Felix find out?"

"The shop that sells those particular special-edition boxes of chocolates is in Greyborne Harbor, and they are only produced at Christmas. Luella Higgins was one of the names on the list of purchasers last Christmas."

"So, someone used her own chocolates against her?"

"That's what I thought. That was until I recalled Tony had told me Luella was fascinated with Maisie's Agatha Christie garden. After some digging, I just had it confirmed that last fall, Luella asked Mrs. Bannerman to come and give a talk to the gardening club members about how flowers, as beautiful as they are, could also be deadly, and which ones they should avoid planting in their home gardens. Then something else Tony mentioned came back to me. Luella had also attended the tea after Maisie Radcliff's funeral in December."

"Of course, she attended." Turner snorted and waved her off. "They had known each other for years. Half the town turned up at the Radcliff estate that day."

"True, but it wasn't until I discovered the chemistry set in her potting shed and looked at some of the plants in her greenhouse that the puzzle pieces all started to fit together and explained why we had hit one dead end after another."

"I'm still confused." Turner rubbed his temple and stared in disbelief at Addie.

Addie glanced back at Paige, then at Marc and Simon before pinning a stare of her own on the sheriff. "Luella Higgins."

"Yes." Turner jeered. "The victim. That is the only fact you've stated so far in this entire soliloquy."

Addie couldn't contain herself any longer. "No, Luella Higgins was the murderer."

It was as though the walls in the room let out a collective gasp.

"You can't be serious." Turner's face paled.

"I am. The victim was, in fact, her own murderer as she unwittingly ate her own tainted treats."

"Explain," said a clearly shaken Turner, rising to his feet.

"My gut tells me that Mrs. Bannerman unsuspectingly taught her which flowers were deadly and with Luella's pharmaceutical background, she had no problem figuring out the rest of it. Everyone knew Luella despised Tony for pulling the funding for the library. She also knew his favorite chocolates were the same as hers. The chocolate-covered cherries contained the poison. However, because Mrs. Bannerman was fiercely protective of the family, she happened to see something no one else did that day of the funeral tea and thwarted Luella's plan by hiding the chocolates. She must have suspected something was off."

"She does seem to have an eerie sixth sense," said Paige.

"She does that," said Addie, holding her head high. "And I think Randy knew what Luella was up to back then, and that was the other thing she was holding over him in her little blackmail scheme. Talk to them. I'm pretty sure they can give you some insight into this whole sordid affair."

Chapter 28

As the minutes ticked by, Addie squirmed and shifted uneasily from one hip to the other in the hard plastic chair. Was it her imagination or did all police stations go out of their way to make the waiting unbearable?

Marc and Sheriff Turner came out of his office. Addie jumped to her feet. Finally, some answers, but when they went next door into the interrogation room, she slumped back down into her seat.

"Have patience," said Simon, his hand patting her knee. "We'll find out soon enough if you dug up the right bone or not."

"But it shouldn't take this long. I just want to pick up my bookmobile and get it home. This has been a ridiculously trying week." She sighed and laid her head on Simon's shoulder. "And I've missed you." She snuggled into the crook of his neck.

He kissed her temple. "Yes, it sure didn't turn out like I thought it was going to."

"What? You expected to bail me out of Turner's jail cell?"

"That did cross my mind a few times." He chuckled, nestled his head against hers, and brought their interlaced hands to his lips and softly kissed her fingers. "I just feel so bad about your birthday. I had a wonderful evening planned and—"

"I think I'll take Pippi outside for walk," said Paige, eyeing the two of them snuggled in their chairs. "I won't be long."

Addie softly laughed and nuzzled closer to Simon. "You were saying about my birthday plans?"

"I was saying that we'll have to—"

"Here's Tony now!" Addie pulled her hand away and leapt to her feet as he and another man headed to the front door.

"Okay, Craig, thank you," said Tony, shaking a man's hand.

The stranger nodded at Addie as he pushed the gate beside the reception desk open and sauntered out the door.

"Addie," said Tony, eyeing her. "You didn't have to wait. I told you everything would be fine."

"Was that your lawyer?"

"Yes, Craig Thornburg. He's the estate lawyer. It seems Sheriff Turner's reputation precedes him, and Craig wanted to be here in case Turner tried to railroad us like he did you."

"So, everything's okay? Where's Mrs. Bannerman?"

"She's just signing her statement, but all's well."

"Were my suspicions right? Did she know something about the chocolates?"

"Yes and no. She didn't know anything for certain, but she said Luella was acting very odd when she set the box on the table in the hallway at the funeral tea."

"She saw her then?"

"Yes, you know Mrs. Bannerman. She has a way of seeing everything without being detected."

"Yes, she does that."

"What was it that made her suspect something might not be right?" asked Simon.

"She said Luella set the box down and then picked it up and stared at it like she was trying to decide if she should leave it or not. Then she placed it at the back of the table behind some flowers. Mrs. Bannerman thought she was trying to make it look like it had arrived earlier in the afternoon."

"Then no one would suspect they arrived about the same time she did," said Addie thoughtfully.

"Right, but I happened to come out of the parlor then and saw the gift table and mentioned to Luella that I could hardly wait to dip into the cherry ones later. Then after the tea, I went back, and the box was gone. I never thought anything about it again."

"So, Mrs. Bannerman removed them before you could have any?"

"Yes, she said she had a funny feeling about it as I just explained. A few months before, Luella had been visiting with Maisie in the conservatory, and she took a strong interest in the poison garden. Then, as you know, she asked Mrs. Bannerman to give a talk to the members of the gardening club about poisonous plants. When

Mrs. Bannerman noticed that the chocolates still had the manufacturer's ribbon around the box but no clear wrap, she got suspicious."

"Why didn't she report it or turn them over to the police if she thought they contained poison meant to harm you?"

"She didn't think anyone would believe her. After all, if what she suspected was right. The poison garden was in Maisie's conservatory, and she was afraid Turner, given his relationship with Luella, would think she had doctored the chocolates. She said since no one had eaten them, she saw no reason to."

"But why did she keep them all this time?"

"As an insurance policy in case something ever did happen to me. Then she'd bring them forward and try to prove that Luella brought them to the house. She said she was just sick about it when I discovered the chocolates hidden in the pantry because I'm never in there." He ran his hand through his hair. "But the police have our statements now, and they seem satisfied after searching Luella's house and talking to Randy Carlyle."

Marc escorted Mrs. Bannerman out of the other interrogation room and through the squad room over to where they were standing. "You're all free to go now. We have what we need, especially from Randy, who confessed to knowing Luella poisoned the chocolates last December."

"So I was right, he did know."

Marc nodded. "Yes. Not only was Luella blackmailing him about not reporting the bogus pharmacy license that she was allowing him to still operate under; she'd told him that if he ever told anyone about their arrangement, she'd also kill Randy's wife, Irene, and make it look like he did it, which as she said, given his criminal record, the authorities would believe."

"But Irene was her sister," said Addie.

"Yes, but there's been bad blood for a couple of years. It seems Irene supported Mayor Bryant in the election and campaigned against Luella, knowing how the power would go to her sister's head. Luella never forgave her for that and told Randy if he said anything about the chocolates meant for Tony, she'd make sure a little something showed up in her sister's food too, to reinforce her little blackmailing scheme and to keep him under her thumb. Since Luella was a regular pharmacist and knew nothing about compounding, she forced Randy to teach her how to extract aconitine from monkshood, which would automatically make Randy an accessory to murder, afterwards guaranteeing he'd stay quiet about all their under-the-table dealings and allow her to continue her political career. It seems that once she got a taste of power, she never wanted to lose it."

"Wow," said Simon. "This quaint little town has more secrets than Peyton Place, doesn't it?"

"Peyton Place?" asked Addie.

"An old television show, never mind."

"Simon, Marc," said Tony, extending his hand to shake theirs. "It's been a pleasure to meet you both, and I hope we can get together again under better circumstances. And Addie, my old friend, as always, it's been an adventure with you."

"Yeah, it's been a reunion for the books, that's for sure."

"Speaking of books, I almost forgot to tell you that I arranged for an old friend of my grandmother's to transport your bookmobile to Greyborne Harbor. He owns A1 Mechanical there, so I've also asked him to complete all the necessary repairs."

"You did what? I haven't even seen it since the accident. Is it worth repairing?"

"Yes, the damage wasn't too bad. It needs a new front end, new engine, and some framework repairs, but they tell me after that's done, it will be better than new."

"You didn't have to do that. I'm sure my insurance would have covered it."

"It would have been a fight since you owned it for less than an hour. Besides, I was happy to do it because you recovered my books that apparently Patricia *had* hidden on the bus to sell at a later date, and for recovering those before she could, I will always be grateful."

"So, Patricia had hidden them."

"Yup, and I must say," said Marc glancing at Addie. "It's been an informative day, that's for sure. Patricia told Turner that she thought after you found them on the bus, since they had been donated to the library in the first place, she'd automatically get them back, and she could still sell them and use the money to buy back the damaged bookmobile from you so she and Bea could run it as planned, but then Tony apparently took them back before she could lay claim on them."

"Yeah," said Tony scratching his head. "I got my knuckles rapped by Turner for not letting the courts decide ownership but, in my defense. I had won the case to stop my grandmother's last bequests, and I felt they still belonged to me."

"All I can say," added Marc, "is it was a good thing you did fight it in court and also bring about that investigation into Luella's finances because with everything coming out now, Patricia's scheming might have worked out for her in the end if the bequests hadn't been revoked."

"I'm glad now too. I knew I had to put a stop to it all, because everything I came back to in Pen Hollow felt so wrong, given the state my grandmother was in. I knew there wasn't much I could do about the money she'd given Luella over the past year, but I hoped I could at least get those books back. Then they disappeared before the auction, and I was afraid they were gone forever."

"I'm just happy," said Addie, "that ultimately we bought the bookmobile and stumbled on them before they *were* lost to you forever."

Tony looked at Addie and smiled. "As you know, they mean the world to me, especially *A Child's Garden of Verses,* and to show my gratitude," he took her hands in his, "I also included a few books just for you from my collection, but you'll have to go through the inventory on the bus shelves, so I can see if you're as good as you think you are in picking out first editions." He gave her an impish wink.

"I really don't know what to say. I'm stunned."

"Just say you'll come and visit me sometime in England."

"Um, I don't know." She glanced at Simon and released her hands from Tony's. "With the shop and everything, I don't seem to have time to get away much."

"Well, if you do, keep it in mind. I think you'd really like Milton Manor."

"You live in an English manor house?"

"Don't get too excited. It's not Downton Abbey or

Pemberley, but yes, it's considered an aristocratic estate, but more like Thrushcross Grange."

"The big manor house in Emily Brontë's *Wuthering Heights*?"

"Exactly like it, haunted moors and all."

"Really? I guess back in the day, I always saw you ending up in a funky New York City loft and never pictured you living on an English country estate."

"I'll take you out for a ghost-walk tour of the moors, and then you can see where a lot of inspiration for my novels comes from. You believe in ghosts, don't you?" He gave a short laugh and glanced at Marc and Simon. "Well, this has been a most enlightening reunion, and I've learned a lot that I can use in one of my books."

"Are you going to change your genre to murder mystery, then?" asked Simon.

"No, but poisons like aconitine have been around for centuries, and I'm pretty sure I can come up with a plotline that incorporates it and some tomb-embalmed cursed relic." He chuckled.

"It's been really great seeing you again." Addie squeezed his hand.

"Don't forget when you want to experience life on the other side of the pond, give me a ring. The invitation to visit Milton Manor is always open." He kissed her cheek, nodded at Simon and Marc, and then he and a complacent-looking Mrs. Bannerman, who bowed her head hastily at Addie as she strutted by her, left.

"Well, since it's all wrapped up," said Marc, "I guess you and Paige are free to leave."

"Aren't you guys coming?" asked Addie, glancing from him to Simon.

"Marc has a few things to tidy up with Sheriff Turner first and he's my ride, so . . ."

"Then why don't you go with Addie," piped in Paige. "I can wait and go back with Marc."

"No, that's fine. You have a little girl to get home to, and you"—Simon looked at Addie—"have someone waiting very impatiently for you in Greyborne Harbor."

"Has Catherine been having problems at the shop?"

"No, she's just fine, but someone else really needs you right now."

"Is Serena okay? You were worried about her. Did her test show something wrong?"

"No, she's fine, but I think she just needs her best friend with her right now because, well . . . I'll let her tell you."

"Stop being so secretive. What's wrong? Is the baby okay?"

"Yes, as far as I know, but go on. Get out of here and go see her. She's waiting for you."

Addie glanced at Paige and hoped the terror inspired by his words didn't show on her face. If Serena was in trouble, she needed to get back to her now.

"Come on. We'll get Pippi's carrier out of the back and get her settled in that," said Addie, charging down the stairs to the Wrangler. "I think she's gotten pretty spoiled lately with being carried around everywhere, and some cave time will do her good." Addie flipped open the back gate and grabbed the doggie carrier, knocking a book off the top of one of the boxes they had filled at the library sale. She picked it up to toss it back in the box and glanced at it. A smile crossed her face. "Before we go, there's one quick stop I want to make." She shoved the book under her arm and closed the back.

* * *

Addie pulled the Wrangler up to the curb and glanced at the woman sitting on the front porch. Addie waved, took Pippi from Paige, and hopped out onto the road. When she got to the end of the sidewalk, she set her little friend down, who immediately let out an excited yip and dashed, hind end waggling, up the front porch steps.

"Hi, Valerie, I hope you don't mind us dropping by, but my friend here wanted to say goodbye." Addie whipped a book from behind her back. "Here. This is my thank-you to you."

Valerie wiped the tears from her cheeks with the corner of her apron. She scooped Pippi into her arms, cuddled her tight, and turned the book over in her hand. "*How to Train Your New Yorkipoo?*" She grinned at Addie.

"I know you haven't made up your mind about whether you'll get a dog or not, or even the breed if you do. However, I found this at the library sale, and it made me think of you and your affection for Pippi."

"Oh, Addie, how lovely, but you really didn't have to."

"I know, but I wanted to thank you for being such a big help with Pippi when we first arrived and . . . well, I thought this fitting."

"The cupcakes were my idea." Paige beamed and handed her a small box of tasty treats.

"Girls, you've made this old woman's day so memorable." She scanned over the book and smiled. "Laurel will be thrilled when she sees this. She said I should find a puppy just like Pippi, and you know what, I'm going to call her right now and tell her to start looking for me."

"Laurel isn't here?" asked Addie. "I have something

for her too." She held up the silver charm of the hands wrapped around a dog and the heart in the background.

"How precious," said Valerie, slipping it from Addie's fingers. "She'll love this, and it's so perfect for her."

"I'm sure she'll be back soon for a visit so you can give it to her then."

"Yes, she's such a dear and worries about me so. I just wish she could get on with one of the animal hospitals in this area, and then she wouldn't have to drive back and forth on that freeway all the time."

"I know Doctor Timmons, Pippi's vet at Harbor View Clinic in Greyborne Harbor, is looking for a partner so he can semi-retire. Perhaps mention that to her."

"I will, thank you. Between the long hours she puts in and running up here all the time to check on me, it would be a great relief if she was closer. That girl works far too hard, if you ask me."

"That sounds like another doctor I know."

"Who's that?"

"Simon, my boyfriend."

"Simon? Funny. Laurel knew a Simon years ago who was going to be a doctor."

"Really? Small world, isn't it?"

"Yes, but I doubt it's so small that your Simon is her Simon." Valerie chuckled. "Thank you again, ladies." She cradled Pippi to her chest and sniffled as she glanced at the book and the box of cupcakes. "And remember, if you're ever back this way, come by. Who knows? By then I may have a little playmate for Pippi."

Addie had to practically pry Pippi from the woman's arms. Her little friend had apparently made herself completely at home at Valerie's. It made Addie recall how

Pippi had a sixth sense about knowing when a person needed to be comforted. She was glad that Valerie was going to get a dog of her own.

"Ah, isn't she the sweetest," said Paige, getting into the Wrangler. "I'd love to adopt her. She always makes me feel so loved. Too bad she never had children. She would have been a wonderful mother."

"I think the really lucky one is her niece. Valerie dotes on her, and I'm sure she has most of Laurel's life. Laurel was doubly blessed with the love of two mothers until her own passed."

"You're right. I guess Valerie's life turned out the way it was supposed to. With her having such a close connection to Laurel, it was easy for her to step in when her sister died and take on a mother role for Laurel."

"Except I think the roles are now reversed, and it's Laurel looking after Valerie."

"Speaking of looking after people, we'd better get back because I have a feeling there's some hand-holding for me to do when I get there." Addie laughed.

Chapter 29

The bells over the bookstore's door jingled. Addie glanced up from the sales report she'd been reading. "Catherine? I thought I told you to take the week off."

"Yes, you did, but I ignored you."

"Why?" asked Addie, eyeing her warily. "After what you went through last week on your own, you've definitely earned it."

Catherine tossed her handbag into the cupboard under the sales counter, gave Pippi a scratch, and turned toward Addie. "Because, my dear, in case you forgot, you're on baby watch, and I knew you'd also given Paige the week off."

"I'll manage. I can close the shop if I have to when Zach calls, but according to Serena last night, she's going to be pregnant forever."

"I can't speak from experience," said Catherine, "but back in the day, I recall all my friends feeling the same way during their last few weeks."

"I only hope it's a quick, easy delivery. I don't think Zach or the nurses could take much more of her mommyzilla mode."

"I'm surprised you're not going in with her. I thought she wanted both Zach and you to be there."

"She did, but I said no. If there was to be anyone besides Zach in the delivery room with her, it should be her mother. After all, she has firsthand experience with all this, not me."

"How did Serena take that?"

"She agreed when I told her I'd be right outside the door."

"I hope Doctor Dowdy's new dates are correct, and this is over for her soon. It'll be nice to have the old Serena we all know and love back among us." Catherine rubbed her hands together. "Now, back to the work at hand, I understand that you need help shelving all those books you got from the library sale. With the bookmobile being ready to go next week, we'll have our hands full with that. So where do you want to start today?"

"Are you sure? I don't want to overwork you. After all, you came to work here under the condition it would be part-time, and lately it's been anything but."

"Just say 'Thank you for coming in today, Catherine.'"

Addie could feel a blush spread across her cheeks. "Thank you, Catherine. I couldn't do all of this without you. You truly are one in a million."

She waved Addie off. "That's what Jonathan told me last night too."

"So, you had *the* talk?"

"We did."

"How did he take it?"

"Better than I thought he would. He said he completely understood. He knows his lifestyle isn't one most women can deal with long term, so if he lost me to anyone, he was glad it was to Felix Vanguard. He said he'd never had such a formidable rival in work, and now love, and I have done well for myself. He wished me all the best. Then in his way, he walked out the door and vanished. Even after all this time, I can't help but think Jonathan was a figment of my imagination," she said with a soft laugh.

"I guess that's why they call them ghost agents." Addie took Catherine's hands in hers. "But seriously, I'm glad that part's over, and I wish you and Felix all the best. He truly is a wonderful man, and I can see that he cares deeply for you."

"Speaking of men and caring, has Simon rescheduled your birthday dinner yet?"

"Yes." Addie beamed. "We're going to Salem on Saturday night for dinner and we're staying at the cutest little B&B."

"Do you want me to take Pippi?"

"Sure, if you wouldn't mind. I was going to take her—"

"Don't be silly." She gave Addie a sly look. "And if my suspicions are right, this might be *the* weekend that finger finds the ring on it that you've wanted from him for so long."

Addie sheepishly smiled. "I know it's silly that I want this so badly, but I can't picture the rest of my life without him. He would complete me."

"Really? You're not a whole person without him?"

"Yes and no. You know what I mean. I have a pretty good life, but I know I would be happier if we had that commitment to each other. You know . . . coming home to him at the end of a long day and snuggling on the sofa, and on Sundays the two of us cooking Sunday brunch together. Then spending the afternoon sipping our coffee and exchanging sections of the weekend newspaper and reading each other little tidbits of interesting articles we come across." Addie sighed and a faint smile touched her lips.

"There's one problem with that romantic fantasy."

"What's that?"

"You can't cook."

"You're right about that." Addie chuckled. "I know I have far too many romantic fantasies about how it *should* be, and I blame David for that because even though our lives were busy, when we were alone together it was like something out of a fairy tale. That's what attracted me to Simon in the first place. Everything with Marc felt like a tug-of-war, but with Simon it was all so easygoing." A sense of comfort came over Addie at Catherine's nod of understanding. "I mean, he still challenges me like David and Marc did, but in a quieter, gentler way and . . ." She stared at her bare finger. "So, ring or no ring, I have to accept Simon's and my relationship as it is and be happy with it."

"Has it been so bad?"

"No, aside from a few hiccups last week." She gave a short laugh. "All in all, it's pretty good."

"Then let fate take its course and I think you might be surprised."

"Do you know something I don't?"

"No, just call it intuition."

"I guess," Addie said, smiling at her old friend. "We'll just have to wait and see if he wants the same things as I do, and if not, then I'll accept that because I'd rather live like that than not have him in my life at all." Lost in a sudden thought, Addie stared out the shop window. "Since I'm so sure about us being right for each other, why can't I ask him to marry me?" She looked questioningly at Catherine. "Why does the man always have to be the one to ask?"

Catherine shrugged. "It's just the way it's always been done, I guess."

"You know what?"

Catherine shook her head.

"That's exactly what I'm going to do. I'll propose to him."

"That's my girl." Catherine laughed and gave Addie's hand a supportive pat.

Addie's phone vibrated on the counter, and she glanced down as *Zach Ludlow* flashed across the screen. A wave of excitement surged through her as she lunged to grab it and swiped Accept Call. "Hello? Is it time? . . . Be right there."

"I knew it might be today." Catherine grinned. "You're back and everything is right in Serena's world again."

"I don't think that has any bearing on Mother Nature taking its course."

"Don't be too quick to disregard it. I think for the first time in a week, she's actually relaxed enough, and knowing you're not in jail and back in town was all it took. Now go, scoot. I got everything here under control."

"Can you watch Pippi?" Addie asked, excitedly dancing a step back to the door.

"Of course, go, your godchild is about to be born."

Chapter 30

Addie screeched to a stop in the hospital parking lot, dashed through the main door, got Serena's floor from the woman at the information desk, and raced into the elevator. When the door opened on the second floor, Addie darted out into the lobby and crashed into a linen cart. "Sorry." She danced sideways and apologized to the housekeeping attendant. "We're having a baby!" She giggled and rushed down the hall to the nurses' station.

"Serena Ludlow's room, please."

The nurse looked up at Addie and checked the computer screen. "Are you family?"

"Not exactly, but Serena made arrangements for me to be outside the door."

The nurse's brow creased. "I'll have to check with the doctor. Meanwhile, please take a seat in the waiting room." She gestured toward a small room across the hall.

Addie paused in the doorway when she spotted Wade and Janis Chandler, Serena's parents. "Janis, I thought you were going in for the delivery?"

She nodded, sending her disheveled red hair swaying about her face. "I was in there, then Doctor Dowdy asked me to wait out here."

"Is everything okay?" Addie asked, taking a seat on the waiting room sofa beside her.

She wrung her hands. "To be honest, I'm not sure. He did an examination, and then ushered me out the door as they brought in all kinds of equipment." She set her tear-filled eyes on Addie. "It looked like operating room type stuff. I'm so worried." She dabbed a tissue at her eyes.

Out of the corner of her eye, Addie caught sight of Simon hustling past the door. She ran out into the hallway. "Simon, where are you going?"

"Doctor Dowdy just paged me and needs a hand in the delivery room."

"But you're a trauma surgeon, not an obstetrician. Does that mean there's something wrong?"

"All I know is this time it's not Braxton-Hicks, and Serena told him the only other doctor she'd allow in the delivery room to help him was me, and he wasn't going to argue that with her at this stage." He placed his hands on her shoulders. "Go and wait with the Chandlers. It shouldn't be long now."

"Simon, I'm worried. This is Serena we're talking about."

"And I will not let anything happen to her." He kissed her cheek. "Now, go sit, I'll be back as soon as I can."

Addie paced the floor and counted the number of tiles across the length and breadth of the small waiting room. When she'd finished those, she counted the number of dots in one of the ceiling tiles. Wade and Janis sat with their heads down, staring at the floor. She knew she should say something upbeat and reassuring, but she couldn't find the words because she was just as anxious as they appeared to be.

Why had the doctor sent Janis away and why did he need another doctor to assist at the last minute? Something had to be wrong. A wave of panic exploded inside her, and the tears she'd been fighting leaked down her cheeks.

"Mr. and Mrs. Chandler?"

"Yes." Wade's face was drawn and etched with exhaustion, but he hauled himself up to his feet.

"Congratulations!" Doctor Dowdy grinned. "You can go in and see your daughter and your new grandbabies."

"Did you say grandbabies?" Addie asked, rising. "Like in more than one?"

"Yes, Mr. and Mrs. Ludlow are the proud parents of two very healthy babies, a boy and a girl."

"Twins! Addie, she had twins." Janis fanned her face, and tears streamed down her pale cheeks.

"Go, go, see them. Tell Serena I'll be in later. But you guys go first." Addie sank back onto the sofa, held her head in her hands. It was no use. She couldn't contain her tears any longer.

"Addie, what's wrong?" Simon asked, sliding in beside her.

"Nothing, nothing at all. I was just so worried and . . . twins, wow. I can't believe it." She wrapped her arms around his neck and bawled into his jacket collar.

He pulled her close and ran his hand through her hair. "She's fine. The babies are fine. Dr. Roberts the pediatrician is in there now. You can stop worrying."

She pulled away and pinned her blurry gaze on him. "Did you know it was twins? Was that the reason for all the secrecy?"

"Let's just say I had a hunch. When I examined Serena in Pen Hollow, I thought I detected an echo of a second fetal heart but couldn't say anything before I spoke with Doctor Dowdy."

"Had he told Serena and Zach they were having twins?"

"No. Sometimes, rarely, when the ultrasound is done, one twin can be tucked up behind the other and can go undetected."

"So, he didn't know either?"

"Not until I brought her back and he did another ultrasound. The babies had shifted position, then it was as clear as day."

"Why didn't she tell anyone then?"

"She was in shock and didn't believe us, but I think when she saw the two of them just now, it finally sank in."

"Oh, what a day. My Serena the mother of twins." Addie giggled and nestled into the crook of his shoulder, her fingers trailing over the sleeve of his white lab coat.

"Yes, and it's times like this that I kick myself for not going into obstetrics. Seeing the look on their faces just now . . . it's a far happier department than emergency and trauma medicine is." He laid his head back on the sofa and sighed, drawing her closer. "I love you so much," he whispered into her hair.

A sharp object dug into her hip bone. She slid her hand inside his coat pocket and pulled out a small blue-velvet box. "What's this?"

"It's . . ." He snatched it from her fingers. "I was going to propose to you Saturday night."

"You were?"

"Yes, I was."

"Why are you speaking in the past tense? Is it because of what happened in Pen Hollow, and why you were so distant? Have your feelings for me changed?"

He gently placed his finger over her lips. "None of that, and what happened in Pen Hollow was simply me being exhausted and running on empty the whole week. The reason for the past tense now is . . . I brought it today because I was going to stop by Serena's house later to check on her and then show it to her to see if she thought you'd like it, and . . . Well, she came in here instead, and now you found it early." He shrugged and tilted her chin up so her gaze couldn't avoid his. "Plus, I just told you I love you, but you didn't say it back. Now I'm not so sure what I should do."

"You know it's not because I don't feel the same. It's just that saying the words is hard for me," she said, searching his face etched with disappointment. "The last time I told someone I loved them, they ended up dead."

"And you think if you tell me you love me, it's going to kill me?"

"No, of course not—well, maybe." She gazed into his sea-blue eyes, and that familiar wave of calm washed over her. "It's only that what I went through after David's death is something I don't ever want to go through again. So if I don't say it, I won't experience it, right?"

"Before David was killed had he ever told you that he loved you?"

"Of course he did."

"Had you told him you loved him?"

"Yes," she said meekly.

"I see." Simon drew in a deep breath. "Then tell me

this. You *could* have easily eaten that chocolate instead of Luella and been the one who died. Is it better to have those words left unspoken? If the worst had happened, I would have been the one left behind, and I wouldn't have had those three little words from you to hold on to; at least you had that from David, right?"

"Simon, I don't know what to say because you're right." Her gaze met his. "The feeling is there, and you know it, but those words . . . I just can't seem . . ." She glanced down at her sweaty palms and wiped them on her jeans. "I don't know. They're just words, I know, and not a death sentence . . . but . . ." She took a deep breath and swallowed hard. "I love you too."

"What did you just say?" He tipped her chin up and stared into her eyes. His held a hint of sparkle.

"I love you, Simon. I know it's been a long time coming, but now, with you, I guess I'm willing to take the chance." She held his gaze with hers. "Because loving you is a feeling I like, and neither of us knows what the future holds. So yes, I can say it now. I love you because I've finally realized that life's too short and there's no point in trying to avoid pain—it's part of living, right?"

"I'm glad you finally see it that way and have stopped wrestling with all your ghosts." He slid his arm from around Addie and got down on one knee beside the sofa and flipped open the top of the blue box. "Addie Greyborne, will you do me the honor of being my wife?"

Addie stared at the tiny, sparkling diamonds that encircled a dazzling emerald as he slid it onto her not-bare-anymore ring finger—and grinned. It was a perfect match to the earrings he'd given her for Christmas.

"Yes, yes!" She flung her arms around his neck. "I'll

marry you. I want to live on this wacky train we call life with you and only you, no matter what our future holds and for as long as we can." She drew back and stared into his tear-dampened eyes, dropping her gaze to his lips . . . so close to hers. "I love you so, so much." She grazed his cheek with feather-like kisses as her lips searched out his.

Visit us online at
KensingtonBooks.com
to read more from your favorite authors,
see books by series, view reading
group guides, and more!

BETWEEN THE CHAPTERS

Visit us online for sneak peeks, exclusive
giveaways, special discounts, author content,
and engaging discussions with your fellow readers.

Betweenthechapters.net

Sign up for our newsletters and be the first
to get exciting news and announcements about
your favorite authors!
Kensingtonbooks.com/newsletter